I0667046

323 Kearny

First Edition

Published by The Nazca Plains Corporation
Las Vegas, Nevada
2009

ISBN: 978-1-935509-10-3

Published by

The Nazca Plains Corporation ®
4640 Paradise Rd, Suite 141
Las Vegas NV 89109-8000

PUBLISHER'S NOTE
323 Kearny is a work of fiction created wholly by *Greg Bowden's* imagination. All characters are fictional and any resemblance to any persons living or deceased is purely by accident. No portion of this book reflects any real person or events.

Cover Photos, DwightL and Vish Studio
Art Director, Blake Stephens

DEDICATION

· ·

To John, who has put up with me for 36 years, and counting.

323 Kearny

First Edition

Greg Bowden

CHAPTER 1

On an unseasonably warm Saturday in early January, 1959, across the San Francisco Bay Bridge at the Orinda Country Club, four men were playing a singularly lackluster game of golf. After the first nine holes they gave it up and repaired to the bar where they took their usual booth. A waiter appeared, unbidden, with a tray of gin and tonics.

"Here's to a lousy afternoon of golf," Charlie said, toasting the others. Charlie Higgins was a Senior Vice President at Pittmann Engineering and was the un-elected leader of the group.

"I'll drink to that," Ray said, lifting his own glass. Ray DeWolf was a doctor and the only single man in the group. He was also the best golfer in the group, aided by his occasional Friday afternoon games with Joe Cox, a dentist who had the office next to his.

Joe, for all his Friday afternoon practice, was probably the worst player among them. He was also the handsomest of the four and, along with Ray, had the distinction of having been to bed with all of the others.

The last of the foursome was Willie Treat, a dedicated family man who had urges he didn't quite understand but gave into quite enthusiastically whenever the opportunity arose.

"Hey, guys, any of you notice that redhead in the foursome ahead of us?" Willie asked.

Joe rolled his eyes. "We all did, Willy." He smiled. "And with the same thought."

"He was nice," Charlie said, "but married. He wore a ring."

Willie laughed. "So are you, Charlie, and I don't see it slowing you down any."

The others laughed but Charlie stood his ground. "No, being married does slow me down. Married guys never have a place to go or, if they do, it's never the right day or the right time or something." He turned to Joe. "Look how long it took for us to get together. Geeze, we finally had to rent a hotel room."

"For which I paid," Joe said with a smile.

"You looking for your money back?"

"Not on your life, Charlie. Just remember though, the next time, you pay for the room."

The conversation turned to politics but Charlie didn't have much to contribute; he seemed distracted, thinking about something unrelated to the topic of the day. Finally, after a second drink, he spoke up. "You know what, guys? I have an idea for maybe solving our problem."

"What problem?" Ray asked.

"Well, you may be single but I bet you don't always want to take someone home. Hell, Pacific Heights is a long way from downtown when all you're after is a quickie."

Ray nodded and smiled. "Yeah, I guess I have missed out on a few guys that way. More than a few, if the truth be known."

"Yeah, me too," Willie said. "So what's the idea?"

"We get an apartment. Downtown. Easy to get to." He looked at Ray. "Bingo, our little problem is solved." He looked around the table, making eye contact with each of them. "It's solved for all of us, be it a quickie of not. Look guys, a thing like this wouldn't need to be expensive. I'll bet we could find a place for less than a hundred a month, apiece." He looked around the table again. "What do you say?"

"I say go for it," Willie said with a grin. "Maybe that redhead works downtown."

Ray and Joe seemed to be thinking about it and then nodded in unison.

"Okay, I'll check the papers on Monday, let you guys know." Charlie looked at his watch. "Come on guys, drink up. I'm taking my wife to the opera tonight and I have to get all gussied up in that damn penguin suit again."

. . . .

The next Saturday was cold and raining so the four men met downtown for lunch. Charlie had news.

"I found a place," he said over drinks. "Close to all of our offices, furnished and available now."

"Where?" Ray asked. "Not down in the Tenderloin, I hope."

"No, no. It's that brick building on Pine and Kearny, you know, where that sandwich shop is, what's it called? Whiskers?"

Willie snapped his fingers. "Oh, yeah, I know the place. Good location."

"How about the other people in the building? We don't need any gossipy old ladies poking their noses into what we're going to be doing." Joe smiled. "And I hope doing a lot of."

Charlie shook his head. "I checked that out. Six apartments, three besides this one empty. This is the second floor front, no one in the back. Third floor back is the landlady, nice old woman named Tan—but she isn't Chinese. Had a Chinese husband I think."

"And above us?"

"That's the beauty of it. No one. It's one of the empty ones. And on the fourth floor only the front is rented, to some hippie guy who sweeps the halls and does whatever maintenance there is to do. I met him and he seemed like he doesn't care what we do as long as we don't get the hall floors dirty."

Ray asked how much.

"Four hundred. And I don't think she trusts the banks much because she wants the rent in cash. That's the way the hippie pays she said, and that's the way we have to pay. I'll bet she keeps it in her mattress."

"Sounds perfect," Willie said. "When do we get it?"

Charlie took a small paper bag from his coat pocket, reached into it and held out a handful of keys. "Now"

. . . .

On Friday night, the 20th day of May, 1960, a young man named Tom Braden rolled over onto his back and tucked his hands behind his head, thinking. Tomorrow was going to be a very good day. Tomorrow he would graduate from college. Yes, a very good day indeed.

While he was thinking, the foghorns at the Golden Gate Bridge began their somber call, surprisingly loud in Tom's Nob Hill bedroom.

The sound of the fog horns took him back two years, back to his summers working for *Bay Tours*, doing a lot of different jobs, the last one of which was giving the narration on the two hour tours of San Francisco Bay. He grinned to himself in the dark, thinking about how many times he had described those self-same horns and the disasters they had presumably averted.

He'd had fun working on the boat, describing to the passengers what they were seeing, the buildings, the bridges, the other traffic on the bay. He'd also learned a lot about himself. He'd learned he was a responsible man, one with a quick mind, one who gave his all to his job. He'd also learned why he wasn't much interested in girls.

It was his second summer and the guy who gave the narration on the two-hour tour showed up drunk one morning. Tom, who was working in the ticket booth then, volunteered to take his place. His boss was a little skeptical but really had no choice so he let him do it on the first tour of the day. He also went along, just to see what the kid could do.

The kid did well. He had the basics of the narration down pat and added a lot of things to make it more informative and, actually, more interesting to the tourists. Tom had the job for the summer.

On his second day, during the break—which was taken mainly so the passengers could avail themselves of the delights available in the snack bar—Tom caught one of the deckhands watching him. When he nodded at the man he received not only a nod in return, but also a smile and a wink.

That afternoon, on the last tour of the day, the man came up to Tom and introduced himself as Mario Lombardi. When they shook hands Tom felt something pass between them, something which caused his dick to get restless in his underwear. Something which made Tom a little excited as well as a little uneasy.

That night, after he'd gone to bed, Tom couldn't get the feel of that handshake out of his mind. He wondered if maybe the deckhand was "that way" and the handshake meant more than he'd understood it to mean. That led him to wonder if maybe *he* was "that way." After all, there had been those times, more than just a few, when he and his college roommate back in Iowa had jacked off together. They'd even sucked each other once, something Tom would have liked to do again but which his roommate seemed to find boring, at least the sucking part. He'd found the getting sucked part quite a bit better.

The idea that he might be "that way" didn't bother Tom so much as it excited him. He imagined himself and Mario doing things which he couldn't quite picture but which, nevertheless, caused his hand to find its familiar place on his dick.

The next day, on each of the morning runs, Tom found himself grinning back at Mario's wink. During the break on the second run they bummed coffee from the snack bar guy and took it out on deck. It had turned cold and windy so the deck had been pretty much abandoned by the tourists. They took seats where they'd be somewhat sheltered from the wind.

"Gonna be cold this afternoon," Mario said. "Captain says the fog is coming in thick through the Gate."

Tom took a sip of the hot coffee, grateful for its warmth. "Great. The folks will just have to imagine they're seeing what I'm describing. If I were them, I'd ask for my money back."

"No need," Mario said with a grin as he moved closer to Tom. "They already got it back. Afternoon's cancelled."

"So what do they do? Send us home?"

Mario looked at him. "Yeah. Unless you want to stay on board, maybe help me with," he grinned, "something." There was a pause. "You like that?"

Tom didn't know what "that" was but he didn't hesitate. "Yeah, sounds good."

That foggy afternoon was the beginning of the best summer of young Tom's life. They started with the basics but it wasn't long before Mario taught Tom to take him inside and showed him what it was like to be made love to. Then he taught Tom to make love to him. By the time Tom had to leave his job to go back to school, he was quite an accomplished—and enthusiastic —lover.

Thinking about Mario and all the things they'd done together drove his hand quite naturally to his dick which welcomed it with accustomed pleasure. It turned into a long, slow session of hovering around that edge of no return until he couldn't do it anymore and then he let the pleasure take him.

When it was done he wiped himself with the little towel he kept just under the edge of the mattress, turned on his belly and went to sleep.

When he woke the next morning he wandered into the bathroom to pee. His dad was in the shower and called out, "Hey, Sport, is that you?"

"No. It's the Creature from the Black Lagoon."

"Well, don't track swamp slime all over the floor. You ready for the shower? I'll leave it running." He pulled the shower curtain back and stepped out onto the bath mat. "Hand me a towel, will you?"

Tom handed him a towel and climbed into the shower, pulling the shower curtain closed before he let go and drained his bladder.

"When do you have to be out at the college?" his dad called over the sound of the shower.

"Ten. Why I don't know. Graduation isn't until noon."

He could hear his dad chuckle. "Probably to see how hung-over you guys are." He chuckled again. "You okay?"

They'd had dinner the previous night with one of his dad's clients. The man had insisted they all have martinis. "I'm fine, Dad. Two martinis and a couple glasses of wine don't give you a hang-over." He ran his soapy hand down the length of his dick which sent little jolts into the middle of his belly.

"I don't know," his dad said. "That's all I had and I needed a couple of aspirins when I got up."

Tom laughed. "That's because you're an old guy. The rest of us handle it fine."

There was a snort but no reply.

They had fried polenta with syrup and sausage for breakfast. Tom's father had become quite a competent cook in the years since Tom's mother had been killed. Tom was seven years old then, old enough to understand what had happened but young and resilient enough to withstand the sudden loss. His dad hadn't faired quite so well but having the responsibility of a seven-year-old son he dearly loved had brought out in him a strength he hadn't known was there. The first year or so had been rough but they had weathered it together and become all the stronger for it.

"So what are you going to do this afternoon? I mean, after the ceremony."

Tom had thought about going over to Bay Tours and seeing if he could bum a ticket on the last tour of the day, the one Mario would be working. "Nothing much. Maybe go down to the coffee shop with some of the kids, lord it over the others that we're now graduates. You know." He shrugged.

"Well, don't forget we're having dinner at Ernie's. Seven-thirty reservation."

"Is Stella coming?" Stella worked in Matt's office and accompanied him on many social occasions. Tom liked her okay but thought she was kind of drab, thought his dad could do better. But then, he figured, they were probably sleeping together and a bird in the hand…

"No, she's got something she couldn't get out of. So it's just you and me Sport—unless you have someone you want to bring."

Tom shook his head. "No, let's make it just you and me. I like that."

His father reached out and put a hand on his shoulder. "Just you and me it is." He looked at the clock above the little window over the sink. "Hey, you'd better get going."

Tom looked up at the clock. "Yeah, okay, Dad." He tousled his father's hair, both out of affection and because he knew it drove him nuts. His father stood and returned the favor—for the same reasons.

In his room, Tom first made his bed. He had begun making his own bed—even to the extent of changing the sheets once a week—right after he had discovered jacking off and the mess that all that cum could make. Even though his dad had explained puberty, sex and masturbation to him he still felt shy about his dad knowing he did it—or at least how much he did it. He was pretty certain that his dad did it too, after all he'd said straight out that most men did it all their lives, but he was still shy about the stains on his sheets and the yellowed rag he kept under a corner of the mattress.

Once the bed was made he got dressed. He and his dad had long ago dispensed with any formality at breakfast and both of them were usually in nothing but boxers and tee shirts and this morning had been no exception. He put on a pair of gray pants, a blue long sleeved shirt and his new penny loafers. Looking in the mirror he decided he should probably wear a tie, just in case. He picked up a light jacket knowing it would probably be cold out at the campus.

"I'm going now. See you at graduation," Tom called as he went out the door. He took the stairs down to the lobby because it was faster than waiting for the elevator, said good morning to Mrs. Clark who always seemed to be sitting in the over stuffed chair by the door. Outside, he turned right and walked the block and a half to Hyde Street where he'd catch the cable car. He could have gone a couple of blocks the other way and gotten one of the busses that seemed always to be coming by on Van Ness Avenue but he loved the cable cars and would gladly wait until one finally came along.

He was in luck this morning. Not only did a car come along in about four minutes, but the gripman was Russ, a giant of a black man who never failed to greet Tom. Tom was partly in awe, partly in lust for the man. He didn't think Russ knew about the lust part.

Tom rode the cable car to the end of the line, where Powell Street runs into Market Street. There he stood on the little island in the street until his streetcar came along. He got on, dropped his coins in the fare box and sat next to a window. He divided his time between looking out at the people on the sidewalk and studying the ones that got on and off the streetcar.

They passed one of the gay bars on Market Street and he smiled, thinking of the first time he'd gotten up the courage to go into one. It had been late March, just after his twenty-first birthday. One of the guys from his statistics class was warning everybody that there was a bar down in the Tenderloin called *The Hideaway* and that it was gay. The guy acted like he was shocked but Tom thought perhaps that was just cover. At any rate, he'd looked the place up in the phonebook and carried the address around in his wallet for a week or so before he got up the courage to go.

It was a cold, foggy Wednesday night and he paced back and forth on the street, working up the courage to go in. A sailor in shore whites pushed past him, yanked the door open and disappeared inside. He was back in less than two minutes.

"Jesus Christ," he said to Tom, "that place is a queer bar! Come on, guy, I'll buy you a drink down the street where there's real men."

"No, I... I think I'll go..." He indicated the door the sailor had just come out of.

"Oh, no. Don't tell me you're one of them!" He took a step back and looked Tom up and down. "Well, you sure don't look like a queer."

Tom nodded and reached for the door. The last thing he heard as he entered was, "Jesus, you can't trust anyone in this town!"

Inside, the place was dim, smoky and hot. Tom managed to get down the stairs without tripping and, looking neither left nor right, went straight to the bar and climbed up on a stool.

"What'll it be?" The bartender took Tom's breath away. He was tall, muscular and redheaded, with a short, reddish strip beard and his shirt was open to his waist, showing a thicket of red hair on his chest. When Tom managed to look up he found the deepest green eyes he'd ever seen.

"B... Beer," Tom managed to stammer.

The bartender grinned at him, showing even, blinding white teeth. "I don't think I've seen you in here before. Your first time?" He opened a cooler, uncapped a beer and handed it to Tom. When Tom dug a dollar out of his jeans the bartender waived it away. "First timers always get the first one on me. After that..." He winked, "...well we'll see, won't we?" He turned away to serve another customer.

Tom drank some of his beer, not really tasting it. He wanted to look at the other men there but didn't know how to do it without being obvious.

"Well, hello there, Tom." It was the man on the next stool and Tom choked on his beer when he turned his head. The man was Dr. Worthington, his advisor at school.

"Here now, careful there," Dr. Worthington said, slapping him on the back. When Tom was finally able to catch his breath again Dr. Worthington put his hand familiarly on his shoulder and said, "Don't worry about it, Tom. We're all here for the same thing."

They talked a little and Tom admitted that this was not only his first time here but it was his first time in any gay bar. He blushed when Dr. Worthington said, "Oh my God, a virgin!" but recovered enough to say, "Well, as far as bars go, I guess."

Dr. Worthington bought Tom another beer and when that was gone Tom excused himself and went home, disappointing the bartender greatly. Tom smiled to himself. He had plans to make that up to him.

Tom came out of his reverie when the car stopped at the college. He had to hold his jacket in front of him to hide the fact that remembering the redheaded bartender had given him a very stiff erection.

He made his way across the campus to the Administration Building where a small crowd of almost-graduates was waiting at the entrance.

"Hi, Tom. Aren't we looking spiffy this morning?" It was Harvey, a good-looking man Tom had had several encounters with. The encounters had always been in restrooms and they had always been fast, dangerous and explosive. Tom wasn't sure he liked that kind of sex but Harvey could always get him to do it.

"Thank you. You're looking pretty good yourself."

Harvey grinned. "The library's open this morning. Want to go over and look something up?"

Tom still hadn't completely lost the erection he'd been carrying when he got off the streetcar and he felt it stiffen up again.

"Well, what do you say?" He looked meaningfully at Tom's crotch. "It looks like you could stand a little relief."

Tom was saved from answering by the arrival of Dr. Worthington. "Hey, Tom, I've been looking for you." He glanced at Harvey and smiled. "You, too, guy. I think you're actually going to graduate."

Harvey looked like he was going to kiss Dr. Worthington. "You mean the calculus final? I passed it?"

It was Dr. Worthington's turn to grin. "More like aced it. If I remember correctly, you got something like an A-. So I guess you're no longer a student here."

Tom thought an odd look passed between the two but couldn't be sure. Harvey let out a whoop and grabbed Dr. Worthington's hand and shook it. "Man, that's wonderful! I'll see you later; I got to go get my cap and gown and do one last thing at the library." He took off toward the table where they were handing out the caps and gowns.

Dr. Worthington smiled to himself and turned to Tom. "How were those job interviews you went to?"

"Okay, I guess." He shrugged. "They all seemed so, I don't know, so dull I guess. Stodgy."

"Yeah, I figured they might. You're looking for something with a little more responsibility, a little more... action maybe."

Tom shrugged again. "Maybe I'm being too picky but..."

"No, I don't think so. I think the right thing just hasn't come along." He grinned. "Or maybe it has." He took a card out of his pocket and handed it to Tom. "Call these people Monday, they're expecting you. Go see them. With your patience and organizational skills, not to mention your common sense, I think you might be a good match."

Tom looked at the card. *"Bay Holdings Group"* it said in raised, engraved letters. Below, in smaller type it said, *"A Real Estate Corporation"* and below that, *Claude Simms* with a phone number. He looked quizzically at Dr. Worthington who laughed.

"I saw Claude at a dinner at the president's home last week. We got to talking and he mentioned a certain problem they have. I told him you might be the perfect man to solve it. Go see him." He glanced across the quad where Harvey was just going into the library. "You better go get your cap and gown. I, uh, I have something to check at the library." At Tom's raised eyebrow he chuckled and said, "Hey, the guy's been after my tail for five years now. He's finally graduating so I guess maybe he's earned it."

Tom smiled. "I'm graduating too, you know."

"Really? Not graduating but... Really? I never thought..." He put his hand on Tom's arm and squeezed lightly. "You can have my tail any time you want it." He waived and turned toward the library.

There was a minor mix-up with Tom's cap and gown but it finally got straightened out and Linda, a piano major, helped him on with it. When she straightened his tie she gave him a light kiss on the lips and said, "I wish we'd gotten to know each other better." Then she ran back to the safety of her girlfriends.

Somehow the staff got them lined up, the orchestra began playing "Pomp and Circumstance" and they began the march to the graduates' section. Parents and well-wishers stood as they passed and Tom scanned the crowd for his dad. He finally found him in the front row, looking very fatherly and proud, pointing Tom out to the man sitting beside him.

It was after the speeches began that Harvey suddenly appeared and sat in the very last seat. Tom thought he looked a little disheveled and breathless.

When the speeches finally ended the graduates were called, one by one, to the platform where they shook hands with the president and accepted the leather folder containing their diploma. Tom noticed that when Harvey crossed the platform he seemed to be crouching just a little but discounted it as just something Harvey would do, for a reason known only to himself.

When it was over and Tom was looking around for his father, Harvey came up to him and whispered in his ear, "Man, that was something!"

"Yeah, I never thought graduation from college would be this emotional. But what's with you? Why were you walking that way?"

"No shoes." He hiked up his gown a little. "In fact," he turned so his back was to the crowd and pulled up the front of his gown, "no nothing. What a trip!" He was naked under his gown and his dick was standing out from his balls, half hard.

"Oh, my God, you walked across there, shook hands with the president and all the time you were naked under there? I can't believe it."

Harvey laughed. "Neither could Dr. Worthington. I got naked over in the library." The laugh turned to a giggle. "I even made him carry my clothes back over here. They're up in his office now. Him too." He leaned in and gave Tom a quick kiss. "I gotta go make him happy again to get them back." He turned and started towards administration. "See ya."

Tom shook his head and scanned the crowd, looking for his father. He found him, still talking to the man who had been sitting beside him. They were with a heavy woman, the man's wife, Tom thought, from the familiar way she rested her hand on his arm. He went over to them.

Even before introducing him, Tom's dad pulled him into a tight bear hug, kissed him on the cheek and told him how proud he was to be his father. Then he introduced him to the couple he'd been talking to, Louise and Hank Devore. They said that their daughter, a math major, had graduated with him and was just now turning in her gown.

At that moment the daughter appeared, a pretty girl who, when she put on another twenty years and sixty pounds, would look exactly like her mother. Tom recognized her from a statistics class.

The two families talked for a moment before the Devores took their leave. They were from Fresno and had a long drive ahead of them. Tom's dad told him again how proud he was and then left, saying he might go to his office for a few hours.

As Tom turned toward the coffee shop he saw a familiar figure just leaving the spectator's area. He hurried to catch up with him.

"Mario! What are you doing here? I thought you'd be working."

"What? And miss seeing my favorite narrator graduate? I couldn't do that so I took the day off."

Tom was flattered that Mario would miss a day of work just to come and see him graduate. He told him so.

Mario got a sudden twinkle in his eye. "You know what? My aunt is spending the day with her friend in Marin and she won't be home until late. If you have nothing..."

Tom began to get hard before Mario even finished the thought.

They took the streetcar and then the cable car to Chestnut Street where Mario lived with his aunt. She was of advanced years and was pleased that Mario would stay with her and help with the things she couldn't manage. It was a perfect arrangement except that Mario could only bring somebody home when she was visiting one of her friends and that was always during the day when Mario was normally working.

They were in each other's arms before the front door was locked and naked before they got to Mario's room. They ended up on the bed, with Tom lying on top of Mario, rubbing their hard dicks against each other.

At one point Mario broke their kiss and said, "Oh, Tom, I really miss you when you're in school."

Tom laughed. "You mean a handsome man like you can't find someone to take into that tool room and play with his tool?"

Mario grinned up at Tom and kissed him. "Sometimes. But they're never like you, always ready for it, always wanting to do it again." He raised his hips under Tom and Tom got the message. He raised up so Mario could lift his legs. "There's stuff in the drawer there." Tom could hear the lust in Mario's voice.

Tom found the slick gel and applied it liberally to his dick. Then he applied some to Mario's ass and began rubbing his finger around the little pucker.

"I don't need that," Mario whispered. "Please, just come in to me."

Tom bent down and kissed him before slowly entering him. Tom's dick was clearly above average in size and he'd had to be slow and careful at first but Mario had adapted to him quickly and now Tom could just slide in without waiting for Mario to get used to him.

Mario groaned as the wide flare of Tom's dick pressed firmly against his prostate. He groaned again when Tom pulled back and used the flare to tug at his sphincter. They went on this way until Tom, even pausing now and again, couldn't do it any longer. He rammed into Mario's prostate a couple of times and then pulled back, pulling the flair of his cock-head barely through Mario's sphincter.

They each let out a loud groan as they came, Mario shooting up into the hair on his chest and Tom shooting inside Mario. For both of them it took a long time. When they'd stretched it out as long as they could, Tom pushed deeply into Mario, resting part of his weight on him.

"You know Tom, you're still the best!"

Tom grinned at him. "Look who taught me."

Mario squeezed his sphincter around Tom's dick. "No, you're a natural. I just gave you a few ideas you might not have had for a few years. You know? If I were twenty years younger or you were twenty years older, I think I'd probably fall in love with you."

"What difference does twenty years make? I *like* older men." He kissed Mario, long and deep. "Especially you."

"And this older man likes you, too, sort of like an older brother.

They stayed as they were until Tom's dick softened enough to slide most of the way out of Mario. Tom had to pull to get it all the way out when the flare of the head got to Mario's sphincter.

"You know, Tom," Mario said when they were lying side by side, touching from shoulder to foot, "I really do feel like your older brother. And if anyone ever tries to hurt you or someone you love, they'll have me to answer to." He laughed. "Me and the Mafia. Come on, let's have a shower. Then maybe it'll be my turn." They were both hard again by the time they'd finished their shower.

Mario was on top the second time. He turned Tom on his belly and covered his back, pressing him into the bed and making him feel both safe and loved. It was a great way to graduate from college.

CHAPTER 2

· ·

It was a great afternoon for Tom's dad, too. Like Tom, he spent it in bed, but not with an old friend. He'd just met this man, walking up Montgomery Street, towards his office. The man was walking in the other direction and as they approached they locked eyes for a moment. When they had passed, they each looked back. Then they both stopped, turned around and approached one another.

"Hi," the man said, holding out his hand. "I'm Clifford. My friends call me Cliff."

"Matt," Tom's father said, shaking the man's hand. "May I call you Cliff?"

The man grinned and didn't let go of Matt's hand. "I think you probably will," he said. "You busy?"

Matt's eyes twinkled. "I *was* going up to my office. Now I'm not."

"Good. I live up there a few blocks. You game?"

Matt looked him in the eye. "I think, with you, I may be game for anything."

Cliff laughed. "Then I have some great ideas."

They walked over to Sansome Street and then up two blocks, to a nondescript gray building. The inside was equally gray and nondescript until they entered Cliff's apartment. It was white with red accents and it was filled with Chinese antiques. Good antiques, from what Matt could tell.

"Yeah," Cliff said, watching Matt look around. "It's very Chinese. My wife was Chinese and when we got divorced, I got the furniture. Some of it is actually more comfortable than it looks."

"And some of it," Matt said, "is very beautiful. Didn't your wife like this sort of thing?"

Cliff laughed. "Oh, my God, no! She hated it. Said she'd lived with it all her life and now that she's free, she's free of this stuff too. She moved to New York and did an apartment over in Danish Modern."

"Well, some of it is quite wonderful."

Cliff pulled Matt into a hug. "Speaking of wonderful..."

They went into the bedroom, undressed themselves and looked each other over. "Now comes the awkward part, figuring out who does what to whom," Cliff said with a little laugh. "You have any no-no's or must do's?"

Matt shook his head. "I think I'm what they call versatile. Well, maybe within some rather broad limits."

"Good. Me, too." Cliff pushed him onto the bed and, starting with his feet, touched him everywhere, running his hands over his body gently, lightly and very excitingly. Matt returned the favor, using his tongue in several places."

They ended up with Matt inside Cliff, making love to him. They both experienced explosive orgasms at about the same time.

After, lying on their backs, touching from hips to shoulders, Cliff pulled out an ashtray and a pack of cigarettes. "You?" he asked, offering the cigarettes.

"No thanks," Matt said, waiving the pack away. "But you go ahead. I kind of like the way a smoker's skin smells and tastes."

Cliff lit a cigarettes and laid back, nestling the ashtray on his belly. He smoked in silence for a while, both of them still savoring what they'd just done.

Finally, Matt said, "So you were married..."

"Yeah. I was young, everyone expected me to marry and Su-Lin's family was very kind to me, made me feel like part of the family. They put me through law school, set me up in practice and paid the bills for a couple of years, until I got the hang of being a lawyer. I'm still family counsel. And friendly with Su-Lin when I see her which isn't often."

"Kids?"

"No. Neither of us could have them." He turned and looked at Matt. "You ever been married?"

"Yeah. Twenty-five years ago. In Des Moines."

Cliff stubbed out his cigarette. "You have kids"

Matt grinned at him. "Yeah. A boy. I just watched him graduate out at State. He's made me very proud."

"What does he think about... You know, this?" he took hold of Matt's dick.

Matt laughed. "I know he thinks about his own a lot. He seems to be something of a stud with the college girls." He thought for a second. "Oh, you mean what does he think about his dad liking men. Nothing, I guess. I'm pretty low key about it. But I wouldn't lie to him. If he ever asked me, point blank, I'd tell him the truth," He shrugged.

They were just about to start again when Matt looked at the bedside clock and realized he had to go if he was going to get a shower and dress before they had to leave for dinner.

They made their good-byes in bed and Cliff watched Matt dress. When he was finished Cliff, still naked, saw him to the door and handed him a card. "Call me," he said. "Please."

. . . .

Tom's dad took him to Ernie's for dinner, a place they'd been once before, at Christmas. Once they were seated and martinis had been ordered, Tom's dad pulled a long box out of his coat pocket and handed it to Tom. "A little something to celebrate your graduation," he said. "Go on, open it."

Inside the box was a gold Rolex watch. Tom took it out of the box and turned it over. *For Tom, the man I admire most in all the world* was engraved on the back. It choked Tom up so much he could only whisper, "Thank you."

They toasted each other and Tom put his trusty Timex in his pocket and put the Rolex in its place. They ordered another martini and consulted the menu. "The fillet stuffed with bleu cheese is excellent tonight, gentlemen," the waiter said and they both ordered it, along with a bottle of Bordeaux.

Over dinner Matt became nostalgic. "You know, Tom, ever since your mother died I've tried to be a good dad to you, to bring you up the way I thought you should be brought up. Evidentially I did something right because as it says on the back of the watch, you've grown up to be the man I'd hoped you'd be. The man your mom wanted you to be, too. She'd be as proud of you as I am."

Tom looked up at his dad. "Thank you. And you know what? I think I've grown up to be the man *I* want to be, too. I couldn't have done that without you."

Later, after the steaks had been served, Matt asked if Tom had any lines on a job.

"Why? You trying to get rid of me? Want me to start paying rent or something?"

His dad laughed. "Not just yet. No, I was just wondering if any of those interviews you went to came to anything."

Tom took a sip of his wine. "Not really. The jobs were all so *boring!* With any one of them I'd be stuck in a room with twenty other guys doing some repetitive make-work job."

His dad shrugged. "Well, you've got to start somewhere. I guess you could come to work at my place but it would have to be down in operations somewhere and I doubt you'd like that either." He paused and gave Tom a grin. "Something will turn up, I know it."

Tom smiled and toasted his dad. "Maybe it already has. I ran into Dr. Worthington this morning and he gave me the name of a man who's looking for someone just like me. Or so Dr. Worthington thinks."

"Doing what?"

"No idea, dad. Dr. Worthington just said the job would be a perfect fit for me. I'm going to call them first thing Monday morning."

And so he did. Mr. Simms secretary said Mr. Simms was expecting the call and put him through right away.

"Mr. Simms? My name is Tom Braden. Dr. Worthington..."

"I know who you are Mr. Braden. Dr. Worthington spoke highly of you. When can you come in?"

"Uh... Today?"

"Good. Right away." He hung up.

Tom laughed to himself. At least there wouldn't be any beating around the bush with the man.

Tom dressed in one of his two good suits and put on one of his father's silk ties for good luck. He arrived at 154 Sutter St. around a quarter to ten, took the elevator up to the sixth floor and entered the door marked *Bay Holdings Group* at exactly ten minutes of ten. He gave his name to the receptionist who said he was expected and pointed him down the hall. "To the end," she said. "Turn right and see Miss West."

Miss West turned out to be a woman in her mid forties. Her hair was cut short, she wore no makeup and, from the way she spoke, Tom knew she'd brook no nonsense. As soon as he gave his name she stood and extended her hand. "Well, I hope you're the one," she said cryptically, knocked once at the door behind her, opened it, announced him and pushed him into the office. He heard the door close behind him.

Mr. Simms pushed his chair back and stood. "Mr. Braden," he said in a horse voice. "Come over here and sit down." He indicated a chair facing the desk.

"Thank you, sir," Tom said, and sat, his back very straight.

Mr. Simms offered a cigarette box and took one himself when Tom declined. He lit it and fixed Tom with a long look. "Bill tells me you have both patience and common sense. That right?"

Tom nodded. "I think so. I certainly try."

"Try's not good enough. Either you have it or you don't. Now which is it?"

Tom nodded. If this was what the man wanted... "Yes sir. I am a very patient man and I have a lot of common sense. My dad has both of those traits and made quite sure that I did too."

Mr. Simms cocked his head. "What's your father do?"

"He's a stockbroker, sir."

Mr. Simms took a long drag on his cigarette and blew the smoke off to the side, toward one of the open windows. "You ever work for a man who was head strong, disorganized, full of himself and not living in the same reality as you?"

Tom thought for a moment, wondering what Mr. Simms was getting at. He gave a mental shrug and said, "Well, I did take physics from Dr. Lowe. I think... " Tom's voice trailed off as Mr. Simms began to laugh.

"That's exactly what Dr. Worthington said you'd say. And you know what? I'm acquainted with Dr. Lowe and know how he is. What sort of grade did you get out of him?"

Tom smiled. "An A."

Mr. Simms nodded. "Okay, you've almost got the job." He reached across the desk and pressed a button on his phone. Miss West immediately opened the door. "Miss West, I want young Braden here to meet with Mr. Diggs. And the sooner the better."

"Yes, sir. I've already spoken to Mr. Diggs. He says he can't possibly see him until next week at the earliest."

"God damn... " He clapped his hand over his mouth for a second and then said, "I'm sorry about that, Miss West. Please forgive my slip of the tongue."

She nodded. "Yes, sir. I'll speak with Mr. Diggs again, tell him how anxious you are for him to meet Mr. Braden." She turned to Tom. "I'll telephone you the moment I get an answer from him. In the meantime, please come with me. You have a few papers to complete." She turned on her heel and left the room.

Mr. Simms stood and Tom took that as a sign the interview was over. He stood, shook hands with Mr. Simms, said he'd enjoyed meeting him and followed Miss West out of the room.

In the outer office Miss West handed him a clipboard with a questionnaire on it, a pen and indicated a chair for him. She then went back to her typewriter. She stopped a few minutes later, just as Tom was signing the form. "He likes you, you know. You have the job if you can get Mr. Diggs to agree to it."

Tom handed her the form, the clipboard and the pen. "Thank you," he said and then laughed. "The problem for me is that I haven't the slightest idea what the job *is*."

She looked up at him. "Why, it's to control Mr. Diggs, of course." She looked at a clock on her desk. "I'm sure I'll be contacting you before the end of the day." She looked back at her typewriter, effectively dismissing him.

Since he hadn't had breakfast, he stopped in a coffee shop and bought coffee and a roll with two kinds of cheese and three kinds of meat. He took a seat at the little bar in front of the window and watched the pedestrians as he ate and wondered what that whole interview had been about.

He was no more enlightened when next he heard from Miss West. All she said was that he was to meet Mr. Diggs for dinner the next night at seven o'clock at the Banker's Club. When he asked his dad if he had ever heard of the Banker's Club his dad let out a low whistle.

"The Banker's Club, huh? They must think mighty highly of you, Son. Sounds like the interview went very well indeed." He went on to explain that the Banker's Club was in the Pacific Stock Exchange, was very exclusive and even more expensive. "Wear your best suit, Son. And polish your shoes."

After Tom described the interview and Miss West's comment that the job was to control Mr. Diggs, his dad just shook his head. "Sounds a little strange to me, Tom. Tell you what, I'll ask around the office, see what anyone knows about this *Bay Holdings Group*. If they have any kind of a presence in this town, someone will have some information."

The next afternoon Tom's dad was home early. "Well, I asked around. It seems that *Bay Holdings Group* is one of the more successful real estate outfits in the state, possibly the country. It's a corporation okay but this Simms guy owns nearly all the stock and none of it is public. They're stable, successful and word on the street is that they are also hugely profitable. Diggs is the number two man and a fairly successful real estate broker." He smiled. "From what I heard, he's well able to afford the Banker's Club." He tousled Tom's hair. "Have a good time and eat well. It's bound be better than the stew we had last night."

. . . .

Taking advantage of the fact that Tom would be out that evening, Matt had called Tony and arranged for a little evening time with him. Tony had been Matt's assistant for his first year in San Francisco. He'd been assigned to Matt to show him the ins and outs of the San Francisco office and they'd hit it off well and had become friends. Since Matt was just coming out then, Tony had shown him the ins and outs of gay life in San Francisco, too.

There was no pretense between the two men and when Matt knocked on his door, Tony answered it wearing only a well worn pair of gym shorts. By the time they'd finished their hello kiss he wasn't even wearing those.

They had their usual good time, first Matt inside Tony and then, when Matt was just this side of his orgasm, Tony inside him, pushing him over the edge by steadily pounding on his prostate. Their orgasms blossomed at pretty much the same time.

When Matt left, they were both happy men.

· · · · · · · · · · · · · · · · ·

Tom arrived at the Stock Exchange building fifteen minutes early and had to walk around the block to kill time. He was so nervous that he didn't even notice the good looking man who followed him half way around but lost interest when Tom didn't acknowledge him.

Tom went into the lobby and was quite impressed by the brass work, the gilt and the high ceilings. He was motioned over to a podium when he started for the elevators. "May I help you?" the man standing at the podium asked. Tom told him he was to have dinner with Mr. Diggs. The man consulted a ledger, looked up and nodded. "Mr. Diggs has already arrived and asks that you to meet him at his table. The maitre d' upstairs will show you. Elevator number five." He nodded towards the proper elevator bank.

Tom went to the indicated elevator and when he pushed the call button the doors opened immediately. He pressed the button with the discreet brass plaque over it marked "Banker's Club. Members only." When the doors opened again Tom was greeted by name by an older, well turned out man who said, "This way please. Mr. Diggs is expecting you."

He was led to Mr. Diggs' table which was also occupied by a stunning blond lady who was introduced as Miss Winters. Tom had an impulse to kiss the hand she offered but managed to suppress it in favor of a light handshake. As the introductions were ending a waiter appeared and held Tom's chair for him. As soon as Tom was seated another waiter appeared carrying a tray of cocktails.

"I've taken the liberty of ordering cocktails," Mr. Diggs said. "Martinis. I hope you don't mind."

Tom grinned. "A favorite, Sir. Thank you." He turned to Miss Winters. "And a favorite of yours?"

She broke into a radiant smile. "Yes, Mr. Braden, they are." She paused for a moment, sipped her drink and then said, "I think I detect an accent in you, Mr. Braden." Then she laughed. "Well, actually all of us have some sort of accent I guess. What I mean is, yours is different from mine."

Tom nodded and sipped his drink. "I must say, Miss Winters, you have a very good ear." *My God,* Tom thought to himself, *I feel like I'm a character in some British "B" movie.* Somehow, though, it seemed to work for him and seemed to give him a framework in which to work.

"Yes," Miss Winters said, "but not good enough to tell just where in the mid-West you come from. Now if it was France, I'd probably know that."

They all had a chuckle out of this before Tom said, "Iowa. Des Moines mostly, two years of college in Cedar Rapids."

They talked about Iowa, a place neither Miss Winters nor Mr. Diggs had ever been and, Tom thought, a place neither of them wished to go. While they were talking Mr. Diggs signaled for another round of drinks. When the drinks were half consumed a waiter appeared with menus and looked at Mr. Diggs, who nodded. The menus were distributed and Mr. Diggs made several suggestions for appetizers and main courses. Since Tom's menu didn't have any prices on it and since he figured Mr. Diggs wouldn't suggest something he didn't want anyone to order, he ordered from Mr. Diggs list. He chose a small dinner salad to start and lamb chops stuffed with pâté and truffles. Mr. Diggs added shrimp to Tom's salad order.

Miss Winters also ordered the dinner salad but with extra shrimp. She had abalone for her main course. Mr. Diggs asked for oysters on the half shell and rack of lamb, rare. He also ordered a half bottle of Riesling for Miss Winters and a bottle of Beaujolais for Tom and himself.

The dinner went marvelously. By the end of the first course they were feeling quite comfortable with each other and by the time the main courses had been cleared they were almost friends.

When the waiter came with dessert menus Tom waived his away. "Nonsense," Mr. Diggs said. "The young man and I will share a Crème Brule and the lady will have one to herself. We'll all have coffee and brandy, from my special bottle."

When they finished, at a quarter after nine, Tom was stuffed and just slightly drunk. He was alert enough, however, to note that no check was presented. Mr. Diggs simply stood, helped Miss Winters with her wrap, beckoned to him and ushered them to the elevators.

At the curb outside Mr. Diggs hailed a cab and, when it stopped, opened the back door and ushered Tom in. Tom started to protest but Mr. Diggs said, "Don't worry about Miss Winters, she is with me." He handed the driver five dollars and told him to take Tom wherever he wanted to go. Then, as he was closing the door, he said, "We start at eight-thirty. Be on time."

The cabdriver, a man in his mid forties, turned and smiled at Tom. "Where to, guy?"

Tom gave his address.

The driver took off. At the first stoplight he turned and grinned at Tom. "You mind if we make a pit stop along the way? I gotta pee something awful."

Tom grinned back at him. "That may save the back seat of your cab. I gotta go, too. Probably worse than you do."

The light turned green and the driver looked at him in the mirror. "You, uh… You know of a place?"

Tom shook his head.

"That's okay. I maybe do. A little alley just up here." He turned left, went up a block, turned left again and pulled into a narrow alley which dead-ended against a building. The driver got out and said, "Come on." In front of the cab he pulled down his zipper and dug around in his pants.

Tom pulled his zipper down and looked at the driver's crotch. The guy's cock was now hanging out and he'd pulled out his balls, too. "Nice," Tom said, nodding at the dick.

"Thanks. Yours too." He reached out and took Tom's dick in his hand. "Big one."

Tom reached for the other man's cock.

"No, no. Not yet. I really do have to pee and I can't do it when I'm hard. And if you're holding it, it'll definitely be hard." He let fly. Tom did the same and they stood together, trying to keep their streams hitting each other. When they were through Tom reached out and took hold of the driver's cock. The driver put his hand over Tom's, squeezed a little and together they milked it down. When it was hard they did the same thing to Tom's only his was already hard.

The driver moved Tom a little away from the puddle they'd made and dropped to his knees, taking Tom's dick all the way in, until his nose was lost in Tom's thick pubic hair. He was very good and it wasn't long before Tom was groaning quietly in the back of his throat.

"I'm gonna come," Tom whispered. The man nodded his head and swallowed down on him. Then it was all over.

When Tom began to go soft in his mouth the man got up and took Tom's hand and put it on his cock, stroking it back and forth. "Help me out, will you?"

"Not that way," Tom said and sank to his knees. The man's cock was slightly musty tasting and Tom thought it was exactly what he needed after all that rich food. The man put his hands on the back of Tom's head and urged him on, pulling him in tight against his crotch. He had very large balls and Tom could feel them against his chin. It was enough to make him hard again.

"Oh, yeah. Oh, yeah. That's the way. Right there. Right there and I'll... " He came. There wasn't a lot of cum but what there was was slightly sweet with an overlay of salt. Tom kept sucking until the man pushed him away.

When Tom stood his dick was still sticking straight out of his suit pants, as hard as before. "Man," the driver said, "I remember when I could do that. Not so long ago, either." He held out his hand. "Come here."

Tom stood next to him but the man pulled him in front. Then he took Tom's dick in his hand and jacked him off. It took a little longer than the blow-job but not much. At the very end the man turned him so he was facing the cab. When Tom came the man laughed softly and said, "Let the guys at the garage figure *that* out." He milked Tom down and gently tucked his dick back in his pants. "Come on, guy, let's get you where you're goin."

. . . .

When Tom went into the well lighted lobby of his building he noticed that the knees of his suit pants were slightly damp and very dirty. He knew he'd have to change before his dad saw him. He was in luck. When he entered the apartment he saw a light on in the little den which opened into the living room. His dad couldn't see the front hall from there.

"That you, Tom?"

"Yeah, it's me."

"Hey, I'm having a little brandy. You want some?"

"Yes, please. I'm going to change. Be there in a minute."

He stripped, put on a pair of jeans and a tee shirt and rolled his suit up and tossed it on the bottom of his closet. Thank God he had another suit to wear tomorrow but he'd have to stop by the cleaners on his way to work. He had a sudden thrill from the thought that he would be going to work. Not school. After all these years, he'd actually be going to work.

When he walked into the den his dad handed him a snifter of brandy. "How'd it go?"

Tom took a sip of the brandy and found it a bit harsher than the brandy he'd had with his coffee after dinner. "Good. I'm pretty sure I got the job."

"Pretty sure?" his dad laughed.

"Well, he had his... his girlfriend, I guess, there and we never did talk about the job. But when he got me a cab he said they start at eight-thirty and not to be late. So I guess I got the job."

"You have any idea what you'll be doing? Or, for that matter, how much they'll be paying you?"

Tom shook his head. "We didn't talk about any of that. He just said to be on time."

"So what did you talk about?"

Tom sipped his brandy and wondered just what they *had* talked about. He couldn't think of much. "I don't know. The mayor, the landscaping in Union Square, accents. A lot of stuff. Just not the job."

His dad laughed again. "Sounds like some sort of nut case. Don't be too disappointed if it all comes to nothing."

"I won't," Tom said with a sigh. "I've already thought about that." He looked up at his dad. "But I did get an awfully good dinner out of it. What'd you have?"

His dad grinned. "I splurged. Corn beef hash out of a can. I did fry up a couple of eggs to put on top of it, just to make it festive."

They spent the next quarter hour speculating on Tom's new job and then called it a night.

CHAPTER 3

The next morning Tom, in his second best—and only other—suit was standing in front of 154 Sutter Street at ten minutes after eight. A sign on the glass door said that the building didn't open until eight-thirty and the door was locked. Tom couldn't think of anything else to do so he just stood there, checking his watch about every thirty seconds. Finally, at eight-twenty, Mr. Simms arrived.

"Got the job, did you?" he asked, unlocking the door. "I kind of thought you would." He opened the door and ushered Tom in. "You'll need a key. See Miss West for that." He pushed the elevator button and the doors opened. They got in and he pushed Six. "Mr. Diggs is probably in by now so you had better go and see him first." The doors opened and Mr. Simms pointed down the hall, in the opposite direction from his office. "Yes, he's in. The lights are on. Go on down and I'll probably see you this afternoon." He strode off in the direction of his office, leaving Tom no choice but to head down the hall towards the door with the light coming through its glass pane.

When he knocked a voice yelled for him to enter.

"Well, well," Mr. Diggs said from behind his desk. "Here comes my assistant. And on time, too."

Ton nodded and said, "Good morning Sir."

Mr. Diggs sighed deeply and pointed to a chair in front of his desk. "You know, Thomas, I haven't the foggiest notion what I'm supposed to do with you. They, Simms and that secretary of his, decided that I needed an assistant so here you are."

Tom decided to take the bull by the horns. "Why? I mean, why me?"

Mr. Diggs smiled at him. "Well, to begin with, you're very pleasant company at the dinner table. You speak well and you have excellent manners. You meet people well. And Miss Winters likes you. I cannot think of a better recommendation."

Tom smiled. "I liked her, too. She's very witty."

Mr. Diggs smiled back. "And can eat and drink both of us under the table. You forgot that part."

Tom blushed and nodded. "But she's pretty, too."

Mr. Diggs waived the comment aside with, "So are a lot of women. Now, what to do with you." He dug through some papers on his desk, pulled up a file folder and thrust it at Tom. "Here. Call this SOB and tell him his offer is a crock of... a crock. Tell him..."

Tom, looking through the folder, interrupted. "You can say that around me, you know. They said it all the time at the college."

Mr. Diggs looked confused. "Said what?"

"That the offer is a crock of shit." He looked at the cover sheet in the folder. "And by the look of this I'd say it probably *is* a crock of shit."

Mr. Diggs threw back his head and laughed. "I think we're going to get along just fine, Thomas" he said, wiping his eyes. "We've had these so called 'sensitive' women around here for so long that it's just an automatic response." He stopped for a moment, thinking. "Okay, I can say things like that to you and you can say them to me but we must never, and I mean never, use words like that in the presence of any of the women who work here. And especially not in the hearing of Miss West or Miss Lynn."

"Miss Lynn?"

"Oh, she's my secretary. She should be in soon. Now go in there," he pointed at a door on his left, "and call the son-of-a-bitch." He paused for just a second. "Oh, yeah, that's your office. Do what you want with it. But get this guy off my back."

The office was more like a large closet and was furnished with a banged up gray metal desk, a wooden desk chair, a telephone and, oddly, a large rubber plant which stood directly in front of the small window, blocking much of the light.

Tom blew some dust off the desk and sat down to read the folder. He quickly figured out that the problem centered around a warehouse owned by a man named Edward Traxler. Another man, William Fall, wanted to lease the warehouse for four years at $8,400 a year. Mr. Traxler, on the other hand, wanted to lease it out for five years at $12,000 a year. There were some penciled notes on the last page, one of which indicated that Mr. Traxler probably would come down a thousand but certainly not $3,600.

Tom sighed, picked up the phone and called Mr. Fall's office. A man who identified himself as Chuck answered the phone and, after Tom had introduced himself, asked what the call was about. When Tom explained the man snorted and said, "I told Bill that offer was a crock of shit but the son-of-a-bitch insisted. What'll they take?"

Tom mentally shrugged and set sail on the uncertain seas of embellishment. "Well, Ed seems to think maybe he *is* just a little high and I agree with him. I managed to get him down a bit but not as much as I'd like."

"Bottom line?"

"$11,000 a year which isn't all that bad for that building. The part you won't like is Ed wants a five year lease. But look, you guys are doing well and in four years you'll be screaming to get that building for eleven-thousand. On top of that, you won't be moving all your stuff out in four years."

"That's it?"

"Yeah. That's it, Chuck. I tried my best."

There was a loud sigh. "I know you did. Let me talk with Bill and see what we can do. I'll call you later."

When Tom took the file back to Mr. Diggs and told him someone would call back, he was sent to lunch. "No point in hanging around here, Thomas. Go have a nice lunch while I try to figure out something else for you to do."

Tom had no idea where he should go for lunch and besides, it was early and he wasn't hungry. He walked around for a while, admiring the men, both young and old, on the street. He thought this might be the best part of the day, walking around and having little fantasies about the more interesting men.

Back at the office he went in to his little space and wondered what to do. Mr. Diggs's door was closed and Tom figured that meant he didn't want to be disturbed so he sat down at his desk and looked out the window. Suddenly there was a sharp rap on the door and Miss West stuck her head in. "Mr. Simms would like to see you as soon as you're free."

At Miss West's desk Tom filled out some more papers and signed up for the office coffee club. Miss West explained how that worked and promised him that his first week would be free. After that it would cost a dollar every week for all the coffee he could drink. Then she sent him in to see Mr. Simms.

In Mr. Simms office Tom was invited to sit and was again offered the cigarette box. He again declined. Mr. Simms selected one, lit it, smiled at him and said, "You must be doing something right, Mr. Braden. You've hardly started and you already have a twenty dollar raise. Mr. Diggs insisted."

"Uh... What *is* my salary, Sir? We haven't discussed that yet."

Mr. Simms laughed. "So we haven't. I guess Mr. Diggs and I each thought the other had done that. Well son, you were to be paid $480 a month but that is now changed to $500 a month."

Tom managed not to let his mouth drop open. He had hoped for $100 a week but certainly didn't expect this. He thanked Mr. Simms profusely and asked why he was getting the raise.

"I have no idea," Mr. Simms said. "Mr. Diggs often does things without telling us why. Between you and me, he's very good at moving real estate so we generally let him get away with it. Part of your job is to make sure he has good reason for the things he does."

When he got back to Mr. Diggs office there was a redheaded lady sitting at the desk by the door. "Oh, you must be Mr. Braden," she said, standing and extending her hand. "I'm Miss Lynn. Oh, but you may call me Susan. I guess I'm not as formal as the others here. Mr. Diggs said he wants you to see him as soon as you get back."

"Call me Tom, will you? I'm not at all used to the formality around here."

She smiled. "You'll get used to it. I did, but it took a while. Now, Tom, go see Mr. Diggs."

Mr. Diggs greeted him with a smile. "How'd the conversation with Bill Fall go?"

A little light suddenly went off in Tom's head. He laughed. "You know darn well how it went."

Mr. Diggs tried to look stern but couldn't pull it off. "I've gotta be careful with you, Thomas. You see through me too well." He leaned back in his chair. "Okay, how'd you do it? And do you really know Ed Traxler?"

Tom shook his head. "First, you tell me what you know."

"Well, for starters, Bill took the place, five year lease and all. Next, you don't really know this Traxler guy, do you?"

"Well, I'll be damned. They really took it?"

Mr. Diggs nodded. "So how'd you do it?"

Tom explained the conversation he'd had with Chuck. "And I didn't actually say I knew this Mr. Traxler. I just said that "Ed" would come down a thousand. It was right there in the file." He laughed. "You know what? That Chuck guy? The one I spoke to? He thought the original offer was a crock of shit too." He looked Mr. Diggs in the eye. "Does this have anything to do with a certain twenty dollar raise?"

Mr. Diggs laughed. "It has everything to do with it." He stood and offered his hand. "Congratulations, Thomas, and welcome to the wonderful world of real estate."

The rest of the day was spent in the files, reviewing them and assigning some of them to Tom. Quite a few of them, actually. Tom couldn't rent or sell any property because he wasn't licensed but he could follow up on things and do research. Since San Francisco and its history were a special interest of Tom's, he really looked forward to the research part. In any case, he had his work cut out for him and by five o'clock he was pretty well exhausted.

Things got easier as the weeks passed and Mr. Diggs was very pleased with him. The other people in the office found him easy to get along with and appreciated his sense of humor. They also appreciated the way he was helping Mr. Diggs because that made Mr. Diggs so much easier to work with.

Tom found time for a bit of a life, too. In June Mario's aunt went stay with her friend in Marin for a couple of weeks and Tom and Mario spent a lot of the time when neither of them was working, in bed. Tom also went back to the Hideaway several times in search of the redheaded bartender but never did find him. Someone told him that bartenders were like that, moving from job to job as the mood struck them.

He did find someone at the Hideaway though: Dr. Worthington, who took him home and showed him how much fun sex with a middle-aged college professor could be. They repeated the lesson several times over the summer.

Tom's dad seemed to think that it was good for Tom to be out sowing his wild oats. They talked about it one night over dinner and he cautioned Tom to get regular check-ups with Dr. Norris and asked him point blank if he was using condoms every time. Tom smiled and assured him that there was no chance of his getting anyone pregnant. He did not, however, specify exactly why there was no chance of pregnancy.

Matt also told Tom that it would be okay with him if Tom wanted to bring someone home some night. Tom said he thought that might be a little awkward for the other person. He did assure his dad that it would be okay if *he* wanted to bring someone home.

"I tell you what, Tom. Let's just keep this," he waived his arm, indicating the whole of the apartment, "for ourselves. If we need to change that, we will, but in the meantime…" he shrugged.

They also agreed to let each other know if one of them planned not to come home so that neither would worry.

The biggest event in Tom's young life occurred early on a foggy August Monday morning. When the cable car got to Vallejo Street, Tom climbed up on the running board at the front of the car. It was crowded, even on the side-facing bench and Tom found himself standing between the legs of the man in the first seat. He nodded at the man and the man smiled in return. In the middle of the block the car gave a jerk as the gripman avoided a car making an illegal U turn. The jerk threw Tom forward, pressing him up against the pole he was hanging on to.

"Don't move," the man in the seat said quietly. "Your heat feels good."

Tom realized that the man's hand was sandwiched between his crotch and the pole. When Tom didn't move the man slowly turned his hand over, cupping Tom's balls. As the ride progressed, the man's hand gently moved until it was holding Tom's dick, giving it gentle squeezes.

Once Tom realized that no one could see what was going on he began to enjoy the little squeezes and quickly got hard. By the time the man removed his hand Tom was on the verge of orgasm.

The man smiled at Tom and said it was his stop. Tom looked around and realized it was his, too. They got off and walked to the curb together, Tom doing his best to hide his erection. "Charlie Higgins," the man said, extending his hand.

Tom shook the offered hand. "Tom," he said. "Tom Braden."

"Glad to know you, Tom. That's quite a piece you're carrying there. Sure would like to get it out, into the light."

Tom glanced at the man's crotch and saw that he had an erection himself. "I'd like to see yours, too. Maybe... Well, you know."

"Yeah, I do know. Do you have a lunch hour?"

Tom hoped he knew where this was leading. "Sure. Twelve-thirty to one-thirty."

"You free today?" When Tom nodded the man said, "You know that sandwich shop on Kearny and Pine?"

Tom nodded. "They make great egg-salad."

"That's the place. Meet me there as soon after twelve-thirty as you can." He grinned. "I know a place." He looked at his watch. "I gotta go. Got a meeting five minutes ago. You'll be there?"

Tom nodded. "I'll be there."

Tom stayed half hard all morning, thinking about what might happen at noon. Unfortunately, Mr. Diggs was in a black mood and even yelled at Tom although he apologized for it later, saying that he had a dreadful headache. Finally, about twelve-fifteen, Mr. Diggs told him to go to lunch. Since Tom couldn't concentrate on anything anyway, he did just that. It took him ten minutes to walk to Kearny and Pine and all the way he worried that the man, Charlie, wouldn't be there.

Charlie was there. Standing in front of the sandwich shop, pretending to read the menu posted in the window but actually scanning the reflection of the street behind him, watching for Tom.

"Well, well. You showed up." He smiled and put a hand familiarly on Tom's shoulder.

Tom nodded, wondering if Charlie had been thinking about this all morning too.

Charlie guided him towards the doorway next to the sandwich shop. Faded letters over the six mailboxes spelled out *323 Kearny Street. No Vacancy.* Charlie pulled out a key and opened the door.

As they were climbing the stairs they were greeted by a man about Charlie's age who was leading a guy about Tom's age down the stairs.

"Hey, Joe," Charlie said. "Anyone up there?"

The man on the stairs shook his head. "It's all yours. Jimmy and I were the last ones out." He smiled and looked Tom up and down and winked at Charlie. "Have a good time." He and Jimmy passed them and hurried down the stairs.

On the second floor landing Charlie opened a door marked *Apt. 2A.* "Here we are," he said, taking Tom's hand and pulling him into what looked like his aunt's parlor back in Des Moines.

Inside, Charlie pulled Tom into a tight hug, rubbing his crotch against Tom's. "Oh, yeah," he said, slipping his hand between them, tracing Tom's erection. He pulled back and looked Tom in the eye. "I gotta see that thing," he said, "see all of you. Naked."

He loosened Tom's tie, leaving it tucked under Tom's shirt collar. Then he slowly unbuttoned Tom's shirt. When Tom put his hand on Charlie's crotch Charlie gently lifted it away and pulled Tom into another hug. "Not yet," he whispered. "Please." He licked Tom's ear. "Just let me get you naked, taste you. Then, if you want…"

Tom hugged him back and let him do as he wanted.

When he got Tom's shirt off Charlie carefully hung it on the back of a chair. Next he sat Tom in the chair and removed his shoes. When they were gone he looked up at Tom. "Can we take these off, too?" he asked, pulling a little at Tom's socks, "or are you one of those guys who has to keep them on, can't get really naked?"

Tom smiled, enjoying the attention. "No. When I'm naked I want to be really naked."

"My kind of man," Charlie said, slipping the socks off and laying them over the shoes. "Stand up."

Tom did and Charlie stayed on his knees, fumbling at Tom's belt. When that was undone he unbuttoned the pants and then slowly pulled the zipper down, being careful not to touch the bulge of Tom's dick. Charlie indicated Tom was to raise one foot, then the other, so he could remove the pants which he carefully laid on the chair. Then he stood and slowly walked around Tom.

Tom, who was wearing his usual standard issue white boxers, made something of a picture, his hard dick straining at the thin fabric which caused the fabric to be pulled tight against his ass. "Beautiful," Charlie said when he'd completed the circuit. Then he reached out and took hold of the waistband. "May I?"

Tom nodded and Charlie got on his knees again and slowly pulled the boxers down. When Tom's dick was freed it snapped up, hitting Charlie in the chin. Charlie took it in his mouth, all of it, although he did choke just a little getting the last of it into his throat. He stayed that way for a long time, tracing the shaft with his tongue and swallowing on the head, until Tom pulled back a little, afraid Charlie would pass out from lack of oxygen.

Charlie did take several deep breaths and then cupped Tom's ass and pulled him forward, again taking in all that Tom had.

This was almost too much for Tom. He felt his balls pulling up tight and knew he was about to come. He patted Charlie on the head, trying to let him know. However, Tom's orgasm was sidetracked by the sound of a key in the door. It opened and a tall man walked in, arm in arm with a shorter, dark haired guy dressed in stained painter's overalls with no shirt under them.

"Charlie, you old reprobate! Couldn't even wait to get him into the bedroom?"

Charlie pulled off Tom and stood. "Could you? Look at him! Is that beautiful or what?"

Both the tall man and the guy in the overalls took a moment to look Tom over, although they both had the courtesy not to ask him to turn around. The tall man put out his hand. "Ray. And this is Stan. You are..."

"He's Tom," Charlie said. "We didn't expect company."

"Obviously," Ray said, not taking his eyes off Tom. "Still, company is here." He turned to Stan and grinned. "Shall we make ourselves comfortable in here and watch the show or," he gently patted Stan's ass, "shall we take the bedroom and get on with our own show?"

Stan nodded, looking intently at Tom's dick.

"I think you're right," Ray said. "This show's probably over for now, at least as far as we're concerned." He took Stan's hand and put it on his crotch.

"That give you any ideas about something we might do? Come on." He turned to Charlie. "Well, carry on. And don't worry about noise. Stan's a groaner too." With that they went through a door and closed it.

Charlie and Tom looked at each other for a few seconds before they both burst out laughing. When he caught his breath Tom said, "A second later and I couldn't have stopped. Wouldn't that have been a pretty picture?"

Charlie wiped his eyes. "And I wanted it so much." He looked at his watch. "But I guess the mood's broken, isn't it?" he asked, a little wistfully. He brightened. "But I could buy you a quick lunch. Maybe talk you into coming back sometime?"

Tom smiled and put his hand on Charlie's crotch. "Only if I can see this thing, see what I'm coming back to."

Charlie blushed but unzipped his pants and dug around inside, bringing out a nicely shaped dick and a large pair of balls. Tom took the balls in his hand and rolled them around in their sack. Then he took hold of the dick.

"I'm definitely coming back," he said. "At least if I'm invited."

Charlie let him dress himself and by the time Tom was tying his tie, Charlie, who hadn't put his dick or balls back in his pants, had a very stiff hard-on. He had some trouble getting it back in his pants, especially when Tom tried to help him. Finally Charley pushed his hands away, saying, "Stop that! Meet me here Wednesday and you can play with it all you want."

True to his word, Charlie bought lunch in the sandwich shop and they ate, sitting on the low wall of a nearby building. After, they agreed to meet on Wednesday, at lunch time.

When Tom got back to the office Susan told him that Mr. Diggs had gone for the day, saying his headache was worse. Her personal opinion was that he was coming down with something and probably wouldn't be in the next day either.

That night when Tom went to bed all he could think about was Charlie, running his tongue along the shaft of his dick and swallowing on the head. As a consequence, his nightly jack-off session was very short, very pleasurable and hugely messy. He didn't care. He just rolled over and drifted off to sleep, enjoying the last shocks of his orgasm.

. . . .

When he got to the office the next day Mr. Diggs wasn't in yet and Tom took the opportunity to cleanup and organize his desk. Shortly after eight-thirty Susan came in and told him that, as she had predicted, Mr. Diggs would not be in. Seeing what Tom was doing, she was just slightly horrified. "He told me never to touch anything on his desk and if I did he'd kill me!" She grinned at Tom. "I think he'd probably just fire me but with him…" She shrugged. "You never know."

Tom laughed. "Well, let him do his worst. I take full responsibility for what we're about to do."

They spent the rest of the morning going through files and the other papers on the desk. More than once Susan said, "So *that's* where that file went. We've been looking for it for a couple of weeks now."

By Susan's lunch time they had most of the paper on the desk in labeled stacks and a goodly number of the actual files back in their proper drawers. "You going to lunch?" Susan asked.

"No, I want to go through some more of these notes. Just bring me back something, okay?" He dug out his wallet and gave her some money.

"I'm going for Chinese with some girl friends. How about some Spring Rolls or fried won-ton?"

Tom thought for a moment. "No, just bring me a container of wor won-ton soup. The kind with shrimp."

"Done," she said, picking up her purse and patting her hair into place.

Tom settled down behind Mr. Diggs desk and began going through the stacks of paper, trying to fit each one with a file or project. It was a tedious job but it had its rewards, too. Several of the neatly handwritten notes actually completed a file so that all that it lacked was a phone call and a signature and perhaps filing a form with the county.

Susan brought him exactly what he had wanted and he savored it while filling out some of the forms that would need to be notarized or filed with some county agency. When Susan came into the office and announced that it was quitting time Tom simply nodded and said, "Yeah, I'll be along."

At seven o'clock he thought to phone his dad. He said he'd be home in a half hour and his dad suggested he stop on the way and pick up something for them to eat.

When Tom got home he was carrying freshly cooked pasta and two cartons of various sauces. Over dinner at the kitchen table, Tom told his dad that he had decided he had to get his real-estate license if he was really going to be useful to the company and especially to Mr. Diggs.

"Well," his dad said, grating a little more cheese on his linguine and meat sauce, "a couple of the guys in my office are licensed in real estate. Let me ask around, see how difficult it is to get and if there's a school or something. You going to pay for it if you have to take a class?"

"I suppose so, Dad. I can't very well ask the company to do it. It's not really part of my job. Besides, Mr. Diggs told me you have to be there a year before they'll even consider it."

His dad laughed. "Actually, that makes sense. Why pay for schooling some guy who's just going to turn around and go to another firm? Anyway, I'll ask around the office. Now, speaking of your job, you need some new clothes. I've noticed that what you call your 'good suit' is getting pretty threadbare and the other one is simply a disgrace. What say we go over to David-Stephan's Saturday morning and get you some decent clothes?"

"Dad, I can't afford to buy clothes in the same stores you do! I'll bet one suit would set me back two weeks salary. No, I do need some clothes but I think I'll have to go back to J.C. Penny."

His dad grinned. "I figured you'd say something like that. How about if you let me pay for them and you pay me back, say twenty-five dollars a week? And it's a good time to shop there. They're having a sale starting Saturday. Okay?"

Tom thought about it and then nodded. "Okay. It's a date."

Later, in bed, Tom decided he'd just go to sleep, not jack-off and take the edge off his anticipation. Or maybe he should, he thought, so he wouldn't be so anxious tomorrow. Then he started worrying that Charlie wouldn't show up. He finally fell asleep on that one and his body took care of itself by giving him a wet dream.

CHAPTER 4

In the morning he found the wet dream had done little to take the edge off his anticipation. If anything, it had honed it to a new sharpness.

He did manage to get some actual work done in the office and was able to take two files down to Mr. Simms office where Miss West said she'd have him sign the certificates as soon as he was free.

About twelve-fifteen he told Susan he was going to lunch and might be a little bit late coming back. She thought that was a good idea after the hours he'd worked the day before.

When he got to the sandwich shop his worries about Charlie not showing up were shown to be pointless. There was Charlie, in front of the sandwich shop window, pacing back and forth. "There you are," he said, putting his hand lightly on Tom's shoulder when Tom walked up. "I was afraid you might forget or something."

Tom laughed. "I was afraid of the same thing, only about you."

Charlie smiled and dug his keys out. "Just shows how anxious we are. Come on, I checked as soon as I got here and the place is all ours. This time we'll take the bedroom and if anyone shows up they can have the little storeroom in the back, or the living room."

He opened the door and waived Tom in, ahead of him. Then, all the way up the stairs, he rested his hands on Tom's ass cheeks. Once in the apartment he lead Tom into the bedroom and closed the door.

From there on it went pretty much as it had on Monday, Charlie slowly undressing Tom and then kneeling in front of him and taking his dick into his mouth, pulling Tom into him by the buns until the dick slid into his throat.

This time there were no interruptions. When Tom warned Charlie that he was going to come, Charlie merely nodded which actually threw Tom into his orgasm. When it started, Charlie pulled back a little so he could work the head with his tongue and help prolong it. When it subsided Charlie stopped moving and simply held Tom quietly in his mouth.

After a minute or two Tom chuckled and said, "It's not going to go soft, if that's what you're waiting for. Not while it's in your mouth at least."

Charlie pulled off and stood. "Too bad. I've never seen it really soft. I'll bet it's kind of pretty that way, too."

Tom laughed. "What about last time, when that Ray guy came in. I got soft pretty fast then."

"No, you didn't. You were still hard when you put your pants back on."

Tom shook his head. "Well, if so, I was hard because you had yours sticking out of your pants and I was thinking about what it'd be like, playing with your balls. Now," he said, reaching for Charlie's zipper, "let's get them out again, see if they're as big as I remember."

They were. A few minutes later, on one of the beds, Tom looked up at Charlie from between his legs and said, "You have beautiful balls, Charlie." He nipped lightly at the smooth, almost hairless sack that contained them.

Charlie groaned and ran his fingers through Tom's hair. "They're yours any time you want to play with them." He groaned again as Tom ran his tongue over them and up the cock standing tall above them. "You can play with that, too. All you..." He sucked in his breath as Tom took it in his mouth and then was quiet except for an occasional "Oh, yes," or "there, there."

Tom prolonged it as long as he could, until Charlie, said, "Sorry Tom. I can't take it anymore, I gotta come, I just gotta." Charlie then held tom's head still and began thrusting slowly into his mouth. It took four strokes before Charlie went rigid, arched his back, let out a low growl and came.

When they were getting dressed, before Tom had put his pants on, Charlie reached out and petted Tom's dick. "You know," he said, "that thing really ought to have prettier underwear to live in." He laughed. "Something silken, maybe with crowns or something to show that he's royalty."

Tom smiled and groped Charlie. "Yours, too. It's a very handsome one."

"Maybe," Charlie said with a shrug. "But he's going to have to live in plain white. My wife buys all that stuff. I just wear it."

Maybe she doesn't think it's as pretty as I do, Tom thought, but didn't say.

"My problem, too," Tom said, "only it's my father who buys it." At Charlie's raised eyebrow he added, "He always has, ever since I was a boy and my mom passed away. And he always buys these," he held up his boxers. "I guess because they're what he wears."

Charlie, who considered himself a pretty good judge of character, looked at Tom and considered. *Oh, what the hell,* he thought. *Why not?* "Hey," he said, "you want to come back here? On Friday, I mean. Meet the rest of the guys, maybe fool around a bit?" His eyes fell and he shrugged. "I'd kind of like to show you off."

"The rest of the guys? You mean like that Ray and that guy, I forget his name, in the overalls?"

Charlie laughed. "Well, I can't speak for the overalls guy. Depends on if Ray brings him. See, there's four of us who rent this place. We use it for... Well, you know."

Tom scratched his head. "Four of you? Doesn't it get a little crowded sometimes. Like if all of you bring someone up, all at the same time?"

"Hasn't so far, and it's happened once or twice. We—we call ourselves The Renters—we're pretty friendly with one another and sometimes it's pretty much of a free-for-all. We sometimes trade guys," he laughed, "and the guys sometimes trade us." He put his hand on Tom's shoulder. "I'm telling you this because I think you're going to become one of the guys we see a lot of around here. That is, if you like this stuff as much as I think you do."

Tom laughed. "Oh, yeah, I love this stuff."

"I thought you were a pretty horny little stud. So will you come? Friday?"

Tom didn't hesitate. "When?"

"Someone's usually here a little before noon. Just buzz 2A. Someone will let you in." Charlie looked at his watch. "Shit. I'm late again. We gotta go."

Back in the office Tom continued with what he'd been doing that morning, making phone calls and completing files. By three-thirty he had four more ready for signatures and filing. When he took them down to Miss West, she handed him the two files he'd brought down just before lunch. "All signed. Mr. Simms said he'd been wondering about that one," she said, pointing at one of the folders with a well manicured index finger. She looked up at him. "I think it safe to say, young man, that Mr. Simms is quite pleased with your performance." She turned back to her typewriter, effectively dismissing him.

. . . .

The next day, Thursday, was more of the same except for two of the files. Both of those had seen fit to look for property with another firm. In both cases the men said they had simply given up hope of Mr. Diggs following through. Tom told each of them the same thing: the firm was very sorry to loose their business, he hoped everything would work out with their new relationship and that he, personally, stood ready to assist them in the future.

By the end of the day Tom felt he had everything on Mr. Diggs desk under control. He was tired but he was also a little apprehensive about what Mr. Diggs might think when he returned. After all, there *was* that warning Mr. Diggs had given to Susan. *Well,* he thought, *it's too late to undo it. We'll just have to see...*

Tom's dad was late getting home that evening so they decided to go out to eat. They went to Alioto's, on the wharf where they had wonderful clam chowder and sautéed sea bass. True to form, they skipped dessert in favor of a brandy. Over dinner Tom told his dad about what he'd been doing the past couple of days and wondered what Mr. Diggs would think about it.

"Well, Sport, if it was me, and if my assistant did what you say you've just done, I'd probably fire his ass." He grinned at Tom. "On the other hand, from what you've told me about Diggs, he might not even notice."

Tom shook his head. "Oh, he'll notice all right. He won't be able to miss it." He shrugged. "Well, we'll see."

. . . .

When Tom got to work the next day, Mr. Diggs was sitting behind his desk, looking a little pale. When Tom asked how he was feeling he waived the question away. "You do all this?" he asked, nodding at his desktop.

"Uh... Yeah."

Mr. Diggs smiled. "You, Thomas, are a man of magic." He looked at the wall, somewhere just above Tom's head. "Could you do this every... say, once a week? Friday afternoon, maybe?"

Tom grinned. "Sure. It won't take long, pulling it together once a week." Tom went on to explain about the two closed files, saying, "We'll get them back one day, though. I could hear it in their voices." He also told him about the files he'd sent to Mr. Simms for signature and the forms he'd filed on behalf of clients. The more he talked the more impressed Mr. Diggs was.

"So I don't have anything to do today, do I? Damn, I could have stayed in bed, which, of course, is where I belong." He thought for a long moment. "In fact, that's where I'm going. Right now. If you think you can hold this place together for the morning I'd appreciate it." He picked up the phone and pressed a button. "Miss West? Mr. Diggs. I'm going home. Thomas will be here all morning but will not in the afternoon. Miss Lynn will handle anything that comes up this afternoon. Good bye."

Tom looked at him quizzically. Mr. Diggs said, "You take the afternoon off, Thomas. It's a reward for this," his hand swept over the desk. "Now, if you'll excuse me, I feel like shit."

The morning went well. When she came in, Susan was amazed that not only was Tom still employed, but he had been given the afternoon off to boot.

It was twelve-fifteen before Tom finally gave in and told Susan he was going for the day. As he hurried down Sutter, toward Kearny, Tom wondered again just what he was getting himself into but by the time he turned up Kearny, towards Pine, he gave up on it and just let the anticipation wash over him.

When he got to the building he found Charlie standing in front of Whiskers. "I figured you might be along at the usual time," he said as he unlocked the downstairs door and ushered Tom up the stairs.

Inside the apartment were four other men, two about Charlie's age and the others Tom's age or a few years older. Charlie took care of the introductions.

"This is Ray," Charlie said, introducing the tall, well built man who had walked in on Tom and Charlie that first afternoon. Ray was sitting in one of the overstuffed chairs with the guy he'd been with earlier in the week sitting on his lap. The guy seemed to be wearing the same painter's pants he'd had on that Monday, although they did look to be just a little cleaner. He still had no shirt on.

"You'll excuse me for not getting up," Ray said, extending his hand. "And you remember Stan." It was obvious from Stan's look that *he* remembered *Tom*. Ray laughed. "And no, we're not connected. Yet."

The next man was introduced as Joe. He was shorter than Tom and had crew-cut gray hair and gold eyes that Tom thought were beautiful. He was pouring Coke into a glass, over ice. He paused and put out his hand. "Pleased to meet you, Tom. Ray has told me a lot about you—all of it good." He grinned. "Very good." He turned to a tall, willowy man who was emptying a bag of potato chips into a bowl. "This is my friend Jeffery."

Jeffery wiped his hands on a paper towel and shook Tom's. "Nice to meet you, Tom." He smiled and his eyes twinkled. "And I've heard nothing at all about you. Perhaps someday we can get together and I can find out."

"I have no doubt that will happen," said Charlie. "And I'm quite sure that the telling," he looked over at Jeffery and winked, "will be very pleasurable. It was for me."

Just then the door opened and two men carrying take-out boxes came in. "Food's arrived," said the shorter of the two, a dark haired man with blue eyes and a catching smile. Jeffery quickly cleared a space on the table and the men put the boxes down. The shorter man opened them and, pointing, said, "Whiskers' famous egg salad, rare roast beef and, by special request, ham and Swiss on sourdough."

"Who's the ham and Swiss for?" Ray asked.

"Why, it's for that young man sitting on your… " He raised an eyebrow. "You guys connected already?"

Ray shook his head and Stan, the young man on his lap, moved his butt around, as though settling into a firm but comfortable cushion. "Not yet," he said with a grin, "but I'm working on it." He turned to look at Ray. "And the ham and Swiss is for me." When Ray started to say something Stan gave him a quick kiss and said, "Don't ask." He turned back to the other man, "Thanks for remembering, Willie."

"And who might this be?" Charlie asked, nodding at the man with Willie."

"Oh, this is George. He drives a truck for UPS." He turned to the man. "George, this is Charlie. Over there, unable to get out of the chair for fear we'll all see the state his dick is in, is Ray and that's Stan in his lap."

George and Stan nodded to each other and it seemed to Tom that the look that passed between them held more than a simple 'hello.'

"And this is Tom," Charlie said, putting his arm around Tom's shoulder.

Tom nodded to the group and said, "Hi, guys." There were smiles all around, and a couple of winks.

"Okay," Willie said, holding out some paper plates. "Who's for something to eat?"

The men, with the exception of Ray and Stan gathered around the table and chose a sandwich and a soda. Stan stood and pulled Ray out of the chair. "In there," he said, pointing to the bedroom. "I'll bring you something."

Ray smiled. "Bring me a sandwich, too."

The men laughed and found places to sit. "Kind of anxious, isn't he?" George asked no one in particular.

"He's a good kid," Joe said with a laugh, "but he seems to be horny all the time, especially when he gets near Ray's cock."

"Aw, he just likes 'em big," Willie said. "Find him a bigger one and he'll be all over it."

"Then you better watch out, Tom," Charlie said, patting him on the thigh and laughing.

Joe and Willie both grinned at Charlie. "That true?"

Charlie smiled. "That's for me to know and for you guys to find out, huh Tom?"

Tom blushed and stammered something unintelligible. Charlie leaned over and gave him a kiss. "Don't be embarrassed, Tom. But if you stay around, they *will* find out." He looked around. "Right guys?"

There was a chorus of ascent and, if possible, Tom blushed even more.

Conversation was lively among the men but Tom and George mostly listened. Jeffery seemed more at ease with the older men and Tom figured he'd been with the group more than once.

After a while George looked at his watch and said to Willie, "If we're going to do what we came for, we have to get started. I still have deliveries to make, you know."

Willie nodded and stood, putting his plate on the table. To the group he said, "If you guys don't mind, we'll take the other bed for a while." He turned to George. "Think all that groaning will distract us?"

George grinned and pushed Willie toward the bedroom door. "Not me, it won't. And you'll be too busy to notice."

Charlie looked at the other men. "Well, I guess that leaves us out here, doesn't it?" He glanced up at the mantle clock. "And I have a meeting in about fifteen minutes so you guys can either watch or get with it yourselves." He turned to Tom, sitting next to him on the couch. "You okay with this? I mean, with them in the room, probably watching?"

Tom reached over and ran his hand over Charlie's crotch. "Let 'em watch if they want. What I want is right in here." He pulled Charlie's zipper down and reached inside, fumbling with his underwear. When he got Charlie's dick out he rolled off the couch, between Charlie's legs, and took him in his mouth.

"I... I thought..." Charlie stammered.

Tom looked up. "You're the one with the meeting," he said. At least that's what he meant to say but it came out kind of garbled since Charlie's dick was still in his mouth. Charlie didn't argue; he just ran his fingers through Tom's hair and groaned. Out of the corner of his eye Tom saw Joe and Jeffery openly watching and playing with each other. He mentally shrugged and went back to pleasing Charlie.

Ten minutes later, when he got up from between Charlie's legs, Charlie was a happy man. Tom tried to tuck Charlie's dick back in his pants but it was too sensitive and Charlie had to do it himself. When he was presentable again he kissed Tom and whispered in his ear, "Stick around and I'll bet someone will take pity on you" Then he was out the door.

A minute or so after Charlie left, Willie and George, the UPS driver, came out of the bedroom, both of them looking very self satisfied. "Have a good time?" Joe asked, still fondling Jeffery.

"Oh, man," said George, "did we ever. I want more of that," he said, running his hand over Willie's crotch. "Think it can be arranged?"

Willie laughed. "Now what do you think?"

"I think I have to go," George said, "if I want to keep my job."

They left together.

"Well," observed Joe, "I guess that leaves just us."

"Don't forget the guys in the bedroom," Jeffery said. "They've been at it for a while now."

"Staying power," Joe grinned. "Ray loves what he's doing and so does the kid. Want to go watch? Perhaps we three could find something to do while we watch the show." He put a hand on Tom's shoulder. "What do you think, Tom?"

Tom could only nod. He'd never been with two men at the same time. Added to that the idea of doing it with two others fucking on the next bed made his mouth go dry.

In the bedroom Stan was on his back with his knees resting on Ray's shoulders. Ray was stroking in him, long, slow strokes. Stan's eyes were closed and he moaned quietly every time Ray pushed into him. Ray grinned at them when they came in, never breaking his rhythm. Then he went back to kissing Stan.

Joe put Tom's hands on Jeffery and Jeffery's on Tom, indicating that they were to undress each other. While they did, he got out of his own clothes. When all three were naked he sat Tom and Jeffery close together on the edge of the bed where they had a good view of Ray and Stan. Then he dropped to his knees and began playing with them. He'd fondle one while he sucked on the other and then, after a minute, switch. Tom was afraid he'd come almost immediately but Joe was very good and kept him—and Jeffery—close to the edge but not close enough to fall over it.

It took almost half an hour and when it was over it was over for all five of them. "Oh, God, I'm going to come," someone had said and that seemed to set them all off. Even Joe, who wasn't being touched by anyone, came, spraying both Tom and Jeffery. Stan seemed to explode and was by far the noisiest of them all, yelping and groaning with abandon. Jeffery made some odd noises deep in his throat and grabbed Tom, kissing him hard. As Joe later told Charlie, "A good time was had by all."

Once everyone was on a even keel again, they made the beds and cleaned up the leavings from lunch. As they were getting dressed Stan pulled Tom into a hug, pressing his crotch into Tom's. "I gotta have that," he whispered in Tom's ear. "Please?"

Ray walked up to them and put his arms around both of them. "Don't worry, Stan. You'll get him one of these afternoons. Maybe both of us at the same time. You think you'd like that?" He patted Stan on the ass. "You think you could take them both up there? At the same time?" Stan nodded. "If you take it slow. Slow and gentle." Ray laughed. "That's the only way I know how to do it baby. Slow and gentle."

As they were leaving Joe stopped Tom at the door. "You want to do that again? Jeffery does." Tom nodded. "How about next Thursday? Noon?" Tom nodded again. Then they were out the door, each going his own direction.

Tom went home, stretched out on his bed and thought about what had just happened. The more he went over it in his mind the more he found he liked it. It had been pure sex. Sex for the sake of sex and nothing more. He wondered if he would ever be in bed with Ray and Stan, if Stan—or anyone for that matter—could actually take both him and Ray inside at the same time and how it could be done. He was going over the possible ways in his mind—and jacking off—when his father came home. He reluctantly put himself away and went out to the kitchen to have a beer with his dad.

"So," his dad said, ruffling up his hair, "you're home early. They fire you already?"

Tom grinned and explained that Mr. Diggs had given him the afternoon off for all the work he'd done.

His dad laughed. "Well, I still think if it was me I would have fired your ass but maybe I'm just too old fashioned. Maybe this is the coming thing, your assistant just sitting down and doing your job. Maybe *his* boss should fire *him*."

They went out to dinner that night, to a steak house they'd grown fond of. Over dinner Tom's dad told him he'd talked to some of the men in his office and, to a man, they'd recommended a place called *Coit Real Estate*. "It's expensive," he said, "but fast and they guarantee you'll get your license or they'll provide a personal tutor until you do get it. All the guys got their licenses on the first pass and Jerry said after the course the exam seemed easy."

"How expensive?"

"A hundred dollars." Seeing Tom's expression he added, "But I got you a fifteen percent discount."

Tom took a deep breath. "That's still a lot of money."

His dad grinned. "I figured you'd balk at it so I already signed you up. Your first class is next Wednesday, six to ten at the Russ Building. Now, you want dessert or a brandy?"

They both opted for brandy.

Chapter 5

. . . .

The next day Matt insisted that they get to the clothing store when it opened at ten. "When David-Stephan's has its' once a year sale, it's an event."

While they weren't the first through the door, once inside they were spotted by Mark, the salesman Matt always went to. Matt introduced Tom as his son. "He needs some work clothes and you're was the only one I trust to help him find the right things."

Mark, who was tall, dark and had a face which reminded Tom of the young Superman, took Tom on a tour of the store and asked a lot of questions about his job. Then he took Tom into a fitting room. "Okay," he said when they were in the room, "peel down to your skivvies and let's have a look at you."

Tom was a little hesitant but did as he was told. When he was clad only in his boxers Mark slowly walked around him. "You'll be easy to fit," Mark said when he finished his tour of Tom. "I'd say you're pretty much a classic 38 regular. You need shirts and stuff too?"

"No. Just a suit."

"You also need prettier underwear, but then, so does your dad. Well, we'll talk about that later. Excuse me and I'll go gather a few things."

When he came back he was carrying a half dozen suits. He had Tom try them on, one by one. As far as Tom could tell, they all fit, they were all nice looking and they were all expensive. He finally held one up. "This one."

Mark laughed out loud. "That's exactly what your father said you'd say. He also asked me to get him when you'd decided. Is it okay for him to come in?"

Tom sighed. "I guess. He's seen me in the buff often enough so he might as well see me in my underwear."

When he came in the fitting room, Matt asked Mark which suit Tom had picked. He nodded when he saw it and said, "Okay, now which ones fit?"

Mark smiled. "Pretty much all of them."

Matt looked at them one by one and set four of them aside. "Okay, he'll have the one he picked out along with these. And don't listen to him when he begins to whine. He needs them and he's going to get them." He grinned at Tom and left the fitting room.

Mark looked at Tom and shrugged. "Shall I get the tailor to mark the cuffs?"

When the fitting was done Mark told Tom he could pickup the suits on Thursday.

Leaving the store Matt began to laugh. "You'll thank me for that, Tom. And even if you don't, your Mr. Diggs will. Now come on. Let's go get a burger and a beer. You look like you could use one.

. . . .

On Wednesday evening Tom started real estate school. As he looked around the room he saw that all of the other men were older, well dressed and looked hungry. Some were also rather handsome and he thought he'd like to get to know several of them.

When the teacher stepped up to the front of the room he said, with a sly smile, that the course was going to be demanding and he expected the students to think things through before jumping in with an answer. The material was complex from the very beginning but Tom had the advantage of having recently been in college. On the other hand, he had the disadvantage of having very little practical experience.

The classes, the teacher explained, would be four hours tonight and Friday night, three hours each on Monday, Wednesday and Friday of the next week. The licensing exam would be a week from Saturday. They'd be given four hours to complete the examination.

The class went rapidly and Tom was quite surprised when the teacher passed out the homework assignment and announced that class was over. There'd been a lot to absorb but Tom had found it interesting and, actually quite enjoyable.

Thursday morning was very busy at the office and Mr. Diggs seemed more disorganized than usual so Tom had very little time to think about what might happen on his lunch hour. Once out of the office and on his way to Kearny Street, however, he was hard almost at once thinking about what could happen.

He'd expected to see Joe or Jeffery waiting in front of Whiskers but neither of them was there. Remembering what Charlie had said, he went to the doorway next to Whiskers and pressed the button underneath the mailbox for Apartment 2A. Almost immediately the door buzzed so he went in and up the stairs. When he knocked on the door to Apartment 2A it was opened by a very naked Jeffery.

"In there," Jeffery said, kissing Tom and then pointing to the bedroom. In the bedroom was an equally naked Joe, lying on the bed.

"Hey," said Joe, with a grin, "you have to be naked to join this party."

Tom pulled his clothes off and laid them out on the other bed, next to Joe's and Jeffery's and then crawled in between them.

For the next hour they played, eventually ending up with Tom behind Jeffery, filling him, while Jeffery and Joe took a classic sixty-nine position. Jeffery came first and his contractions finished Tom off. Joe didn't take much longer, especially with Tom playing with his balls.

Dressed and ready to leave, Jeffery said, "That was great, guys. It would only have been better if we had more time."

Joe laughed. "We'll get you up here on a Wednesday or Friday sometime when we all have the afternoon off. Sometimes everyone's here with someone." His eyes took on a twinkle. "What would really be fun would be to throw a mattress or two on the floor and all of us get on it and everybody play with everybody."

"Count me in!" Jeffery said with a grin.

"Me too," Tom said. I'd love to try a group thing."

Joe ushered them out of the apartment. "I'll talk to the guys about it, see what we can arrange."

When Tom got home that evening he was carrying five suit bags and a shopping bag from David-Stephan's. "Hey, you got your clothes, huh?" his father said when he came through the door.

"Yeah, and a present. One for you, one for me."

"What…"

Tom shrugged. "Mark just handed me this," he held up the shopping bag, "and said half of it is for you. On the house since we're such good customers."

Matt laughed. "Well, let's see what he's up to."

Tom reached into the bag and found underwear, ten pair, in bright, jewel like colors. They seemed to be made of silk. "Well, I guess he wasn't kidding," Tom said.

"Kidding?"

Tom grinned. "Mark said we, both of us, need prettier underwear. I guess this is his way of taking care of the problem." He laughed. "Did he ever say that to you?"

Matt thought for a minuet. "Yeah, I guess he did, once. I didn't think much about it." He sorted through the packages. "So I guess we each get one of each color, huh? One pair for each day of the week?" He looked at Tom and laughed. "What does he think, we don't wear underwear on the weekend?"

"Maybe. Anyway, it was nice of him, to give us these."

"Yeah, it was. We should send him a thank-you note. I'll take care of it in the morning."

After dinner Tom hit the books. There was no way he was going to be unprepared for class the next night.

Tom wore one of his new suits to work on Friday, with a pair of the "pretty" underwear. Mr. Diggs only comment was, "New suit?"

Sue was a little more effusive. "Neat suit, Tom. Looks expensive." She fingered the coat. "Oh, I love material like that. And it doesn't get dirty fast." She stood back and looked him up and down. "Good fit. Looks like it was made for you. Wait until Barbara sees it. Mr. Simms is going to think they pay you too much!"

Tom wondered what she'd say if she knew about the sapphire blue silk shorts he was wearing under the suit. *On the other hand,* he thought, *maybe I don't want to know!*

That afternoon Tom straightened up Mr. Diggs desk while he was at a meeting. He found three folders he'd been looking for and completed two of them. When he saw what Tom had done, Mr. Diggs was a happy man.

Real estate class that evening was, if anything, tougher than the one before. But Tom got through it and felt he was making real headway learning the material.

Saturday morning, over breakfast, Matt asked him if he'd worn a pair of the new underwear the day before.

"Yeah, Dad. Didn't you?"

"Yeah." There was a long pause. "Did you notice... Did they feel... uh, different to you?"

"What do you mean, Dad? Different."

His father sighed. "Well, I guess you young studs don't notice how often you... Or maybe you don't care, but the silky, cool cloth against... me... "

Tom suddenly understood and broke into a huge grin. "They gave you an erection, didn't they? That cool, silky cloth, against your dick." He laughed. "Did the secretaries all shriek and avert their eyes?"

Matt finally laughed. "Not hardly. But I was a little uncomfortable a couple of times. I really like them and I know I'll get used to them but what do I do in the meantime? I can't sit behind my desk all the time."

"I know," Tom said, suddenly serious. "It can be a problem. Even for young studs like me. My advice? Always carry a file folder with you. Not one you have to get into. And move around. The more you let nature take it's course, the faster you'll get used to them."

"That how you deal with it?"

"Yeah, but it's not actually bad for me. Not like when I was still in high school."

"What'd you do then?"

Tom smiled. "Mostly I went in the boy's bathroom and jacked, uh, masturbated."

Matt raised an eyebrow. "That's okay. I know what jacked-off means. But in school? Wasn't that... I don't know, dangerous?"

"Nah. All the guys did it. We mostly didn't talk about it but we all knew we all did it."

Matt grinned. "Well, I don't think that'll work for me. I mean..."

"Dad, do you really think the guys in your office don't go into the men's room sometimes, just for a quickie hand-job? I'll bet they do, most of them."

"Well, I'm not going to be one of them. But I do like the idea of the file folder. Thanks for your expertise."

. . . .

The next week went by rather quickly for Tom. He had the real estate class Monday, Wednesday and Friday and he had to study hard before each class. The licensing exam, on Saturday, was coming up fast. Then, too, things were happening at the office and Tom had to spend a lot of time shepherding the paperwork through the office to keep Mr. Diggs from losing it on his desk. By the time he got into bed each night, he was too tired to engage in his nightly pleasure.

But it paid off. The Saturday licensing exam went like a well rehearsed play; answers came easily to Tom and he was finished early. So early, in fact, that he had time to go over the entire thing again. He made very few changes to his original answers. He was pretty sure he'd aced the whole thing.

When he got home, his dad, who'd had a pretty good day himself, grilled lamb chops for dinner. He served them with tiny red potatoes in garlic butter with parsley, and a green salad. At dinner Matt asked Tom what he had planned for Sunday.

"Not much," Tom said. "Sleep, mostly."

"Good for you. After the work you put in this week, you deserve it." Matt sipped his wine and grinned. "You'll have peace and quiet, too. I've got to be out with a potential client most of the day. Tell you what, though. Let's plan to have dinner at Giordano's, okay? To celebrate getting through this thing."

"Sounds good, Dad. Hey, maybe they'll have those little steamed clams that are so good."

Tom did, in fact, sleep late the next day, finally getting out of bed and into the shower near noon. When he woke he found himself both very hard and very horny. He played with his dick for a few moments but quickly realized that that wasn't going to do it for him. He needed a man.

Showered and dressed he went he went out to see what he could find. It was a clear, warm day and he decided to walk over to a small park near the waterfront and see if there was anyone there who might be in the same mood as he was.

On the way he stopped at a little coffee shop and had coffee and a sandwich. Sitting at the counter, he made eye contact with a man sitting two stools away. The man smiled at him and he smiled back. They held each other's gaze until it became obvious to both of them that each was looking for the same thing.

The man finished his coffee and went to the cash register to pay. As he passed Tom he said, "You about ready?"

Tom nodded, pushed his plate away, grabbed his check and followed the man to the register. "You have a place?" Tom asked, standing close enough for their thighs to touch.

The man turned and grinned. "Yeah, just up the street a ways."

Tom paid his check and nodded. "That's good. I'd hate to miss out on this."

The man laughed and put out his hand. "I'm Clifford," he said, holding the handshake a bit longer than strictly necessary. "I'd hate to miss out on it, too."

As they left the guy behind the counter laughed and said, "Have a good time, boys."

Outside Tom introduced himself. "I'm Tom," he said, "what brings you out on such a pretty day?"

Clifford turned to look at him. "The truth? I'm horny."

Tom laughed. "Me, too. It's about all I can think about."

"We're a matched pair. This way, up the hill. Oh, and I'm Clifford but call me Cliff, okay?"

As they walked they talked about what each of them liked to do in bed. It turned out there was just about nothing either one of them *didn't* like to do and talking about it made them even hornier. When they got inside Cliff's apartment they were both so excited that Tom hardly even noticed all the Chinese furniture.

Naked and on the bed, they easily fell into a classic sixty-nine and, by unspoken agreement, brought each other off with no finesse, no artfulness, nothing but sheer lust. It took about three minutes and it wasn't the best orgasm either of them had ever had. But it *was* an orgasm and it got them over their need for immediate relief.

After, lying together, touching from leg to shoulder, Cliff said, "Now that that's done, we can take the next one slow and easy. You smoke?"

Tom shook his head. "But go ahead," he said. I kind of like the smell on a guy's skin." He leaned over and kissed Cliff. "And the way he tastes."

Cliff pulled back and looked at him. "You too, huh?"

"Me too what?"

"Nothing," Cliff said. "I just remembered someone who said that same thing. About the way a smoker's skin tastes and smells." He waived his hand, dismissing the subject.

While Cliff had his cigarette Tom spent the time gently playing with him, holding his balls and touching his nipples. By the time Cliff stubbed out the cigarette, he was as hard as he'd been back at the coffee shop, wondering if he could get it on with the handsome guy at the end of the counter.

Putting the ashtray aside, Cliff rolled on top of Tom and wedged in between Tom's legs. Almost as a natural reaction, Tom moved his feet until they were flat on the bed and then lifted his ass up, giving Clifford easy access to it.

It was a slow, easy entry which had Tom groaning and urging Cliff to hurry.

"Can't do that, Tom," Cliff whispered. "I'm way too close and I really want this to last. You mind?"

Tom shook his head, unable to speak around the pleasure Cliff was making him feel.

True to his word, Cliff made it last a long time. He nearly lost his control when Tom came but, at Tom's urging, was able to stave off his own orgasm. When it finally was his time, when he simply couldn't hold out any longer, he took Tom over the edge with him. That lasted a long time, too.

A little later, in the shower, Cliff pulled Tom into a slippery hug and said, "You *were* horny, weren't you, Stud? I mean, three times in one session!" He pulled back and looked at Tom. "We definitely have to do this again."

Tom laughed and kissed him. "Any time, Cliff." He reached down, between them and grasped Cliff's dick. "You ready now?"

Cliff sighed and shook his head. "I'd need a couple of hours, I think, after that one. But maybe sometime very soon?"

Tom nodded. "You serious?"

Cliff nodded and shut off the water. "Very serious." They got out of the shower and Cliff handed Tom a towel. "How about Saturday, here, one o'clock?"

Tom grinned. "I'll be here, probably with a hard-on preceding me."

CHAPTER 6

. . . .

When Tom got home it was late and he was glad he'd had his shower already. Matt came in right after him. "Gotta change, Sport. Be right with you."

They went to Momma Giordano's, an Italian restaurant, run by a family who had somehow escaped the Fascists during the war. Momma herself commanded the kitchen and her four boys and two girls ran the restaurant under the direction of their father, a heavyset, balding man who spent his evenings on a stool, behind the cash register, with a glass of red wine.

Matt and Tom were well known by the family; they were welcomed warmly and their drinks were at the table almost before they were. After the salad and over bowls of Linguine Carbonara, Matt said, "Well, Sport, how'd the exam go, any idea?"

Tom looked up and grinned. "On a scale of 1 to 10, from God awful to very good, I think I'm somewhere between an eight and an eleven."

His dad laughed. "Then I can assume that my son is now a licensed real estate operative?"

"Well, we won't actually know until Friday, when we pick up our grades and the actual piece of paper won't be mailed out for a week or two. But, yeah, I think I'm now a real estate man."

. . . .

The next week was a rough one at work. Mr. Diggs, who was obviously feeling fully recovered from his bout with the flu, decided Tom should accompany him when he went to assess new listings. The reason for this, he said, was to give Tom some new experience in the business. Tom thought it was also because then Tom could write up the assessments, which was a rather tedious job. But it was fun getting out of the office and actually seeing the buildings they were going to rent out or sell.

The report writing was not such fun. Since the reports were often looked at by others, including the owners, there were certain words and phrases which couldn't be used—for example, "impossible to get to" or "run down." There were, however, other words which could be used in their stead—such as "unusual location" or "vintage construction." Tom had to learn the codes before he could write a proper report.

On Saturday Tom rang Cliff's doorbell at exactly one o'clock. Cliff, who opened the door naked, greeted Tom with, "You're overdressed." He then led Tom to the bedroom and helped him with the problem. They fell into bed and over the course of the next three hours, each managed to bring the other off twice. It was a greatly satisfying afternoon for both.

. . . .

The following week was not so bad—and far more satisfying. At least for Tom.

Monday morning was cold and foggy and all Tom could think about was getting to his nice, warm office for a nice, hot cup of coffee. When he got on the cable car he found Charlie sitting in the front, outside seat. Tom situated himself between Charlie's legs, hanging onto the front handgrip. Charlie looked up at him while slowly turning his hand over and finding Tom's dick.

"Hey, Stud, haven't seen you in a while," he said, feeling Tom begin to harden.

Tom grinned. "Been busy, Charlie." He quickly added, "At work."

Charlie laughed. "You got a lunch hour today?"

In his head, Tom quickly ran over his schedule. "Yeah, probably around noon." He leered at Charlie. "You got something in mind?"

Charlie squeezed Tom's dick. "Now, what do you think?"

Then didn't talk much for the rest of the ride, listening instead to a couple of women complaining in loud tones about what appeared to be a friend whose boyfriend or husband, Tom couldn't tell which, was cheating on her with her best friend. The consensus was that the best friend had better watch out because if the guy cheated on one, he'd cheat on the other. "It's in the man's blood," was the way she put it. The general tone of the conversation was *Men are no damn good.* Tom smiled to himself thinking that, on the contrary, men could be very good.

Meanwhile, Charlie continued playing with Tom's dick until Tom was seriously afraid he was going to come in his pants. He was saved by the car's arrival at their stop. As they got off Charlie looked at Tom and grinned. "Noon at the apartment?" When Tom nodded he added, "You got a book or something you could carry in front of you? Gonna make a lot of guys jealous if you don't."

Tom looked down and blushed. Charlie handed him the newspaper he'd been carrying and laughed. "Now get to work and save that thing for me. I'll take care of it later."

In the office Mr. Diggs looked hung over but claimed he had a touch of allergy. As a consequence, Tom was pretty much on his own that morning and got a lot done.

At eleven-thirty Mr. Diggs announced that he was going home and take some antihistamine. Since antihistamines always put him to sleep, he would be gone for the rest of the day. He put Tom in charge.

A couple of minutes before twelve, Tom told Sue he was going to lunch and might be a few minutes late getting back; then he had to wait until she left his office to get up from behind his desk. He grabbed Charlie's newspaper and held it in front of him as he went out and walked up Sutter Street.

Charlie was just coming out of Whiskers carrying a couple of lunch sacks when Tom got there. "Thought you might be hungry," he said. With a grin he added, "After."

Tom put the newspaper under his arm. "Well, certainly not before," he said, pushing his crotch out.

Charlie looked at Tom's crotch and said, "You been carrying that around all morning?"

"Well, let's just say I had to sit behind my desk all morning. Come on."

The apartment was empty when they went in, a good sign Tom thought. Charlie stashed the lunch sacks in the old refrigerator and took Tom in his arms. "I've been looking forward to this," he said, running his hand over Tom's fly. Tom backed off a little and unzipped Charlie's pants. "Oh, no," Charlie said, taking Tom's hand out of his fly. "Naked. That's the way it should be. Come on, let's go claim one of the beds."

In the bedroom Charlie undressed Tom and then played with his dick while Tom undressed him. They lay down on the bed in a sixty-nine position and played with each other for a few minutes before Charlie said, "Not this way. I never can do it this way. I don't know which to concentrate on, my dick or yours. How abut this?"

He climbed over Tom, pushed him up on the bed and nestled in between his legs. He took Tom's dick in his hand and looked at it for a long moment and then took it in, all of it, well into his throat.

Tom let out a great sigh. "I don't know how you do that, Charlie. Even just trying, most guys would be choking and gagging.

Charlie lifted off and grinned at Tom. "Practice, my boy. Practice."

"Well, practice makes perfect they say, and believe me Charlie, you are perfect."

Charlie kissed the head of Tom's dick. "No, desire makes perfect. Now shut up and let me enjoy this."

If desire makes perfect, Charlie had a great desire and very quickly had to be careful not to push Tom over his edge. Tom, for his part, tried to let Charlie know just where he was and how close he was getting. Their teamwork kept Tom on the verge for a good ten or twelve minutes, until Charlie swallowed down on him one time too many and Tom lost all control. Then it was a long fall to a soft landing.

They were just trading places when Willie came in with a good looking man. "Hi, guys," Willie said. "You mind if we..." He nodded at the other bed in the room.

"Not if you don't mind us," Charlie said.

"Yeah," Tom said, "we're only half way through." He sat up and extended his hand to the good looking man with Willie. "Hi, I'm Tom and this," he said. taking hold of Charlie's dick, "is Charlie."

"Oh, sorry, guys. I've forgotten my manners." He took hold of the good looking man's hand. "This is Bet." He turned to the man, "I hope you're not shy, Bet." He patted Bet on the belly, "But if you are, you'll soon get over it around here." He began to unbutton Bet's shirt and Bet returned the favor.

Tom and Charlie went back to what they'd been doing, Tom playing with Charlie's dick and sucking on his balls. Charlie groaned and fell back on the bed, seeming to be in ecstasy.

It didn't take long before Charlie came in Tom's hand. Tom wasn't actually counting but he later thought Charlie had fired seven or eight shots. As Charlie explained later, his balls were the most sensitive part of his "equipment" and once Tom started sucking on them Charlie just couldn't bring himself to stop him.

When Charlie was finally breathing somewhat normally, Tom slid up behind him, put his arms around him and they watched Willie and Bet who had gotten into a sixty-nine position and were enthusiastically sucking on each other's dicks. After a bit Charlie looked at his watch and motioned Tom that they had better get dressed. They picked up their clothes, patted Willie on the ass and went out into the living room to dress.

"Hey," Charlie said as Tom was pulling on his shorts, "pretty underwear. You buy it or did your dad get a look at your dick and realize it needed to be in a prettier place?"

Tom laughed. "My dad's seen my dick I guess ever since I was born; we're not particularly shy about that stuff. But no, I bought a couple of suits and the salesman thought I needed—just as you said—prettier underwear. So he gave them to me."

"Uh huh," Charlie said, tying his tie. "I'll bet he just wants to get in your pants."

Tom shrugged. "Doubtful. I mean, he gave the same ones to my dad, too."

Charlie rolled his eyes. "If your dad is anything like you are I can see why. The guy has good taste. You hungry?"

Charlie got the lunch sacks out of the refrigerator. "Hope you like egg salad and chips," he said, handing Tom one of the bags. He grinned, "It's my favorite."

Over the sandwiches Charlie asked Tom if he'd been with any of the others yet. Tom admitted that he'd been with Joe and his friend Jeffery in a three-way a couple of times.

"Good for you," Charlie said. "But you gotta try all of them. You know, we each have our talents, like Ray's dick and my ability to take all of a guy in, and you'll find that everyone has something to offer." He grinned, wiping a bit of egg salad off his lips, "As do you. You're bright and fun to be with, not to mention that thing you carry around between your legs."

"And nobody minds?"

"Not at all, and that's the thing about this place. There's absolutely no strings attached to anyone. Nor can there be. Look, Tom. We—the renters—we're all married, except for Ray, and we all love our wives and our families very much. But, you know, we sometimes want the touch of a man, just for fun. This," he swung his hand around, taking in the entire apartment, "is a place for fun, a place where we can safely have what we might not be able to have otherwise. That's all."

"So no one gets... involved?"

Charlie got very serious. "No. That's the cardinal rule. If you get involved, you get out because if you get involved, it's not just for fun anymore and it becomes dangerous, both for yourself and for your family." He smiled at Tom. "Okay?"

Tom nodded. What Charlie had said not only appealed to him, it felt right.

"Hey," Charlie said, looking at his watch, "we better get out of here. As usual, I have a meeting and, as usual, I'm going to be late."

They left just as loud noises started in the bedroom. One, the other, or perhaps both of the men were having a very satisfactory time of it.

Just as Charlie was late for his meeting, Tom was late getting back to the office although no one, including Sue, seemed to notice.

. . . .

The rest of the week went by both fast and pleasantly. Tom thought perhaps Mr. Diggs was making up for his lost afternoon. They spent Wednesday and Thursday "out in the field" checking on properties so Tom had plenty of work to do on Friday and well into the next week.

On Saturday Tom and his Dad went down to Monterey, just to look around. They discovered the quaint little village of Carmel and spent the night there. It was a good trip and they had fun looking in the shops and eating in good restaurants but, as Matt put it, there was just a bit too much *cute* about the place.

A week later, on Tuesday, Tom ran into Ray on his way to Work. After greeting each other, Ray invited Tom to have a cup of coffee with him in a coffee shop just down the block. Tom, who was always early getting to work, had plenty of time and took him up on it.

At the counter they each ordered coffee and Ray asked for a Danish. "It's pretty much a no-no for me but if we split it I guess it'll be okay," he said with a weak smile. It was obvious to Tom that something was on his mind.

Once they were served and the Danish had been split, Ray said, "You know, Tom, I've only seen you a couple of times, up at 323, and both times you've been with Charlie. Uh... Charlie's pretty damn good at what he does but I was just wondering, well... You like it the other way, too? I mean..."

Tom grinned at him and wondered if the counterman, who was hanging around their end of the counter, was listening to them. He said, "You mean fucking?"

Ray smiled back. "Well, yeah. That's exactly what I mean. You like to Fuck? You like to be fucked?"

Tom shrugged. "Doesn't everyone?"

"Well, some more than others, I guess. And a lot of guys will pitch but they won't catch."

Tom smiled again. "Not me! When it comes to sex, I love it all, Ray. What I give, I take and what I take, I give."

The counterman evidentially was listening to them because he dropped a newly filled cup of coffee on his foot. Tom hoped he hadn't burned himself.

"Well then, Stan and I will be at 323 tomorrow at lunch. You want to join us?"

Tom smiled. "Sure, if it's okay with Stan. I'd love to."

"Oh, it's okay with Stan, for sure. He loves it when there's another guy or two. And I think, based on what we saw of you that first time, Stan will think he's in heaven."

It turned out to be a long day for Tom because Mr. Diggs was having another one of his allergy attacks and had lost a lot of his civility. He went home early in the afternoon which gave Tom some time to actually get things done.

When he got home he found a note from his dad telling him he wouldn't be home until late. Tom made himself a sandwich for dinner and hoped his dad was getting lucky.

. . . .

The next day Mr. Diggs seemed much better and apologized to Tom for being such a bear the day before. He even suggested that Tom take a long lunch hour and maybe go shopping or something.

When he left for lunch, Tom, taking his own advice and casually carrying a file folder in front of his crotch, thought maybe he should get some baggier pants to help hide his anticipation of afternoons like this.

When he buzzed the apartment the building door immediately clicked open. Upstairs the apartment door was open and Stan came out of the bedroom to greet him. Stan was naked and his sizeable organ was already pointing towards the ceiling. "We're in here," he said, turning back into the bedroom, "we waited for you."

In the bedroom Ray was just pulling off his underwear. "Hi, Tom. Glad you could make it, aren't we Stan?"

"What do you think?" Stan pulled his erection down and let go. It snapped up and hit his belly with a sharp sound. "Well, come on Tom, get with the program."

While Tom undressed, Ray said, "Let's make ourselves a Stan sandwich. You want the front or the back?"

"New guy has to be in back," Stan said, fondling Tom's dick. He looked Tom in the eye. "Okay?"

Tom patted him on the ass. "Very okay," he said.

Ray put a thick coat of KY on Stan's dick and then on Tom's. They arranged themselves on the bed and Stan slowly pushed into Ray who let out an appreciative moan. When he was well into Ray he reached behind himself and pulled Tom towards him. As the head of Tom's dick went into him he let out a groan. "God damn that thing is big," he said through clenched teeth. "Let me do it." As he pushed slowly back, Ray moaned again. It took a couple of minutes but Stan eventually found his rhythm, bringing great pleasure to all three of them.

Stan came first and took Tom with him almost immediately. Afterward the three of them lay in companionable quiet for a few minutes, Tom's arms around Stan and Stan's around Ray.

Once disengaged, both Tom and Ray kissed Stan. "You ready to go again?" Ray asked, taking hold of Stan's dick.

"Yeah," Stan said, his inflating dick confirming his word. "But I can't. Got to get to work. It's already after one." He untangled himself from them and reached for the damp towel on the bedside table.

Tom and Ray sat up on the bed and watched Stan pull his overalls on and put on his shoes. "Don't you ever wear underwear?" Ray asked.

Stan shook his head and grinned. "Don't own any. Can't afford it like you rich professional guys." He bent down and gave each of them a kiss. "I'll let myself out."

Ray turned to Tom and said, "I suppose you have to get going too."

Tom smiled. "Not yet. I'm supposed to be out shopping or something. Besides, you haven't come yet."

Ray rolled Tom over on his belly. "And you, young man, haven't been fucked yet."

It was a long, easy coupling, one in which each man tried to being the other the maximum possible pleasure.

Leaving, kissing goodbye at the door, Ray said, "We'll do that again, I promise."

They did, and within three months Tom had become a regular at 323 Kearny. So much so that he thought perhaps he should be paying a share of the rent. When he mentioned this to Charlie he dismissed it with a "Nonsense!" Charlie also gave him a key and told him the place was his to use, any time he wanted it.

Things at the office were quite different. Mr. Diggs allergy attacks seemed to come on more and more frequently and with greater severity. When Tom mentioned them to his father, Matt thought they sounded more like hangovers than allergies but kept his own counsel.

On the last day of October, Charlie called Tom at work. "Could you do us a big favor?" Charlie asked. "I've been so damn busy that I forgot all about paying the rent at 323. Could I send the money over to you and ask you to deliver it?"

Tom agreed. Mr. Diggs was in another of his foul moods and Tom figured he could use a little time away from him. Promptly at eleven o'clock a very good looking lady stopped at Susan's desk and asked for Tom. She was carrying a small package which she said she was to deliver to him personally. When Tom came out of the office she handed him the package and had him sign a receipt.

When the lady had gone Tom turned to Sue and said, "I tell you what. I think I'll take an early lunch, okay?" He glanced at the clock on her desk. "Like right now." Sue thought it was kind of unusual but didn't say anything.

CHAPTER 7

. . . .

Tom went directly to 323 Kearny and let himself in. Charlie had told him that the landlady, Mrs. Tan, hardly ever went out so he was fairly confident he would find her in her apartment. He actually had little choice in the matter since he had no way of contacting her.

When he knocked on the door to the third floor rear apartment someone called out, "Who is it, please."

"It's Tom, from the second floor, delivering the rent," he called.

"Well then, come in. Come in."

Tom tried the door and found it unlocked. He entered a short hallway and Mrs. Tan called out, "I'm here. In the living room."

Tom turned right and found himself in the strangest room he'd ever seen. Half the furniture was massive, dark and kind of English looking. The upholstery was mostly leather with a little needlepoint thrown in to soften it. The rest was of Chinese design, delicate and upholstered in silk, in bright, jewel like colors. Sitting in a brocade covered wing chair was a small redheaded woman, barefoot and wearing a housecoat.

"Come here, young man and let me look at you. I don't remember anyone of your name downstairs."

Tom went and stood in front of her. "No ma'am, I'm just a friend of Mr. Higgins. He's in an important meeting so he asked me to deliver this." He handed her the package he was carrying.

"Well bless his heart. Always on time, that man. Always. You tell him thank you for me." She slowly stood and Tom had the impression she might be in some pain. She crossed to a huge ornate desk and put the package in one of its drawers.

"Now then," she said, turning to Tom, "may I offer you tea? I was just sitting here thinking it was about time for tea and perhaps a biscuit or two."

Tom, thinking about Mr. Diggs black mood, said, "If it's no trouble. And if you allow me to help with it."

She shook her head and smiled. "No need, young man. I may look old and frail but I'm not." She smiled again, here eyes picking it up this time. "Frail that is. I suppose I must be quite old to a boy like you, barely out of school."

Tom laughed. "Let's just say that you're older than I am and let it go at that. Now, what can I do to help?"

She took him into the kitchen, put a kettle of water on the stove and directed him to a cabinet containing a set of very thin, delicate china cups and saucers. Then she had him add some small plates while she arranged some cookies on a larger one.

"They're fresh yesterday," she said of the cookies. "From Wings, a little bakery up in town." Without thinking about it Tom understood *up in town* to mean Chinatown, a block or two to the North and West.

When the tea was ready Tom carried the tray out to the living room and placed it on an ornately carved Chinese side table, convenient to Mrs. Tan's chair.

With the tea poured and a couple of cookies on a plate by his side, Tom sat in a rather more delicate chair indicated by Mrs. Tan. "Don't worry," she said, seeing his expression as he went to sit down. "It's much sturdier than it looks and it's survived the rumps of many men bigger than you in its two hundred years."

Tom mentally shrugged and sat. The chair turned out to be much more comfortable than it had looked to be. "You have so many beautiful things," he said, looking around.

She laughed, a high pitched sound that reminded Tom of the upper notes on a church organ. "I suppose I do, too many of them. We, Mr. Tan and I, we had very different taste, as you can see. But now let me hear about you. You're from somewhere else."

Tom started to briefly tell her about coming from the Midwest but she was a very good listener and a half hour later he was still describing his life in Iowa. When the small enameled clock on the mantel struck the hour he stopped and looked at his watch. "I think I've bored you for far too long, ma'am. I'm sorry, I didn't mean to be so long winded."

Mrs. Tan smiled and shook her head. "Not at all, young man. It's always interesting to hear about people's lives."

"Well, now you know more than you ever wanted to about mine. But I have to go before my boss gets into an even blacker mood than he was in when I left the office."

"Surely Mr. Higgins..."

Tom laughed. "Oh, no ma'am, I don't work for Mr. Higgins, he's just a friend and I've never seen him in a bad mood." He looked around. "May I carry the tea things back to the kitchen for you?"

She shook her head. "Thank you but I can manage. If you'll just see yourself out?"

Tom nodded, shook her hand and left thinking what a nice old lady she was.

On the way out he decided that he could afford the time to stop in at the apartment, just to see who was there. It turned out that the place was empty except for Joe who was sitting on the couch with a book and playing with himself. "Well, well, well," he said when Tom came through the doorway. "Am I to be rescued after all?"

Tom smiled. Ever since he'd met him he'd thought Joe was pretty sexy and now, watching him play with himself, he was quickly getting hard. "Rescued from what, Joe?"

Joe laughed. "Rescued from a solitary jerk-off while reading Henry Miller, that's what. I got stood up."

Tom sat down next to him, took the book and put it on the coffee table, leaned over and took Joe's dick his mouth, sucking it in until his nose was in Joe's tightly curled pubic hair.

Joe put his hands on the back of Tom's head and held him still. "Let's... Let's go in the bedroom, Tom, okay? I've got to get you up to where I am before we go any farther."

They got up and Tom lead Joe by the dick into the bedroom. When they were naked they got on the bed in a sixty-nine position and spent a delicious quarter-hour playing before neither one of them could contain it any longer. Then, together, they let it go.

Tom felt just a little guilty getting back to the office so late but no one seemed to notice.

. . . .

Two weeks later, for the very first time, Tom voted in a National Election. He felt very proud as he went into the polling place just down Vallejo Street. He and his dad had talked a lot about this election and Tom had learned a lot about the candidates, both from the newspapers and from his dad, who had very strong opinions about it. He finally voted for Kennedy and Johnson even though his dad had grave doubts about Johnson. Voting was a milestone in his life and his dad made sure he knew it.

On Thursday Tom and his dad went to Ernie's for Thanksgiving dinner. They had cocktails before, wine with and brandy after and then another brandy when they got home. Neither of them was feeling much pain or sense of inhibition which allowed Matt to bring up a subject which he normally avoided.

"You know, I was over in Operations the other day, Tom, and met the new guy, the one they're grooming to take it over."

Tom wondered where this was going but mentally shrugged it off. It was just nice that he and his dad could sit and talk together. "So what's he like?"

"Interesting. Has an encyclopedic knowledge of brokerage operations and Bob, his boss, told me he's... Well, he's one of those, you know, a guy who, uh... who likes guys."

Tom, who was in the same relaxed state as his dad and so didn't panic at the subject being discussed, said, "Gay?"

"Yeah. Gay. But what makes it interesting is that he's been living with the same man for fifteen years. I didn't think those guys ever stayed together for very long. I mean, not like a real couple."

Tom took a swallow of his brandy and thought for a moment. "You know? I knew a couple of those guys in school They were pretty much like everyone else." He chuckled. "Well, except for who they... who they went with."

Matt sat up straighter in his chair. "Any of them... I mean... Oh hell, did any of them ever make a pass at you?"

Tom thought about Harvey and the library men's room. "Maybe. But I probably wouldn't know it if they had. They've got to be careful I guess and can't just come out with *Hey Bud, you want a blow job?*" That last shocked Tom, that he could actually say 'Blow Job' in front of his dad.

Matt was equally shocked that his son would say those words like they were just regular words. "No, I guess they can't. They say there's more of them around than we know. Most hide it."

Tom finished his brandy. "Wouldn't you?"

"I suppose. But wouldn't it be lonely to be that way? I mean unless you had a partner or something." He drank the last of his brandy and looked at Tom. "That's it, unless you want to switch to scotch or something. I forgot to put it on the shopping list."

Tom tried to suppress a yawn. It didn't work. "No, I think I want sleep." He smiled. "Unlike you, I have to go to work tomorrow."

Matt laughed. "Slave drivers." He stood and pulled Tom into a tight hug. "See you tomorrow, Son. But I probably won't see you at breakfast."

Sleep didn't come right away to either of them. They'd never discussed *Gay* before and they both had a lot to think about.

. . . .

Things went along smoothly at the office for the next three weeks or so. Mr. Diggs still fell into black moods now and again and his allergies were getting worse, causing him to take time off more and more frequently but otherwise things were going okay.

One day in early December Tom overheard Mr. Diggs say to Sue, "…and burn the damn thing in Hell!" He then heard the outer door slam. When he went out to Sue's desk he asked what the commotion had been about.

"This," she said, waiving a thick folder. "He's all bent out of shape because he thought he had a deal and the other guys didn't think so. Now he's gone God only knows where. Probably the bar at the Palace."

Tom took the folder from her and opened it. It was jammed with little scraps of paper, a cocktail napkin with notes on it and a number of uncompleted forms. "Let me take a look at it, Sue, and see what I can make of it. In the meantime," he looked at his watch," why don't you take the rest of the afternoon off. I know he's been a bear today and you've earned the time off." He laughed, "Just stay out of the bar at the Palace."

Sue smiled. "Not a chance I'll be there. Macy's is having a pre-Christmas sale!"

Ten minutes later she stuck her head in his door and said, "I'm off. Thanks Tom. I really mean it."

Tom put the file in order but still couldn't make sense of any of it. Finally, in frustration, he called the man listed as principal. Mr. Tickson answered his own phone and sounded quite pleasant. Tom identified himself and said that he was having difficulty figuring out what was going on.

Mr. Tickson said it was complicated and then asked Tom to have lunch with him and his assistant the next day to discuss it. "You, not that Diggs character. Okay?" It seemed to Tom that he had little choice but to agree so he did. He figured he could always cancel in the morning if Mr. Diggs wanted to do the thing himself.

The next day, of course, Mr. Diggs didn't come to work, claiming an allergy attack, so Tom went to lunch with Mr. Tickson and his assistant, a Mr. Wilding. When they sat down the waiter asked about drinks. Tom ordered iced tea and the two other men did the same.

Over a very nice crab salad lunch, Tom saw that there really weren't any problems to be ironed out. It was a perfectly straight forward transaction of the sort that was done all the time. At the end of lunch all three of them signed the forms Sue had typed up that morning and the deal was done. Done at a quite advantageous commission to Bay Holdings Group.

As they were leaving the restaurant, Mr. Tickson shook Tom's hand and said, "It's been a pleasure doing business with you, Tom. We'll do more of it."

Then, as they were getting in a cab, he quietly said, "And tell your boss to lay off the sauce, okay? If not, his deals are all going to go South."

Back at the office Tom took the folder to Mr. Simms office for his signature. Then he went to his office and wrote a short *Thank You* note to Mr. Tickson.

Later that afternoon Mr. Simms came into Tom's office and told him what a good job he'd done. "Diggs has been working on that thing for a month now and you finish it up in one lunch. By the way, who paid for lunch?"

"Mr. Tickson did. I thought perhaps I should have but I didn't know if I was allowed..."

"Son, closing a deal, you're always allowed. Next time, you pay for it and put in an expense report."

Thursday, when Tom got to work Mr. Diggs called him into his office. He waived Tom into a chair and handed him a file.

"You responsible for that?"

It was the Tickson file. Tom nodded and started to explain but Mr. Diggs held up his hand. "I know, I know. Simms told me all about it." He laughed. "You even got them to pay for lunch! You're something else again, Thomas. Now, a job that well done deserves a reward and you shall have one." A slightly leering grin came over his face. "Hold New Year's Eve open, okay?"

Tom went back to his office debating with himself as to whether or not he should have told Mr. Diggs what Mr. Tickson had said. He finally decided that Mr. Diggs didn't much like Mr. Tickson so it wouldn't make much difference to him in the greater scheme of things.

The day was a busy one and it was quitting time before he knew it. At home, over a before dinner cocktail—which had become something of a ritual when they were both home—Tom mentioned Mr. Tickson's comment to his dad.

"Lay off the sauce, huh? Sounds like this Tickson guy thinks your boss has a bit of a problem. And I'll tell you, Tom, from what you've told me I have to agree. He's out a lot, has these 'allergy attacks' after lunch, classic signs of a guy who's climbing into a bottle."

Tom nodded. He'd begun to think the same thing after Sue said it looked more like a hangover than an allergy attack. "Well," he said to his dad, "I'm only glad that it's Mr. Simms problem to deal with and not mine."

"Yeah, the mess always falls to the guy in charge. How well I know that! Anything else interesting going on?"

Tom told him about Mr. Diggs saying he'd get a reward for closing the Tickson deal. "I don't think it's money though. He told me to hold New Year's Eve open. Maybe it's dinner or something."

His dad laughed. "Well, if it is, my advice is to eat well. You deserve it."

. . . .

At lunchtime a week or so later Tom bought a sandwich and ate it while sitting on the steps of the Crocker Plaza. He loved sitting there because it seemed that sooner or later the whole world passed by the place. A nice looking guy about Tom's age stopped at the base of the stairs, pretending he was just watching the people going by but actually watching Tom, his right hand in his pocket making small, careful movements. When Tom realized the man was playing with himself he smiled and winked at him.

"Hi," the man said, coming up the stairs and sitting next to Tom. He still had his hand in his pocket.

"Hi," Tom said. Then, after a moment of silence, "You got a hole in that pocket?"

The man laughed and blushed at the same time. "Yeah." Then, after a moment, with a grin, "If we had a place you could put your hand in and see."

Tom looked at his watch. "Too late today. How about tomorrow?"

"Really? Yeah, I'd like that. You too maybe."

Tom laughed. "No, me too definitely. You know that sandwich shop over on Kearny, Whiskers?" When the man nodded Tom said, "Good. Tomorrow? Twelve thirty?"

The man nodded again, pulled his hand out of his pocket and extended it. "Bill Jones, folks call me Jonesy."

Tom shook his hand. "Tom Braden." He looked at his watch again and stood. "See you tomorrow, Jonesy. Twelve thirty, in front of Whiskers. Gotta get back to work now."

Mr. Diggs didn't come back from lunch and called in late in the day complaining of an allergy attack. It was Sue's opinion, based on his voice, that he probably wouldn't be in for a couple of days.

The next day Jonesy was standing in front of Whiskers when Tom got there. "Different pants," Tom observed. "No hole today?"

Jonesy laughed. "I'll tell you, every pair of pants I own has a hole in the right pocket." He shrugged. "What can I say, I like playing with myself. Like to play with other guys too."

On the way up the stairs Tom explained that there might be some others in the apartment but if there were, they were all there for the same reason. Sure enough, inside the apartment they found both Ray and Willie. Ray was with the same man he'd been with two weeks before, the one who was always ready to go and Willie was with an Italian looking man about Tom's age.

Tom introduced Jonesy and while Jonesy was shaking hands with Ray, Tom stuck his hand into Jonesy's right pocket. Just as he'd said, there was a hole in it and a warm, circumcised dick hanging beside it.

Introductions over, Tom and Jonesy took the large bedroom along with Ray and his guy who was simply called Stud. Willie and his Italian took the little storeroom in the back.

In the bedroom the guys undressed each other and Tom and Jonesy fell into a classic sixty-nine position. Ray stretched out on the other bed and Stud unceremoniously mounted him, slowly pushing into him without stopping. Ray let out a long sigh of pleasure as Stud began moving in him.

Tom and Jonesy tried to stretch it out but they were both very horny so it didn't last as long as they would have liked. When it was over they simply watched Ray and Stud. Ray had turned on his side and Stud was playing with him and Tom could tell Ray wasn't going to last very much longer. Sure enough, he let out a loud groan and came in Stud's hand. Stud said, "Oh, boy, here it comes," and obviously came too.

When they were breathing normally again, Ray got up and said, "Well, guys, it's been fun but I've gotta go. I know, I know, Stud. You're just getting started but I've gotta go. Maybe you can talk one of these fine men into helping you out for a while." He grinned and grabbed his pants and shorts.

Stud looked over at Tom and Jonesy and Jonesy raised his hand. He turned to Tom, "if you don't mind?"

Tom kissed him. "Go for it, guy. I'm going out and have a coke, maybe I'll get a turn later, huh Stud?"

"Oh, yes, definitely," Stud said, pulling Jonesy down on the bed. "After him."

Tom and the now dressed Ray went into the living room where Willie was sitting in the easy chair, drinking some tea. "Hey, where's the other guys?" he asked. Before Ray or Tom could answer, he nodded and said, "Oh, yeah. I know. God, how do these guys do that? Two or three times in an hour."

"They're young," Ray said. "When you were their age, couldn't you do two or three times?"

Willie laughed. "Two or three times a day maybe. I can still do that, sometimes. But not in an hour."

Ray took his leave and Tom, who still hadn't dressed, poured himself a cup of tea and sat on the couch. "So how's it going, Willie? Where's your guy?"

"Had to leave. It was just a quickie. How about you?"

"About the same I guess. Except he's still in there. Stud'll get him off again I imagine."

Willie laughed. "Yeah, once or twice. How come no body takes time with it any more?"

"Don't have time, maybe," Tom said, sipping his tea. "Ought to make time though. Take it slow and make it last."

Willie nodded. "Yeah. Make it really good. You want to do that Tom? Maybe take an afternoon off and devote it to a long session of good sex?"

"With you? There's nothing I'd like better."

Willie sat up, nearly upsetting his cup. "Then let's do it." He got a far-away look in his eyes, visualizing his calendar. "Can't be next week or the week after. I've got to be in Atlanta for a meeting. How about Tuesday the nineteenth? It's pretty close to Christmas but..." He shrugged. "There's one advantage. we'll have the place to ourselves; all the other guys are out of town most of that week. Okay?"

Tom crossed the room and sat on the arm of Willie's chair and put Willie's hand on his dick. "The nineteenth it is." He kissed Willie and flexed his rapidly hardening dick. "We'll have fun."

. . . .

Saturday Matt took Tom to a ball game and they had a fine father-and-son afternoon. Afterwards they went to Tommy's Joint on Geary Street for a drink.

"You know, Tom, I've been thinking. One of these days you'll be getting married and settling down to start a family. I'm getting on in years and probably should be thinking about what I'll do when you're gone."

Tom mimicked Matt's voice, a thing he did very well, much to Matt's annoyance. "I'll be getting on in years…" He switched back to his own voice. "Good lord, dad, what are you forty-two? Forty-three? That's hardly old in my book." A fleeting thought crossed his mind: *I've been to bed with men older than you. I wonder what you'd think if you knew that?* "Besides, unless you want me out, I have no plans to leave the nest, as it were."

Matt laughed. "Well… Maybe not for a year or two but a man needs a plan, don't you think?"

"Maybe. But… Wait a minute! Have *you* met someone you want to settle down with? You thinking about getting married again?"

Matt sipped his scotch. "Well, maybe thinking about it. Not seriously I guess but, yeah, it's crossed my mind."

"Anybody I know?"

Matt snorted. "Not even anybody *I* know. It's just that a man doesn't want to grow old by himself."

"But… "

"Oh, I know. You'll be there, with a wife and a family and you'll try to include me in your life. But a man wants a life of his own and somebody of his own to share it with."

Tom signaled the bartender for another round. "Yeah, I suppose I see what you mean, Dad. It probably applies to me too but, like you, I haven't met anyone I'd really like to spend my life with." He thought to himself, *But there are a couple…* He dropped the thought.

"Well, she'll come along and you'll know it when it happens. I sure knew it when I met your mother." He finished his drink and decided not to go there. He looked at Tom, "Not even any prospects?"

"None. But don't worry Dad, you'll be the first to know."

Chapter 8

· ·

The next couple of weeks were busy. Mr. Diggs was a bundle of energy and passed a lot of paper around the office for Tom and Sue to process. A few times he sent Sue out to bring in lunch for them and often kept them an hour after quitting time.

All that activity made it easy for Tom to ask for the afternoon of the nineteenth off. Mr. Diggs, in an uncharacteristic mood, said yes and gave Sue the afternoon off as well. They found out the next day that he gave the afternoon off to himself also.

When Tom got to 323 the apartment was empty. He changed the bed but didn't bother with the lubricant because he'd never seen Willy do anything but suck and get sucked. Then he changed his mind and put it out anyway.

Just as Tom was finishing, Willie came in carrying a shopping bag. He put the bag down on the little console table and gathered Tom into a hug and then kissed him. "I've been looking forward to this for a while," he said.

"Me, too," Tom said. "What's in the bag?"

"Ah, good things." He pulled out a couple of bottles of wine and held one up. "Red, for before, to fan the flames." He held up the other one. "And white, for after, to cool the over-heated senses." He took the bag into the kitchen, put the white wine in the refrigerator, opened the red and poured two glasses which he took to the bedroom and placed on the bedside table. "But first, a shower. It's been a dirty morning."

They stripped, without artifice, looked each other over and walked to the bathroom, holding hands.

In the shower they washed each other, taking special care in the erogenous areas. When Tom had washed and rinsed Willie's little pink bud, he squatted down and kissed it. Willie groaned and pushed back against him.

In the bedroom they sat cross-legged on the bed, facing each other and sipping their wine. Every few seconds one or the other of them would bend forward and kiss the other. It wasn't long before the kisses became longer than the intervals between them. Finally Tom touched his wineglass to Willie's and said, "It's time, Willie." He drained his glass and put it on the bedside table.

Willie said, "And so it is," and did the same thing.

It was a long, sweet afternoon and it soon became apparent that Tom had done the right thing in putting out the lubricant. "You know," Willie said to Tom, who was putting the lubricant on his dick, "in all my years, I've never done this. Until you came along I guess I never wanted to. Now I wish I had, so I'd know how to do it, how to make it best for you."

He needn't have worried. He took to fucking like fish takes to tarter sauce and managed to bring Tom to orgasm, just before he took himself to the same place.

The other way went the same. Tom tried to talk Willie out of trying to take him inside but Willie insisted. Tom was slow and very gentle but once he was fully inside, Willie was having none of it. He wanted it a little rough and told Tom so. The way he put it was, "Come on, Tom, I want to be *Fucked*." Tom did his best to accommodate him.

Over the course of the afternoon they showered twice, finished the red wine, had five orgasms between them and used up nearly all the lube.

Around seven Willie laughed and kissed Tom, his tongue sharp with the white wine. "Are you hungry? I am."

Tom agreed so they showered again, dressed and Willie took him to Tadich Grill. The maitre d' seemed to know Willie and they had to wait only a few moments at the bar, just long enough to order martinis and have them served. As soon as they were, they were picked up by a waiter who escorted them to a private booth at the back. When he left, pulling the curtains over the doorway, he called Willie by name and said he'd be back soon to take their order.

Tom was impressed. He'd never had a meal in a private booth with a curtain over the doorway and the only time a waiter had called someone at the table by name had been the dinner at the Banker's Club with Mr. Diggs.

"Well, Tom," Willie said, touching his glass to Tom's, "here's to you. And to the end of... I don't know what, but to the end."

Tom knitted his brows. "The end..."

"Think about it, Tom. I'm at least twice your age and half again..." He held up his hand to stop any comment from Tom. "I have a wife whom I love very much, I have a son who could be your younger brother and I have two young daughters whom I adore. I have no right to... well, to fall in love with you, which is exactly what I'm doing."

Before Tom could react and as if on cue, the waiter stepped in and asked if they were ready to order. "Oh, we haven't even looked at the menu," Willie said. "But wait. Tom, you like crab?" At Tom's nod he turned back to the waiter and said, "A cracked crab, I think. With regular melted butter, not that drawn kind that has no flavor. French bread and a bottle of whatever you think will go with the crab." He turned back to Tom. "That okay? We'll order another crab if one's not enough." Tom nodded and the waiter left.

They sat in silence for a moment, absorbing what had been said. Finally Tom said, "you're serious, aren't you? About falling in love with... with me?"

Willie smiled. "Yes, Tom, with you. It's been coming on for a long time and this afternoon just made it clear. And I can't do that, I really can't do that to my family."

Tom thought for a time. "What are we going to do about it?"

Willie laughed. "That is so like you, Tom. What are *we* going to do about it. One more reason..." He paused while the waiter served the cracked crab and poured the wine.

When the waiter was gone and they'd sampled the crab, Willie said, "I was in Atlanta last month, Tom. I guess it's actually what prompted our afternoon today."

Tom gave him a questioning look and he smiled. "Sorry. I guess you can't read my mind after all." He peeled a crab leg and dipped it in the melted butter before putting it in his mouth. "Wonderful!" He selected another leg before he continued. "When I was in Atlanta, the Chairman of my firm asked me to take over our Cincinnati office. It's a great opportunity for me. It's the biggest office we have and it's tradition that the head of that office generally becomes president after a couple of years. Anyway, I told him I'd think about it. Then I did something I've wanted to do for months now. I asked you to spend the afternoon with me. I knew I was breaking the first rule we set up when we rented that apartment but I did it anyway."

"What rule?"

"It's always play. It's never serious. Serious is dangerous. As I found out this afternoon, the rule is one hundred percent correct. That decided me, told me what I have to do."

"And you thought about that this afternoon?"

Willie laughed. "Not *all* afternoon, Tom. Mostly I thought about... about the pleasure we were bringing each other. That decided me."

"And?"

"And, I'll call him tomorrow and accept the offer. I'll probably have to leave right away because the man in Cincinnati is going to another firm."

Tom got up, went around the table and kissed him. "I'll miss you, Willie. I really will."

"Go sit down and eat your crab," Willie said, rather brusquely. Tom did, because he could see the tears beginning.

After a long silence Willie said, "I'll tell the others just after Christmas," He paused for a moment. "I'll tell them about the job in Cincinnati, Tom. I won't tell them about you. That's just between us, okay?"

Tom nodded. "I'll stay away from 323 for the rest of the week, give you time to... To do what you need to."

When they were finished, Willie hugged Tom and kissed him. Then they left. When they stepped out of the restaurant Willie quietly said, "Goodbye Tom," and hurried away, down the street. He didn't look back.

Tom wasn't sure how he felt about Willie and the reason he was leaving. On one hand, he was flattered that the man thought he'd fallen in love with him. On the other he'd never heard of such a thing lasting very long and wondered if Willie wasn't making too big a thing of it. But what bothered him the most was that he hadn't seen it coming. He'd had no idea of Willie's feelings for him. He liked Willie and he'd been sure they could have a great time in bed but falling in love enough to endanger his family? That was something completely new to him.

. . . .

He saw Charlie on the cable car Wednesday morning and Charlie asked him to come to 323 for *a lunch hour conference.* He wouldn't say more but Tom assumed it had something to do with Willie.

Mr. Diggs was in one of his black moods and both Tom and Sue were happy to get out for an hour. On the way out Sue said she figured things would be better in the afternoon because she doubted Mr. Diggs would come back from lunch. She was right.

When Tom let himself into 323 he found Charlie and Ray already there and Joe came in just a moment later.

"Okay, guys, we have a bit of a problem," Charlie said. "Willie has been promoted to manager of his Cincinnati office and is leaving us. He told me he has to leave next week so we won't be seeing him around here again."

"Damn shame," Joe said. "He was fun in the sack."

"Yeah, but not very versatile," Ray added. "God knows I wanted to fuck him in the worst way but he wouldn't even try. Said he'd never done it and never would. I even offered to catch for him but he still turned me down. Not interested."

Tom thought that made his afternoon with Willie all the more special, but of course he didn't say anything.

"Well, he may have been a little inhibited that way," Charlie said, "but he was a good pal to us and he sure seemed to make the boys he brought around happy."

"Not as happy as you can," Ray said with a laugh. "You've got real talent there."

Tom thought Charlie blushed a little as he went on. "Well, I don't know about that but anyway, we still have a little problem: there's one fewer of us paying the rent here. We have to either find someone who'd like to take Willie's share or we each have to cough up an extra thirty-three,"

Tom spoke up. "Hey, how about me? I think I kind of fit in with you guys and I'm around so much I might as well be paying rent. I even have a key."

Joe nodded but said, "Yeah but you're just starting out, Tom. It must be hard, you know, making ends meet." The other two expressed general agreement.

It suddenly occurred to Tom just how much he wanted to be a real part of the group. He liked these guys, liked being around them, liked being in bed with them. "No, really, I'm doing okay. I live with my dad and he doesn't charge me much and I just got a raise and besides, you guys are friends. On top of everything else, I like the arrangement. I never would've have gotten in Jonesy's pants if it weren't for this place."

"Yeah, and nice pants they were, too," Ray said. "Did he really have a hole in that pocket?"

Tom nodded. "More like no pocket at all. I stuck my hand in it and found nothing but warm dick."

There was general laughter and without further discussion the decision was made: Tom was now a rent paying tenant of 323.

Back at the office Tom found that Sue had been right: Mr. Diggs didn't return from lunch. Since it had been such a tough day Tom took it upon himself to tell Sue to take the rest of the afternoon off. He figured he might be overstepping his bounds but he doubted anyone would even notice.

. . . .

On Thursday Tom went up to 323 just to see if anyone was there. The place was empty except for Ray who was setting up a small Christmas tree on the table next to one of the easy chairs. "Hey, merry Christmas," Ray said, giving Tom a kiss.

"Merry Christmas yourself," Tom said, groping Ray and finding him with the beginnings of an erection. "What's with the tree?"

Ray stepped back to admire his work. "Well, they were on sale at Macy's and I thought we should have a bit of the Christmas spirit around here. Looks pretty good, huh?"

Tom nodded. "Yeah, it does. Glad you thought of it."

"So what are you doing here, alone?"

"I don't know. I just came up to see who was here."

Ray pulled him into a hug. "Well, I'm here. I'm also horny," he said, finding Tom's dick and taking hold of it. "You got time for a quickie?"

Tom kissed him. "Oh, yeah, that'd be nice."

They spent the rest of the hour in the bedroom, making each other happy.

When he got home that evening, Tom found his father putting up the identical tree that Ray had. "Found it at Macy's," he said, "on sale. I thought we needed a little something to remind us it's Christmas."

Tom laughed. "As if we could forget."

Matt grinned at him. "Well, I wanted to make sure you didn't forget my present."

Tom hugged him. "Had it for weeks," he said. In the back of his head he thought, *No wonder I like Ray so much. He and dad are so much alike.*

. . . .

On Friday Mr. Diggs called Tom into his office. "I think perhaps, in light of the good work you have done, it would be appropriate for you to take Miss Lynn out for lunch. I've made reservations for you at Gianini's and lunch will, of course, be on my tab. Normally I would accompany you but I have other obligations this afternoon. And take the rest of the afternoon off. You'll be no good back here." He made a small gesture, essentially dismissing Tom.

Outside, Tom stood in front of Sue's desk and grinned at her. "Come on hard worker, lunch is on Mr. Diggs and we can stay as long as we want because he gave us the rest of the day off."

Gianini's was a quiet, and expensive, place downtown and they ate cracked crab, sourdough bread and drank a very good white wine. Both were just a little tipsy when they finished.

After lunch Tom went up to 323. In the living room Joe was pouring eggnog, well spiked with brandy. "They're in there," he said, pointing at the bedroom. "Ray brought in that guy Stud. You know, the one who can't get enough and is always ready?"

Tom nodded and wondered if he might get to try out the guy. Jonesy had said he was very talented. "Nice tree," he said, sampling his eggnog. "Makes the place kind of festive, doesn't it?"

"Yeah. Ray does that sort of thing every once in a while. So," he pulled Tom into a gentle hug, "you got to get back to work?" His hand slipped down to Tom's crotch and fondled the dick he found there.

Tom put his eggnog down on the table and kissed Joe. "You suppose the bedroom will hold two more? Or shall we just use the couch?"

"Bedroom," Joe said, kissing Tom back. "Better scenery in there."

. . . .

On Christmas Eve Tom and his dad went to Ernie's for dinner where they enjoyed four courses of incredible food and a bottle of a wine neither one of them could pronounce. They went home in a cab and Tom was pretty sure the driver was the same one who had taken him home from the Banker's Club. He was sure of it when the man winked at him and patted him on the ass when he got out of the cab.

Christmas morning found the two men exchanging gifts. Matt gave Tom the same gift he always gave him: a hundred shares of stock in some company. Tom got to look at it, finger the heavy paper it was printed on and read all the fine print. Then, when his dad went back to work the stock went with him and got put into an account Matt had set up for him. He'd been doing this for Tom since he was born. Tom knew the account was sizable but paid little attention to it since his dad managed it. He couldn't even get into it until he was twenty-five and then only a quarter of it. He got a second quarter when he was thirty and the rest when he was thirty-five.

Matt also gave him a good briefcase saying that no self respecting business man would be caught dead without his briefcase, even if it did hold nothing but a clean shirt, a change of underwear and lunch.

Tom gave his dad a thing called a Silent Valet. It was polished wood gadget that sat in a corner of the bedroom, ready to receive keys, change and all the other stuff men filled their pockets with. It had arms so a coat could be hung up, a holder for a hat and a little compartment containing shoe polish, brush and wax. Matt loved it and nothing would do but they had to place it in his bedroom and sweep the change and handkerchief off the dresser and put it on the little shelf.

"That is great," Matt said, pulling Tom into a hug. "I should have had one of these years ago."

"I don't think they had them years ago," Tom said. "You were supposed to employ some old guy who would put your stuff away for you."

"Well, this is better," Matt said with a laugh. "At least he won't talk back to me. I'll have to think up a name for him."

Monday was a holiday and Tom spent much of it in bed with Mario who's aunt was spending the day with her friend in Marin.

The rest of the week was fairly productive considering it was the week between Christmas and New Year's and a short week at that. On Wednesday Tom was again summoned into Mr. Diggs office. "Well, Thomas, did you reserve New Year's Eve for me? Well, not for me exactly, because I have to be in Los Angeles over the long weekend but, did you reserve it?"

"Uh, yeah, I guess so. Yeah."

"Good. You shall have a New Year's Eve to remember. You will have dinner at the Garden Court in the Palace Hotel. After dinner you will pass the night in a small, but I think rather elegant, suite upstairs. So that you needn't dine alone you will have Miss Winters for dinner table conversation. She will also keep you warm in the cold of the night."

Tom was so stunned that he hardly remembered to thank Mr. Diggs.

At noon Tom skipped lunch and went over to 323 in hopes there would be someone there to talk to, because he needed to talk in the worst way. He found Ray and Joe, each with a young man, and Charlie who had just come up to hang around and see if anyone might need some help. Ray and Joe took their young friends into the bedroom but Charlie poured Tom a Coke and sat with him on the couch, casually playing with Tom's dick through his pants.

Tom explained what Mr. Diggs had done and then said, "I can't do it, Charlie, I can't. I've never done it with a woman. I don't even know how!"

Charlie laughed and squeezed Tom's dick. "It comes naturally, Tom. And with this thing and the way Joe says you use it, you won't have any complaints."

Tom gave Charlie a kiss. "Thanks Charlie, but I can't do it. I wouldn't even be able to get it hard."

"Unlike now," Charlie laughed.

Tom put his hand over Charlie's. "I'm hard because it's you! Not her!"

Ray came out of the bedroom, buttoning his shirt. "Hey, Tom. You want a turn? He's one of those guys who's always ready and frankly, I need a little rest. He'd be happy if you did."

"Yeah, Tom, go on. It'll take your mind off your problem," Charlie said.

"What problem?" Ray asked. "Tom?"

"Nothing, I think, you can help him with, Ray," Charlie said. "Come on Tom, tell Ray all about it."

Tom did. When he was through Ray didn't laugh the way Tom had thought he would. Instead he looked off into space for a couple of minutes and then said, "The way I see it, Tom, you have only three courses of action to choose from. First, you could just tell your boss that you prefer men to women and thank him for the offer."

"Sure," Tom said, "and then listen to him fire me."

"Not necessarily," Charlie said. "Guys who have women they can offer up as a reward often know of men they can do the same thing with. Maybe he'd just get you a man instead."

"Doubtful," Ray said, "but possible. Your second choice of action, and this one I seriously don't recommend, is to drink too much and pass out as soon as you hit the bed. She would probably get disgusted and leave you alone. Possibly she'd simply leave and go home."

Charlie laughed. "Yeah, but you can be sure your boss would hear about it. And not as a funny story."

Tom nodded and looked hopefully at Ray. "And the third?"

Ray shrugged. "Go through with it. Give her a fucking she won't soon forget and one she'll compare to his and find his wanting." He held his hand up, cutting Tom off. "You *can* do it, you know. It'll be different and you might not actually like it much but you can do it."

Charlie nodded. "We do it all the time with our wives and we love it, don't we Ray?" He paused and then went on, "Well, you've never been married so you wouldn't know but the rest of us do." "He turned back to Tom. "You can, Tom. You really can do this."

. . . .

That night, lying in bed, Tom tried to jack-off picturing Marilyn Monroe, trying to imagine what it would feel like being inside her. The image wouldn't cooperate though and Marilyn kept shifting into Ray or Cliff and his orgasm came when the image twisted into Russ, the black cable car gripman. His last waking thought was *I can't go through with this!*

. . . .

At lunchtime on Friday Tom went over to 323 to leave his part of the rent for Charlie to deliver on Saturday. He found all three of the guys there.

"Ah, just the man we need to see," Charlie said. "But first, some champagne?" He handed Tom a flute glass of wine.

"See about what?" Tom said. "And champagne?"

"Sure," Ray said with a grin. "It's New Year's Eve. Time for a toast."

"It's tomorrow, guys. But what the hell." He sipped his champagne and found it wonderful. Joe read his mind.

"It ought to be good," he said. "It's Deutz. Now, give us a kiss."

They did. Everyone kissed everyone, and not brief little friendship kisses. By the time they finished every one of them was well on the way to an erection.

Charlie laughed and ran his hand over his crotch. "Damn, now I'll be carrying this thing around for the rest of the day."

"Aww, poor Charlie," Joe said. "Here, let me take care of that for you." He reached for Charlie's crotch.

"I wish you could, Joe," Charlie said, "but I've got to get out of here or I won't have anything at all down there to carry around. We're off to Mexico for a week and Mary will chop it off if we miss that plane." He turned to Tom. "Hey, could you deliver the rent to Mrs. Tan tomorrow? I won't be able to and I don't trust these clowns to do it."

"Sure. Guys? The money?"

"Oh, yeah," Ray said, "you don't know about that, do you? There's a canister on the second shelf in the kitchen marked 'flour.' The money's in there."

Joe spoke up and added, "We do that because some of us put it in a week's worth at a time. Saves explanations at home." He smiled. "Nifty, huh?"

Charlie left shortly after that, leaving Ray, Joe and Tom to finish the champagne. They toasted one another until Joe said, "Okay guys, who's up for a blowjob?"

Both Tom and Ray raised their hands. "Well, not up yet," Ray said, "but I will be in a second."

They ended up on one of the beds, Joe on Tom, Tom on Ray and Ray on Joe. It was quick but thoroughly satisfying.

. . . .

Saturday afternoon Tom went down to 323, glad of something to do to keep his mind off the coming evening. He retrieved the rent money and went up to Mrs. Tan's, rang the bell and identified himself. When asked to come in he found Mrs. Tan in her accustomed brocade covered wingchair, a bottle of champagne set in a silver cooler and a plate of cheese and crackers by her side.

"Well, isn't this nice," she said, nodding at Tom, "a kind young man come to share my little celebration." Noting his look of confusion she added, "Oh, I knew someone from downstairs would be along with the rent this afternoon. I hope you can stay long enough to share a toast to the New Year with me. Just put the rent on the desk there, will you?"

Tom did so and then, at further direction from Mrs. Tan, opened the champagne and filled two heavy crystal flutes. They toasted the New Year and each other.

"Are you able to spend a few minutes?" she asked. "I know you young people are so busy these days but..."

Tom grinned at her. "But never too busy to spend a little time with a lady such as you," Tom finished for her. He looked around the room for a moment and then said, "Could you tell me about your furniture? I mean, it's very different..."

Mrs. Tan let out a whoop of laughter. "Oh yes, it is that. As I think I may have said, Mr. Tan and I had quite different backgrounds and quite different tastes in furniture. You see, Mr. Tan was Chinese, born here, of course, but of a Chinese family. I, on the other hand, though born here also, came from an English background. Thus," she waved her hand, taking in the entire room, "the furniture."

She went on to explain that they, she and Mr. Tan, had decided they each liked furniture from both cultures and so furnished their home with practicality: a sturdy English desk but a delicate Chinese lamp, things like that. "We were very dissimilar in our tastes and backgrounds," she said, "but we were very much in love and that made all the difference."

"It must have been very interesting for both of you, marrying into such a different culture," Tom said.

Mrs. Tan rolled her eyes. "Oh, you don't know the half of it. And it was hard on our families as well. You know, neither his mother nor his father ever set foot in our home. On *their* New Year Mr. Tan was invited to the celebration but never I. And of course he wouldn't go." She laughed. "So you know his solution? We stayed home and he cooked all the traditional dishes. He was quite an accomplished cook by the time he died."

"Well," she said, glancing at the little ormolu clock on her side table, "I've kept you twice too long. I'm sure you have plans for the evening." She winked at him. "And the night. You'd better run along. Can you see yourself out?"

Tom nodded and stood, gathering the champagne glasses and cheese plates. "I'll put these in the kitchen if you like."

"Well, thank you. And thank you for letting an old women run on about her life. You are very kind."

Tom came out of the kitchen and pulled her into a gentle hug. "I enjoyed every minute of it and I hope to hear more. Truly."

CHAPTER 9

. . . .

At home he found his dad in the den. "Well, I'm glad you're home, Tom," Matt said. "How about a little New Year's toast?" There was a bottle of champagne on the table, chilling in a glass cooler. "I also got some very nice little sandwiches and things from the deli. I figured you'll probably be eating late and," he laughed and winked, "you'll no doubt be needing your strength."

They opened the champagne, *Piper Heidsieck, Brut,* and laid out the little sandwiches, spreads and crackers. "This should keep us until dinner," Matt said.

"Hey, Dad, what are you doing tonight? Going to some party with Stella"

"She's busy with something. But I have a date. Can you believe it? Your old man on a real date?"

"Gosh," Tom said with a grin, "I hope she'll walk real slow so your shuffling steps can keep up with her. Old man, my foot! You gonna get lucky?"

Matt laughed. "Isn't that the idea? It's what New Year's Eve was invented for. You?"

Tom nodded. "Looks that way. We'll see."

He dressed in the sapphire blue silk boxers, the ones he liked best, his favorite white shirt and the black suit from David-Stephan's. He borrowed a pink and gray stripped tie from his dad, put on his newly polished shoes, his Rolex and a splash of lime cologne. He even remembered to put a new box of condoms in his inside coat pocket.

"Well, aren't you the snazzy one," his dad said when Tom came out of his room. "Must be quite an important date. Here," he said, digging in his pocket and handing Tom a twenty dollar bill, "have a drink on me." He winked. "And be careful!"

Tom nodded, smiled and pulled the box of condoms partially out of his coat pocket so his dad could see them.

"Good man," his dad said, hugging him. "Now go and show 'em how it's done."

Tom, as was usual for him, got to the Palace Hotel early. He was supposed to meet Miss Winters in the bar across from the Garden Court at six and he was there at a quarter of. He sat at the bar and ordered gin and tonic. He really wanted a martini—a double—but he was afraid to drink too much. He was pretty sure he'd need all of his wits about him.

At five after six Miss Winters stepped into the bar, a vision in bright red silk and eggshell linen, wearing the highest heels Tom had ever seen. She came up and hugged him. "I'm sorry to be late," she said, "traffic was quite bad. Please sit." She rather delicately sat on the stool next to the one he'd occupied.

"I hope you don't mind," she said, "but I've run into an old friend and, as it's New Year's Eve, asked him to join us for a drink. He'll be along shortly."

The bartender came over and, after a brief conciliation, Tom ordered Miss Winters a martini and then thought *Oh, what the hell,* and ordered one for himself.

Miss Winters smiled and said, "My, we are compatible. I believe my friend will have a martini as well." She looked towards the door. "Oh, here he comes now."

Tom looked up and very nearly fell off his barstool. Her friend was the red-headed bartender from Tom's first time at the Hideaway. He was dressed up in a dark suit and a tie but he was still the redheaded bartender.

Miss Winter slipped off her stool and hugged the man. She then turned to Tom and said, Tom Braden, I'd like you to meet Dan Davis."

Dan extended his hand and said, "Miss Winters, that is, Irene, and I are old friends and she's been kind enough to ask me to have a drink with you. I hope you don't mind."

While he spoke Tom could see the recognition in his eyes; they never wavered from Tom's. The moment was broken by the bartender, serving the martinis.

After a quarter hour or so of meaningless conversation Dan looked at Miss Winters and said, "My dear, are you feeling ill? You seem so pale."

Miss Winters nodded. "I believe one of my headaches is coming on. I don't know what to do."

"Well, I do," Dan said. "You must go home, take one of those powders the doctor gave you and go immediately to bed with a hot water bottle and an extra blanket."

Miss Winters looked at Tom. "I'm so sorry, Mr. Braden, but he is, of course, correct. If I don't this will last for several days." She got off her stool and put her hand on Tom's shoulder. "Perhaps Mr. Davis will be kind enough to share the evening with you. And you may be sure that Mr. Diggs will hear what a lovely evening it was, how good the food and how enjoyable the night. Again, I apologize but I must go."

She picked up her coat and quietly left the bar. Tom, who was just a little shaken by this turn of events, turned and looked at Dan who had a wide grin on his face.

"Don't worry, Tom," Dan said. "She'll tell him all that and more. By the time she's through he'll be nervous about his own abilities. And you," he said, touching his glass to Tom's, "had better live up to what she's going to tell him!"

Just then the maitre d' came up to them and said, "Your table is ready gentlemen. Do I understand that the lady will not be joining you?"

"Yes," Dan said. "She has been taken suddenly ill."

"Oh, I'm so sorry," the waiter said. "I'm sure she will be missed." The way he said it made it quite clear that he knew the lady would *not* be missed. "Please come this way."

When they were seated and a bottle of California Pinot Noir ordered, Tom looked at Dan and asked, "What just happened?"

Dan laughed. "Look, for a straight female, Irene has very good gaydar and can generally spot a gay man before he finishes his first sentence. When... that guy, whoever he is, hired her..."

"My boss. She was... well, she was supposed to be a reward for getting things done."

"Even worse," Dan said with a broad smile. "Anyway, I just happened to be in town so she asked me to come along and confirm her judgment. She said you weren't ugly so if you really were gay, I could take her place if I liked." He shrugged. "Hey, free drinks, free dinner and get laid in a hundred dollar hotel room? Of course I liked. And then, just in case all that wasn't enough, the guy who's going to do the laying turned out to be you. What a deal!"

"What a deal," Tom echoed. "And I was so worried."

"Worried?"

"Yeah. I've never... well, you know. I wasn't sure I could do it." He caught Dan's eye. "Shall we eat? Then we'll go upstairs and I'll show you what I do know how to do. Okay?"

Before Dan could answer, the waiter appeared with the wine. Right behind him was another waiter with menus. If Tom had looked, however, Dan's answer was right there, forcing a large bulge in his pants. The wine waiter did see it and was quite envious. Of both of them.

. . . .

While Tom and Dan were ordering crab cakes and lobster turnovers in the Garden Court at the Palace Hotel, Tom's dad and a lady named Monica were ordering Mai Tai's and Cashew Nut Chicken with Fried Rice in the Tonga Room at the Fairmount Hotel.

Monica was an accountant who worked for a CPA firm on the same floor as Matt's offices. They had become acquainted one afternoon when the elevator they were riding became stuck between the seventeenth and eighteenth floors of their building.

Matt had been thinking for some time that Tom was probably going to be moving out of the flat one day soon. After all, a good looking, intelligent and soon to be very successful man couldn't live with his dad forever. Besides, it was getting towards the time when Tom would stop being a stud-about-town and begin looking at his women with an eye to settling down and starting a family.

This had led Matt to think that perhaps he should be doing the same. He'd done it once and he figured—especially at his age now—he could do it again. Beyond that, he didn't want to end up a lonely old man, living alone, dependent on his only son for the joys of family life. He was beginning to consider his current way of life as simply an interlude, a time of easy pleasure with like-minded men.

Therefore: Monica.

When dinner was finished Matt suggested a drink in the Hurricane Bar and, as he'd expected, Monica countered with an invitation to have a drink at her apartment. They took a cab out to the Marina where Monica lived in the guest house behind one of the grand homes that lined Marina Boulevard.

Entering the living room, Monica pointed out the bar cabinet, went to the kitchen for ice and then to the bedroom to change. Matt made a pair of highballs, removed his coat and thought about taking his shoes off but then decided that would be too obvious.

It went off like clockwork, each of them knowing their parts, each of them working towards the common goal of the bedroom, the bed and it's pleasures. It was perfectly done, except for that last part.

Once in bed Matt found that he couldn't get an erection. Monica said she understood that things like this happened to men now and again and she thought she knew a way to help things along. She was right, her mouth doing what Matt's mind couldn't.

Once they started in earnest Monica seemed to enjoy it, making all the right noises and thrusting back at all the right times. For Matt it was pleasurable enough to maintain his erection but nothing more. In the end, once Monica had climaxed, he had to fake his, making what he hoped were appropriate movements and sounds.

When Monica pointedly didn't ask him to spend the night, asking instead if he wanted her to call a cab, he dressed, hugged her and thanked her for a lovely evening. The cab arrived just in time to keep things from being awkward.

. . . .

While Matt and Monica were being carefully civilized with each other, Tom and Dan were rutting like the fine young animals they were. They'd started quietly enough, undressing each other, carefully handling and admiring the parts that caught their attention and generally bringing each other gentle pleasure. This lead to a three word discussion of who would do what to whom first and that lead to Dan lying on the bed with his calves pressed against Tom's shoulders and Tom doing his best to be slow and gentle as he entered him. He succeeded, too, until Dan suddenly pushed back and took into himself everything Tom had.

"God damn that thing is big," he whispered, and then he came. His contractions brought Tom off. "That," Tom said when he was finally coherent, "took exactly three and a half minutes."

Dan smiled. "That's okay. It means the next round will take longer. There will be another round, won't there?"

"I think so," Tom said, fondling Dan's dick. "Several."

There were and at about the time Matt was stepping into a cab, Tom and Dan were well into their second bout of love making.

. . . .

"Where to, Mac?" the taxi driver asked.

"Home, I suppose."

"Oh, good," the driver said somewhat sarcastically. "And just where would that be?"

Three thoughts occurred to Matt, nearly simultaneously. The first was that he was nearly life threateningly horny. The second was that his right hand wasn't much of an option. The third was that someone, somewhere, had mentioned that the baths were virtually a sure thing if you wanted a blow job. Matt wanted a blow job.

He'd never been to the baths but he didn't hesitate. "Forget home. Take me to the baths."

"Which one?" When Matt hesitated the driver twisted around in his seat and looked at him. "You ever been to the baths?"

"No, but I think I need to go."

The driver turned back to his steering wheel and pulled away from the curb. "Okay, we'll go to Dave's. It's clean and there's always a big crowd on New Year's Eve. We'll get lockers; you got twenty dollars?"

Matt caught the driver's eye in the mirror. "What for?"

The driver laughed. "Look they're not in this business just for the fun of it, you know. Lockers are ten dollars. Two lockers: twenty. No group discount."

"You're... You're going with me?"

"Look Mac, somebody has to look out for you, being your first time and all. Besides, standing out there, before you got in the cab? Looked like you have something very nice down there between your legs and I'd kind of like to get a piece of it." He pulled over to the curb, into a space marked *No Parking at Any Time.* "Here we are."

They went into a fairly nondescript building that in other circumstances Matt would have taken to be some sort of light industrial plant or a small warehouse. Inside, the attendant seemed to know the cabdriver and Matt wondered if he got some sort of commission for bringing men to the place. Matt paid for their two lockers and they went to take their clothes off.

In the locker room the cabdriver openly watched Matt as they both undressed. When Matt slid his boxers down—the sapphire blue silk ones, the same as Tom was wearing—the cabdriver let out a low whistle. "That's bigger than I thought it'd be," he said, reaching out to touch it. "Must be huge when it's hard."

"Keep that up and you'll find out," Matt said. "But you'll be disappointed. It'll maybe grow a little but mainly it'll just get hard." The cabdriver, in an attempt to verify Matt's statement, hung on.

Another man, naked but with a towel slung over his shoulder, came into the room just in time to hear the driver exclaim again about how big Matt's dick was. The man laughed, looking at Matt's dick with an appraising eye. "It's nice," he said to no one in particular, "but it sure isn't the biggest one here."

"You're shitting me," the cabdriver said to the man.

"You don't believe me? Go take a look at the guy in 319." He chuckled. "But not now. Some guy is sitting on it at the moment."

Matt laughed and turned to the Cabdriver. "Now what?"

The first thing they did was take a shower. The shower room was interesting. It contained a large stainless steel column with six shower heads coming out of it. It was designed, Matt was pretty sure, so everyone got to see everyone.

After the shower they took a look in the steam room, which the cabdriver said was for later, for relaxing, and then went to the main playroom. There, the cabdriver had Matt sit on the large, raised platform, kneeled between his legs and gave him a blowjob which Matt could only describe as a near religious experience. The guy was that good.

After, when Matt tried to return the favor, the driver shook his head. "No, Mac, save that for a guy who really needs it, like you did. Me? I'm going to check out room 319." He gave Matt a quick kiss and was gone.

Matt, still in the afterglow of his orgasm thought he'd just explore a little but was stopped by a man who looked at him and then, without a word, pulled him into a hug and kissed him for a very long time. When they broke the kiss they were both hard. They hugged again, pulling their dicks up so they were lying beside each other and Matt put his hand on the man's butt. The man moaned and pulled Matt closer.

A moment later they were on the platform, Matt lying on the man's back, slowly entering him. They took their time with it, savoring the pleasure, until an unknown hand slid up between Matt's legs and found his balls. It was so unexpected and so sexual that Matt simply lost all control and came. The other man, the one receiving him, followed suit almost immediately.

After that Matt took another shower, spent some time in the steam room and then discovered the small, dark room where they were showing porn.

· · · · · · · · · · · · · ·

In the Palace Hotel things had slowed down somewhat and, in fact, Tom and Dan were curled together spoon fashion, sleeping. In time, Dan half woke, found himself hard and Tom still slick so, almost by instinct, he gently slid back inside Tom. Tom let out a contented sigh and continued with the extremely erotic dream he was having.

· · · · · · · · · · · · · ·

At the baths, Matt, too, was taking a hard dick inside himself. He hadn't actually seen the man, it being so dim in the room but the man was very enthusiastic about what he was doing and brought Matt as much pleasure as Matt was bringing him.

· · · · · · · · · · · · · ·

And so it went, well into the morning, until they had all had enough. Matt took a final shower, dressed and decided to walk home and enjoy the cool morning. Tom and Dan took their room service coffee into the bathroom and took a final shower as well, although theirs was more active than Matt's and resulted in orgasms for both of them. They left the hotel with each other's taste still in their mouths.

Dan, who was attending Stanford, forty miles South of San Francisco, promised to call Tom the next time he'd be able to get away to The City. They were each feeling a little soreness in the ass and both were savoring it, remembering what had brought it about.

At home, Matt was just opening the door when Tom walked up. "Well, well," Matt said, looking Tom up and down, "it sure looks like someone got lucky last night. From the looks of you, several times."

Tom laughed. "As do you, Dad. As do you. You have fun?"

"Yeah, I did. More than I have in a while. You?"

"Oh, yeah. Hey, Dad, you hungry?"

"Very. You want to go to Arthur's and have bacon waffles?"

Tom laughed again. "The perfect ending to the perfect night. Yeah, let's go."

Chapter 10

At work on Tuesday Mr. Diggs was late but seemed in a jovial mood. When Tom went into his office he said, with a laugh, "So. I hear you have talents well beyond the business world. I wonder if I should be worrying?"

At lunch time Tom went up to see who might be at 323. All the renters were there, Charlie, Ray, and Joe, and they all wanted to know how Saturday turned out.

Tom laughed and gave them a slightly edited version of the evening. When he was through Joe said, "So essentially you jumped into a barrel marked "Shit" and it turned out to be Channel Number Five, right?"

Tom laughed. "You might say that. Oh, and to add to that, that I really enjoyed my time in the barrel."

On Tuesday of the next week Mr. Diggs handed Tom a file to be put in the "Completed" drawer and said, "It's a good thing I managed to close that one. Your little reward cost me a bit more than I expected."

Tom cocked his head. "We didn't eat that much, did we?"

Mr. Diggs laughed. "No, no Thomas, it wasn't the dinner. It was the fir jacket."

"Fir jacket?"

"Never mind, Thomas. As you gain experience with women, you still won't understand them. Now let's get to work."

. . . .

The following Tuesday morning, the shit hit the fan.

It started innocently enough with a visit from Miss West, Mr. Simms secretary. Since Miss West never came back to Mr. Diggs area, that in itself should have given them a clue that all was not well. She went into Mr. Diggs office and told him Mr. Simms wanted to see Tom at nine o'clock. Sharp. She left without speaking to Tom, leaving Mr. Diggs to pass along the message, which he did.

Tom was on time and was told Mr. Simms was waiting for him.

"Good morning, Mr. Braden," Mr. Simms said, holding out the cigarette box. Tom shook his head and waived the box away. Mr. Simms took one and lit it before offering Tom a chair.

"I don't have time to beat around the bush young man, so I'll get directly to the point. Are you registered? Have your real-estate license?" He looked directly at Tom and Tom could almost hear the unspoken: *And don't lie!*"

Tom nodded. "Yes sir, I took a course and got registered maybe six months ago. Is... Is there a problem with that?"

Mr. Simms ignored the question. "And just who, Mr. Braden, paid for your course of study and your fees?"

"Well, technically I guess my dad did. But I'm paying him back, sir. It's nearly all..." A sudden thought occurred to him. "Wait a minute. What does it matter who paid for it?"

Still ignoring Tom's questions, Mr. Simms asked, "Mr. Diggs didn't pay for it? For any of it?"

Tom shrugged. "No. Why would he?"

Mr. Simms sighed in exasperation. "I'm asking the questions here if you don't mind, Mr. Braden. What did Mr. Diggs say when you told him you were registered and licensed?"

"Nothing. He doesn't know."

"Doesn't know? You didn't tell him? Come now, Mr. Braden."

Tom was doing his best to control himself but he could hear an edge of anger come into his voice. "He told me, when I first started working for him, he told me that it was company policy, *your policy, Sir*, that employees could not be registered until they'd worked here for a year. If I'd said anything, I supposed he'd have to fire me."

Mr. Simms shook his head. "So why'd you do it?"

"I was fired up, I wanted to understand what we were doing. I figured it'd help me be more of a help to Mr. Diggs. That's all."

Mr. Simms put out his cigarette and lit another. He fixed Tom with a look which did nothing to break the tension in the room. "Then tell me, Mr. Braden," he said in a quiet voice, "why you rented a suite of offices in the Russ Building. The ones on the fifth floor." This last was added to show that he knew exactly what he was talking about.

Tom gave him a blank look. "The Russ Building?"

Mr. Simms smiled for the first time since Tom had come in. "You really don't know what all this is about, do you?"

Tom shook his head. "No sir."

Mr. Simms didn't hear him; his eyes were focused far away, on something Tom couldn't see. Then, without warning, he slammed his hand on the desk, making a sound like a gun shot. "That bastard," he roared. "That God damned bastard." He thought for a few more moments before picking up the phone.

"Miss West, coffee please, for Mr. Braden and myself. Thank you." Then he turned to Tom. "I'm sorry to have put you through this, Son, but I had to know." He smiled. "My wife, Mrs. Simms, with whom I often discuss business, said it would turn out something like this. But I had to know for sure. You see..."

Just then Miss West came in with a silver coffee service and two China cups. Once she had poured Mr. Simms waived her away with a thank-you. Then he turned to Tom.

"You see, Son, the real-estate business in San Francisco is quite a tight knit community. It's very difficult for any of us to do something without the rest of us, or at least those of us who might have an interest, knowing about it. When a suite of offices in the Russ Building was rented to a registered real-estate operative, and that operative worked in my office, I was among the first to know."

Tom sipped his coffee. "But I didn't..."

"Of course you didn't. Mr. Diggs did; in your name. Not knowing you are registered, he thought no one would be the wiser, especially me."

"But why..."

"Think about it, Son. Why would a man with a lucrative group of clients rent an office? In the Russ Building or anywhere else in town?"

Tom laughed. "I get it. He's going to jump ship, isn't he. And he didn't want you to know it because you might do something to keep those clients with *Bay Holdings.*"

"Exactly."

"So, if I may ask, what are you going to do?"

Mr. Simms grinned. "Exactly nothing. There's no point. If a client wants to go with Mr. Diggs, there'll be nothing *I* can do to stop him. He'll go where he's comfortable. But if he's not comfortable, he'll stay with us. And many of those that go will come back. It's the way people are." He finished his coffee and with a gesture asked Tom if he wanted more.

Tom shook his head. "Anything I should do?"

"I don't think so. You might watch out for missing files, that sort of thing, but there isn't much he can really do. We have copies of nearly all his files up here. He's probably forgotten that so please don't remind him of it. When he does leave, *and not before it,* you and I will get together and chart a path of action for you. That is if you are still with us. I think he depends on you a great deal and will no doubt offer you a job. You may take it or not, as you see fit and with my blessing."

Back in his office, Mr. Diggs wanted to know what was going on. Tom made up a little story about missing files which Miss West needed help in finding. Mr. Diggs complemented him on his organizational abilities and asked him to lunch on Thursday.

Tom didn't know what to make of this development. When he talked to his dad about it that evening his dad laughed. "Happens all the time in my business, Tom. Some firm offers one of the guys more commission or better trading rules or better coffee or some damn thing and off he goes. Your Mr. Diggs is just trying to beat the odds by starting up his own office. After all, his own office will mean his own profits although I don't particularly like the way he's gone about it, renting offices in your name. You'd better get that one straightened out rather quickly. And your Mr. Simms is right. Diggs will no doubt offer you a job. You going to take it? He'll probably offer you more money."

"I don't know, Dad. I'll have to think about it, I guess. I mean, he's okay to work for but he does have his moods. They're sometimes pretty hard to deal with."

"Well, give it some thought. You know better than anyone what will be best for you. In the meantime, that's my special lamb stew you're smelling. Want some?"

Tom did. His dad made the best lamb stew in the whole world.

In bed, after a short but explosive session with his hand, Tom decided not to worry about Mr. Diggs and his potential job offer. He'd deal with it when—and if—it came.

. . . .

It came at lunch on Thursday. Mr. Diggs said he was going to start his own office and he very much wanted Tom to join him. "What we'll do," he said, "is get you registered right away. That way you can have part of my commissions and eventually make your own. At first you'll be on salary—say seven-hundred dollars a month. Then, as you make commissions, for a year I'll make up any difference between what you make and seven-hundred dollars. When your commissions are more than seven-hundred dollars a month I'll take half of everything over seven-hundred. Believe me, Thomas, it's a good deal for both of us."

While Mr. Diggs was pouring wine Tom suddenly remembered a conversation he'd overheard on the cable car one day and the words echoed in his mind: "If he cheated on one, he'll cheat on the other. It's in the man's blood."

He realized that by renting offices in Tom's name, Mr. Diggs had cheated on him and by keeping it a secret he'd cheated on Mr. Simms. He now knew what his answer would be.

"Well, Tom, what about it?"

"I don't think so. I think I'll take my chances and stay at *Bay Holdings*. But I wish you luck, I really do."

A dark look passed over Mr. Diggs face for a moment but then he smiled and said, "Your choice, Thomas, but I think you're making a big mistake. No matter. The offer stays in effect for the next two weeks." Again the dark look. "And you will keep my plans confidential, won't you?"

"Yes, of course, sir. But they aren't exactly a secret. Mr. Simms knows about them."

Mr. Diggs turned white and began to shake. Tom thought he might fall off his chair but he didn't; he summoned the waiter and ordered a double gin.

"How?" His voice was choked.

"The offices in the Russ Building."

"B... But they're in... Well, they're not in my name."

"No sir, but they're in the name of someone registered with the Real Estate Board. He found out that way."

"Christ," Mr. Diggs mumbled under his breath. Then, looking at Tom, "You'd better go now." He gave a brief waive of dismissal.

Back in the office Tom went to see Mr. Simms. "Well, Mr. Braden, how was your lunch?"

"Uncomfortable. But you were right, he offered me a job. Seven hundred a month. I turned him down."

"Oh? What made you do that?"

Tom laughed. "Partly out of loyalty to you and the firm, sir, but mostly I guess because of something I overheard on the cable car a while back."

Mr. Simms looked perplexed. "I beg your pardon."

"It's not really important, sir. Just something about men who cheat on their wives."

"I see. Well Son, we'll talk about your position here as soon as I speak with Mr. Diggs. In the meantime, please carry on as you have been." He stood, signaling that the meeting was over.

In his own office Sue came in and said, "What the hell is going on?"

Tom wasn't sure just how much he could tell her. "Why?"

"Well, for starters," she said with a strong edge of sarcasm to her voice, "there's a guy out there changing the locks on the doors. At least on Mr. Diggs office and I think he's already done yours. So what gives?"

Tom rolled his eyes and was suddenly tired of secrets so he told her the whole story. "But for some reason it's a secret and I'll probably lose my job when they find out I told you but I don't care. I'm tired of this."

Sue smiled. "How will they find out? Certainly not from me."

"Thank you Sue. I appreciate that." He laughed. "Mr. Simms said I was to carry on as usual so I suppose we should. Let's see what's on Mr. Diggs desk."

Tom spent the rest of the afternoon working the files, making phone calls and even setting up an appointment or two.

That night he told his dad how the lunch had gone. When he explained the pay arrangement his dad said, "Well, I hope you turned him down, Son. Seven hundred isn't much for what he'd have you doing."

"Yeah, I turned him down but not because of the money. I did it because he's a cheat and I don't want to work for a cheat."

His dad grinned and went over to him. "You have paid attention, haven't you? I'm proud of you Son. Very proud." He pulled Tom into a bear hug and held him for a moment making Tom feel very safe and warm.

. . . .

It took over a week, a week in which Mr. Diggs did not come to work, for things to finally get settled. On Friday, first thing in the morning, Mr. Simms called a meeting of all the staff and explained that Mr. Diggs would no longer be part of *Bay Holdings.* Tom was put in charge of Mr. Diggs former area and Sue would report to him. He was to move into Mr. Diggs office as quickly as possible. Tom didn't see that this involved much change. He'd been doing pretty much all of Mr. Diggs work and, without paying much attention to it, had been using his office.

After the meeting Mr. Simms motioned Tom to remain. When the others had gone he offered the cigarette box to Tom. When Tom refused it he took one himself and lighted it. "Mr. Braden, I…"

"Please sir, call me Tom."

Mr. Simms looked perplexed. "I know other businesses do that, but I'm not sure it is appropriate to us, here at *Bay Holdings*." He looked out the window, lost in thought for a moment. "But I shall think about it and talk with my wife, Mrs. Simms, about it. In the meantime, Mr. Braden, we must discuss the question of your salary."

"Yes, sir?"

"I know what Mr. Diggs offered you, both from what you told me and what Mr. Diggs himself told me. I'm prepared to offer you eight hundred dollars a month. You would keep all of your commissions for the first year and, after that, the firm would take the standard twenty-five percent. Your salary would stop after the second year."

Tom was floored; Mr. Simms was offering him more than he'd ever hoped for. Tom couldn't quite figure out what to say and Mr. Simms took that as a bad sign.

"I'm sorry, Mr. Braden, but that is the best I can offer."

Tom gulped and found his voice. "No, No, Mr. Simms. That is more generous than I could ever hope for. I'm just... Well, I'm just a little overwhelmed."

Mr. Simms chuckled. "Well, then, Mr. Braden, shall we shake hands on it?"

Both men stood and rather formally shook hands. "That is effective immediately," Mr. Simms said, "so I suggest you get on with it." Tom took this as dismissal and acted accordingly.

When he got home that evening, Tom told his dad about his new position at work and his new salary.

"You mean he's going to pay you eight hundred dollars a month for two years? Regardless of the commissions you make? You know what I think?"

"That he's crazy?"

Matt grinned. "No. I think he's a very canny business man. First he rewards you for your loyalty, then he sews you up for two years because only an idiot would leave a deal like that. After a couple of years you're going to make him a lot of money for providing you with essentially nothing but an office, a phone and someone to type your stuff up. My hat's off to him." He gave Tom a long look. "Just make sure you don't get lazy and coast along on his money." Then he smiled. "You won't. I know you and that's not in your blood."

Tom shrugged. "Hey, look who brought me up and taught me all the important stuff about life."

"Flattery will get you anywhere. To Momma Giordano's, for instance. You up for some steamed clams?"

"Oh, yeah. But I pay this time. Share the good fortune."

Matt turned serious for a moment. "Good fortune plays a small part I guess, but most of the credit goes to you and the man you've become." He smiled. "My son, the real estate magnate. Sounds good."

. . . .

On Friday a couple of weeks later, just before quitting time, his phone rang. He thought of just ignoring it but then thought better; it might be Mr. Simms and not answering would look worse in his eyes than giving Sue the afternoon off. He was very glad he did answer: it was Dan Davis, the redheaded bartender and, though Mr. Diggs didn't know it, Mr. Diggs New Year's present.

"Hey, Tom. I've got to be up in town tomorrow and wondered if... well, if you might have some time or something..."

Ton laughed. "For you, Dan, I've always got time." He unconsciously ran his hand over his crotch. "I've got something else for you, too, but... Well, you know."

"Yeah, I know. I've got one for you, too." Tom could hear the smile in his voice. "Look, I have to give a little talk tomorrow morning but from about eleven to three, when my ride leaves, I won't have much on. My friend Bob is away and I have his key. You interested?"

"You won't have much on?"

Dan chuckled. "Not if you take it off."

"I'm interested! Just tell me when and where."

Dan gave him the address, an apartment building out on Geary, and said that if Tom got there around eleven they could save some water by showering together.

They didn't actually save much water because they played in the shower until the hot water ran out. Then they played in the bed for a while and ended up with a quickie while standing at the kitchen counter waiting for the coffee to brew. It was a fine afternoon for both of them.

CHAPTER 11

. . . .

In mid-February, on Valentine's day, Tom gave both Sue and Miss West each a small bouquet of roses and a box of See's candy. Sue, when she saw them on her desk, swept Tom into a hug and kissed him on the cheek. In contrast, Miss West stood behind her desk and shook his hand. However, Miss West also sent him a handwritten Thank You note.

The day after, Miss West called to say that Mr. Simms would like Tom to come down to his office for a moment. In his office, after offering the cigarette box to Tom and then taking one for himself, Mr. Simms said, "I must say, Mr. Braden, that Miss West was quite pleased with your little gift yesterday. I've always thought it improper for a married man to present a gift to an unmarried woman so I'd like to thank you for your kind gesture. Both Miss West and I had a very pleasant day because of it." He then turned back to the papers on his desk, giving Tom a little waive of dismissal.

About this same time Tom took to visiting Mrs. Tan once or twice a week. Her stories of her life with Mr. Tan and of her life earlier, as a child, were fascinating. Beyond that, she was a master storyteller and always kept Tom deeply interested.

In March, on the Wednesday before Tom's birthday, he had a call from Dan. "Look, I know your birthday is Saturday and I imagine you'll be tied up with a big party that night but how about the night after, Sunday night?"

Tom laughed. "Gosh, Dan, I don't know. I have a date with my right hand. But maybe I could postpone it or something."

"No, no. Don't do that. Invite your hand along and I'll give him something new to play with. Like maybe this little thing trying to bust out of my pants."

"He'd be honored, although he already knows that that little thing grows into a monster pretty darn fast."

"Especially for you. Can you meet me at The Copper Lantern around seven-thirty? That guy I stay with will be out until Monday morning so we can go to his place after and see what that hand of yours can do."

"Among other parts of my anatomy," Tom said. "Yours too."

At home, after work, Matt said, "Did you know your birthday is Saturday?"

"Yeah, actually, I did. Why?"

"Well, I thought maybe we could go to dinner at Ernie's to celebrate."

Tom smiled. "Like last year? Just you and me? Or is there…"

"Just you and me. Unless there's someone you want to invite to come along."

"Not that I can think of," Tom said. "Not yet, at least. Maybe one of these days."

Thursday and Friday were quiet at the office and Tom felt like he was really getting some things done. On Friday Sue brought in a homemade birthday cake which turned out to be very good and which they shared with Mr. Simms and Miss West. Miss West presented him with a small card, suitable for any male between the ages of nine and ninety. Mr. Simms gave him the afternoon off.

At lunchtime Tom went up to 323, not to play because he had some vague idea of "saving himself" for Dan, but just to see who might be there. He found Charlie, Joe and Ray there, drinking champagne.

"Well, well," Joe said, "here's the birthday boy now." He gave him a kiss and handed him a glass of champagne. "Guys?"

Ray and Charlie each got up and gave him a hug and a kiss. "Welcome to twenty-two, kid," Charlie said. Ray laughed. "Yeah, twenty-two. I remember it but not very well. I think I was horny all the time."

Tom laughed. "I'll bet you were, seeing as how you're horny all the time now." He sipped his champagne and unconsciously ran his hand over his crotch. "Me too."

"See?" Joe said. "I told you it was the perfect birthday gift."

Tom looked at him. "Huh?"

Ray laughed. "You'll see. It's in the bedroom there. Go on, go get it."

Tom drank down his champagne, set the glass on a table and started towards the bedroom. "Really, guys, you shouldn't have done anything." He opened the doors and was face to face with three, obviously horny, naked men.

"Surprise!" they said, in unison. Tom recognized one of them as Stan, a guy Ray had brought up to 323 fairly often. Then Tom remembered the time Ray had put him between himself and Tom. He was suddenly very hard.

"Well, go on in," Joe said. "We're not part of this but we are going to watch so make it good!"

Tom stepped into the room and the guys immediately began undressing him. When he was naked all three of them began to lick him, from his toes to his forehead. When someone got to his ass he let out a groan, his brain shut down and he just gave himself up to them.

A short time later he found himself stretched out on the bed, on his back, on top of someone who was working a very large dick into him. His head was hanging over the end of the bed and suddenly there was an uncut dick in his mouth. He was working his tongue under the foreskin when he felt a sudden hot wetness on his own dick. At the same time the dick working into him hit his prostate and sent a jolt of pleasure through him that he was sure everyone else felt right along with him.

The man in Tom's mouth was the first to come, his dick so far down Tom's throat that Tom couldn't really taste him. He stayed, slowly riding Tom's mouth until he began to soften. Then he traded places with the man who was sucking Tom's dick.

The new cock in his mouth wasn't as big as the first one and it was cut, but it had a taste and smell that Tom's brain interpreted as *Man*. It drove him nuts and it drove him to orgasm. Tom's contractions set off the man in his ass and they groaned un unison. The man in Tom's mouth came too, and, as Tom knew he would, he tasted like *Man*.

When they'd untangled themselves Tom saw that it was indeed Stan who had fucked him. Tom gave him a special kiss of thanks. The other two were Mike, whom Tom had not seen before, and George, the UPS driver Willy had brought up to 323 a couple of times.

"Thanks, guys, that was one hell of a birthday present," Tom said, kissing each of them again. He nodded to Charlie, Ray and Joe, "And thanks to you for arranging it. This is a birthday I'll always remember."

They had just time for sandwiches and Cokes before the guys had to leave. When they were gone, taking whatever sandwiches were left over with them, Joe turned to Tom and said, "It's a damn shame you have to go too, being the birthday boy and all."

Tom grinned. "I don't. My boss gave me the afternoon off."

The men crowded around him and Ray said, "Really? You guys think we can do as well as those studs just did?" He patted Tom's ass. "I do. Shall we have a go at it?"

It wasn't long before all of them were naked and crowded on and around one of the beds. Not only were they as good as the young studs, they lasted longer.

That night, over a dinner of pasta, meat sauce, salad and garlic bread, Tom's dad commented that Tom looked a little tired. "Been a hard day?" he asked.

Tom grinned at him, thinking *You don't know the half of it.* and said, "The morning was okay it's the afternoon that was hard. Really hard." He thought for a moment and added, "But it was a good day, too."

The next night's birthday dinner at Ernie's was wonderful: butter lettuce and shrimp salad, lobster Thermidor, apricot mousse, coffee and brandy. Very good brandy.

For his birthday Matt gave him the usual hundred shares of stock and a beautifully made gold fountain pen. "Every man should have a special pen for his signature," he said. Treated right, this one will last you a lifetime."

Sunday night's dinner was good too: hamburger steak, onion rings, peas and carrots (which neither Tom nor Dan ate) and coffee ice cream. Over dinner they talked about their weeks and Tom told Dan about his birthday present at 323.

"Oh, wow," Dan said, "that must have been something, three guys all together."

"Oh, yeah, it was. Especially since it was followed by three more. Of course I've been with all three of them before but not at the same time. It was pretty sensational."

"So tell me about this apartment, 323."

Tom did, explaining how he got involved with the guys and that 323 was a convenience for them, especially for the two who were married. "There were three married guys at first but one moved away, I think because he broke the rule."

"The rule? They have just one rule?"

Tom thought for a moment and then nodded. "That's all we've ever talked about, at least as far as rules are concerned. The rule is: Never Get Emotionally Involved With Anyone."

Dan raised his eyebrow so Tom explained. "It's for fun, for casual sex. I guess if you're married and love your wife but still have certain urges, this is an ideal solution."

"How about the guy who isn't married?"

"It helps him stay in the closet, I guess. He's a doctor, lives on Russian Hill and it'd be hard to take a guy out there just for a noontime quickie."

Dan reached out and laid his hand over Tom's. "God I wish we didn't have to be in the closet! Why can't we just be like everybody else? Live our lives, love who we want to love and it's nobody's business but our own. Wouldn't that be great?"

Tom looked around the restaurant. "Well, we do have places like this, where nobody cares if you're gay or dating another guy. That's a start."

Dan sighed. "Yeah, I guess it is. I just wish it'd go faster, that's all." He got a twinkle in his eye. "Come on, let's go where we can be us."

Tom grinned. "You mean to bed?"

"Man, you *can* read my mind."

While Tom and Dan were being themselves in bed, Matt was being himself at the baths and having a fine time of it, too. He completely surprised himself by having three almost overwhelming orgasms in the first four hours. The third one, brought on by four men who played like a team and couldn't seem to get enough of him, left him panting and exhausted. He decided he'd had enough and went home, a satisfied man. He hoped Tom was in the same condition as he was.

Tom was contentedly asleep in Dan's arms.

In the morning Tom and Dan didn't have time for proper lovemaking so they contented themselves with blowing each other in a sixty-nine position. They were beginning to learn each other's hot buttons and they pleased each other in record time.

"You know," Tom said as they were washing each other in the shower, "I really like sleeping with you." Dan ran his hand over Tom's dick which began to harden. "No, no, not just because of that. I seem to sleep better. I always feel really rested when we wake up."

"Me, too," Dan said. "We ought to do it more often."

"Yeah, we should." Something flitted through the back of Tom's mind but was gone before he could catch it.

. . . .

Tom and Dan managed to spend a night together twice in April, both times mid-week and both times because Dan was conducting a seminar in town. Each night was remarkably similar: they had dinner at The Copper Lantern, shared a quick cocktail with Bob, the man Dan stayed with, and went to bed. They didn't get a lot of sleep either time but were always rejuvenated the next morning.

. . . .

By May Tom was beginning to feel really comfortable with his job. He leased several properties, including one known as the *Basement*, mainly because that's exactly what it was, a basement under an empty grocery store. The man he leased it to painted the entire place flat black, put dim red bulbs in a few of the light fixtures, installed a trough urinal along one wall and called it *The Meet Market*. It was an instant success.

Tom also continued dropping in on Mrs. Tan each month as well as delivering the monthly rent money. He always enjoyed sharing tea with her as he learned more and more about her life which had been a very colorful one.

On the Wednesday morning of the first full week in May, Tom had a call from Charlie asking him if he could come up to 323 at lunchtime. "Don't bring anybody," he said, "we have a little problem to discuss."

Curiosity got him to 323 early where he found both Charlie and Joe already there. "Ray will be here in a minute," Charlie said. "He's getting sandwiches."

Before Tom could ask what the problem was, Ray arrived with sandwiches, some chips and Cokes. Once the food was passed out, Joe began to talk.

"Last week," he said, "I went to Macy's for a new sport coat. A cute little guy was helping me try things on and somehow my hand kind of brushed over his crotch. Honest, guys, I really didn't mean it to happen."

"Sure you didn't," someone said.

"No, really. Anyway, it happened again and he didn't move away, he just kind of stood there and said, 'Nice.' Well, one thing lead to another and I invited him up here. He couldn't that day but said he'd like to the next day. So I met him at the store and brought him here. You were here, Ray. You remember him? Black curly hair. Stocky. Pretty eyes?"

"Oh yeah, I do remember," Ray said. "Like you say, cute little thing. I saw him for just a minute, as he was leaving. Aren't you going to eat anything?"

Joe shook his head. "Not hungry," he said. "So anyway I went in to Macy's yesterday and asked if he wanted to do it again."

"And after one of your patented super blowjobs he jumped at the chance for another one," laughed Tom.

"I guess... I don't know. Anyway, we came up here and had some fun. I mean, he loved getting his dick sucked, even if he wouldn't do anything back. I should have known, I should have known right then."

Charlie wadded up his sandwich wrappings and said, "Are we getting to the point any time soon? I got a meeting."

"You've always got a meeting, Charlie. Is that all you guys do over there, have meetings?"

"The point of this is that he asked me if I liked sucking his cock. I said yeah, I did. He then said he really liked it too and it was too bad I couldn't afford to do it anymore."

"Oh, God. Here we go," Ray said. "How much did he want?"

"Five hundred dollars! Two hundred and fifty for each time." He looked from one to the other of them. "I don't have five hundred dollars, guys! I'm lucky to have five." He was developing a slight edge of hysteria to his voice.

"Hold on, hold on." Ray said. "What's the threat?"

Joe got up and began to pace. "He said he'd tell my boss and you know, my boss hates homosexuals more than he hates the Communists. I'd be fired instantly. And then he said he'd tell my wife. I can't..."

"Wait a minute. Your boss and your wife? Come on, Joe. Your boss wouldn't let him in the building. And how's he going to get to your wife?"

"No, Ray, wait. He knew their names. He knew my address. He even knew where my wife works. No, he was serious. He followed me around for a couple of days, he said." He looked at them, visibly trying to keep the panic down. "What am I going to do?"

"You're going to stop pacing like a caged animal and we're going to figure something out." Charlie poured him a Coke. "Here, drink of this. The caffeine will calm you down." He turned to Tom and Ray, "There has to be something..."

Something clicked in Tom's head. "Can we leave this until tomorrow? I know someone who might be able to help. Anyway he'll know what to do." He turned to Joe. "Is there a time limit or anything?"

Joe shook his head. "He didn't say anything about time. Just that I'd better show up with the money pretty quick."

"Okay. I'll see my friend tonight and meet you all back here at lunch tomorrow."

Tom went back to the office, got his coat and told Sue he was gone for the day. It was nearly two o'clock when he got to Fisherman's Warf and the Bay Tours *Bay Queen* was getting ready for the two o'clock, two hour tour. Tom hurriedly bought a ticket and went aboard with the other tourists.

After the flurry of activity involved with leaving the dock was over, Tom stood at the back of the main deck. It took ten minutes or so before Mario came by, looked at him and did a double take.

"Tom! What are you doing here?" He grinned. "You looking for your old job back?"

Tom laughed and shook his head. "Not likely. I have trouble and I came to see my older brother." He lowered his voice to a low whisper. "Also I want to kiss you."

Mario laughed. "Oh, you can do that all you want if you can wait a little bit. Let me see who I can find." He went forward and Tom saw him talking to another deckhand. When he returned he said, "Come on," and lead the way to the tool room.

When they were inside and he'd locked the door, he pulled Tom into a hug and gave him a kiss that wasn't at all brotherly. When he ran his hand over Tom's crotch he found an erection that wasn't very brotherly either.

"You are in trouble, little brother?" he asked when he pulled back to look at Tom.

"No. But a friend of mine is and I need you to give me some advice." He went on to explain briefly about 323 and Joe being blackmailed.

When he was through, Mario said, rather fiercely, "Blackmail is a crime worse than murder. We will do something." He looked thoughtfully at Tom, "Perhaps murder." Seeing the expression on Tom's face he smiled and said, "Only if all else fails. Only then. Let me go back to work. I think best when I'm busy with work and not with thoughts of," he ran his hand over the bulge in Tom's pants again, "this."

They went outside and Mario told Tom to wait for him. Then he went forward and disappeared down a gangway. Tom sat on one of the benches with the other passengers and watched the familiar scenery.

After a while, Mario came back, talking to one of the deckhands. It sounded like Mario was giving him instructions.

"You sure you don't want your old job back?" Mario asked him. "This narrator is terrible. I think he makes up half the things he says and a lot of them are just plain nonsense."

"No, I really enjoyed it when I worked on the boat, Mario, but I really enjoy my job now." He grinned. "And I make a lot more money now. Did I just hear you giving directions to that hand?"

It was Mario's turn to grin. "Yes. They made me the deck supervisor. Now I make more money too." He put a hand on Tom's shoulder. "Come forward with me so we can talk. We can't go back to the tool room because if we do we won't talk."

Mario told Tom he had a pretty good idea how to deal with the blackmailer. First he wanted a description of the man but all Tom could do was say he had dark, curly hair and was stocky.

"Wait. I tell you what." Mario said. "I'm off after we dock so maybe we could go to Macy's and find him so I can see him for myself."

A light went on in Tom's head. "And afterward I could show you the apartment, you know, where he threatened Joe."

Mario laughed. "And," he said, "you could also show me just what was done to prompt this threat."

Tom's dick immediately came back to life and they had to sit and talk about Mario's aunt until they were both presentable again.

At Macy's they had no problem finding the man; he was the only salesman in the suit department under sixty. He wore a plastic name tag which said 'Philip Watson.' Mario took a good look at him and then indicated they should leave. "I didn't want him to see us," he said as they made their way out. They stopped at the bank of pay phones by the Powel Street entrance so Tom could call his dad and Mario could call his aunt and say they would be late getting home.

They then went up to 323. The apartment was empty and Tom showed Mario the bedroom first. That visit turned into a long, slow session of lovemaking.

"Do you want to tell me your plan?" Tom asked as his softening dick was slowly being pushed out of Mario's ass.

"No," Mario said in a husky voice. "I want to be inside you."

Tom wiped his dick and straddled Mario. "Like this?" he said, sinking down on Mario's hardness.

"Oh yes," Mario said, pulling him down for a kiss. "Just like this."

An hour later, in the shower, Mario asked Tom if he still wanted to hear the plan. Tom, on his knees in front of Mario, nodded his head, bringing Mario even more pleasure. Mario's response was a ragged sigh, "Later."

Over a dinner of sautéed perch, fried potatoes and spinach, Mario told Tom to have Joe tell the blackmailer to go up to 323 at lunch time Friday to get his money. Mario said he had that day off and he'd be there to greet the man.

The next day Tom relayed what Mario had said to the other men.

"So what's he going to do?" asked Joe.

Tom shrugged and said he had no idea. Mario never had explained to him what he was going to do. "Besides," he said with a grin, "we were busy with other things. At any rate, I think your Philip will find Mario very persuasive."

"Well, I hope whatever it is, it works. I haven't been able to sleep since this thing happened and both my wife and my boss have told me to see a doctor because they think I'm sick." He turned to Ray. "Well, Doctor? Do you have a diagnosis?"

"No, but I have a cure. Trouble is, you don't do it enough to really like it."

Joe actually laughed. "My God, Ray, do you really think that fucking is a cure for everything?"

"Of course not, Joe. Sometimes a cure requires you to *get* fucked."

On that note they all went back to work.

. . . .

On Friday, when Mario arrived, all four of the guys were already there. Mario was dressed in a dark blue pinstripe suit, a black tie and highly polished black shoes which could only be described as 'substantial.' Tom made the introductions and Mario herded them into the bedroom. "We'll leave the door slightly open but you mustn't make any noise, no matter what happens. And stay back from the door. I don't want him to know you're here." He went into the living room and hung his coat neatly on a straight backed chair, allowing the black leather holster under his arm to show just a little.

When the knock came, Mario looked through the peephole and nodded to himself. He opened the door, grabbed Philip by the crotch and yanked him into the room. "Well, well, well," he said, squeezing Philip's balls hard enough to cause him to cry out and try to double over; only Mario's hand on his shoulder kept him upright. "So you're the one giving my boy trouble are you?" He tightened his grip on Philip's balls, causing Philip to cry out again and his eyes to water.

"Well, let me tell you something Mr. Watson." His voice took on a low, menacing tone. "If you want to keep your little *cogliones* here, you will never, do you understand me Mr. Watson? *never,* let me see you in this town again. Not in a store, not on the street, not in a restaurant." He punctuated each location with a rather harder grip on Philip's balls. "If I *do* see you then twenty-four hours later your little *cogliones* will be resting on my mantle in a jar of formaldehyde. Do you understand Mr. Watson?"

Through his haze of pain, Philip nodded.

"No, Mr. Watson. You must *say* it. Do you understand?" He squeezed a little harder and Philip's knees gave way and he sank down to the floor, pulling his balls out of Mario's hand.

In a strangled voice Philip managed to croak out, "Yes, Sir. I... Yes, Sir."

"Good." Mario yanked him upright and it was obvious that Philip had wet his pants. Mario opened the door and growled, "Get out of my sight!"

Philip managed to get through the door before the pain doubled him over.

It was four very subdued men who came out of the bedroom.

"Remind me, Mario, never to get on your bad side," Tom said, giving him a kiss. "That was an incredible performance."

Joe came up and shook Mario's hand. "I can never thank you enough, Sir. Never."

Mario pulled him into a hug and kissed him on the mouth. "I'm very glad I could help. I doubt you'll be having more trouble from him." He stood back and looked Joe up and down and grinned. "As to thanking me, perhaps we can think of a way."

"Anything you want," Joe said. When Ray raised an eyebrow Joe looked directly at him and again said, "Anything."

Ray leaned in and gave Mario his own kiss. "The shoulder holster was a stroke of genius. Scared the shit out of the little bastard. Is that a real... "

"This?" Mario laughed, pulling the gun out of the holster. "Not quite. My aunt gave it to me when I was a child. It came filled with candy but alas," he shook the gun, "the candy is all gone now."

"Well, I for one need a drink. Anybody want to join me?" Charlie said, going to the kitchen. It turned out they all did.

Over drinks, Charlie, speaking for the group, told Mario that he'd be welcome at 323 any time. Then Joe, speaking for himself, asked Mario to come up on his next day off, which turned out to be Monday.

An hour later, when Joe, Ray and Charlie left the apartment, Philip was nowhere to be seen. Nor was he ever seen again by any of them. Tom and Mario stayed behind to continue what they'd started Wednesday evening.

CHAPTER 12

. . . .

The next Wednesday Tom was horny and went up to 323 just to see if anyone was there and maybe needed some help. No one did, according to the sounds coming out of the bedroom, so Tom got a Coke out of the refrigerator and sat on the couch, imagining what was happening in there. His imagining, of course, made him hard almost immediately.

It wasn't long before the bedroom door opened and Charlie came out, leading a naked, red-haired man by the hand. The first glance told Tom the man was just coming down from an orgasm. "Oh, hello Tom," Charlie said. Then, pushing the red-haired man forward, "Tom, I'd like you to meet Gil. Gil, this is Tom." Given the purpose of the flat, this wasn't as awkward as it might seem. Tom stood, making the erection in his pants all the more obvious, and shook Gil's hand.

"The bath is right down that hall," Charlie said, pointing. "Second door on your right." Gil started down the hall and Charlie gave Tom a kiss and a long grope. "God I love that thing," he said.

"It's yours whenever you want it, Charlie. You know that."

"Yeah, I know," Charlie said, reaching for his clothes. "But the fact is, I have a meeting." At Tom's look he went on, "I know, I know, when don't I have a meeting? Anyway, I think Gil would like to go around again but I can't stay. You want to do the honors?"

Tom shrugged. "Well, maybe as a favor to you, Charlie. Sure."

Charlie rolled his eyes. "He's yours then."

Just then Gil came out of the bathroom and started towards them. Charlie whispered in Tom's ear, "Fuck him. That's what he wants." Turning to Gil he said, "Tom is going to take over for me if you don't mind." He smiled broadly. "He's not as good as me but he's okay." With that, Charlie was out the door.

Tom grinned at Gil. "The hell I'm not." He toed off his loafers and gave Gil a brief kiss. "You game?" Gil nodded and Tom took his hand and lead him back into the bedroom where Joe and an older man were curled up on one of the beds, kissing.

When Tom began to unbutton his shirt Gil pushed his hands away and did it for him. Then he removed Tom's tie by lifting it, still knotted, over his head, then taking his shirt off and hanging it neatly on a chair. He ran his hands over Tom's chest and then pulled him close so he could lick Tom's nipples. Tom sucked in his breath and moaned very quietly.

By this time Joe and his man were openly watching them. "Come on," the man said, "get his pants off so we can go back to what we were doing."

Joe laughed and nuzzled the man's neck. "Doesn't matter to me. I've seen it." He then bent down and took the man's dick in his mouth making the man groan. "I haven't," the man said in a thick voice, "and I want to."

Gil smiled and kissed Tom lightly. "Shall we satisfy his curiosity?" he asked. "And mine, too?" Tom nodded and it wasn't long before he was naked, lying on the bed, playing with Gil's dick.

Joe rolled his man onto his back, crawled down between his legs and slowly took his dick into his mouth, clear down to the base. The man closed his eyes and seemed to drift off to some unknown, but very pleasurable, place.

"You like to watch?" Tom whispered in Gil's ear. Gil nodded. Tom took a bottle of lube off the night table and showed it to Gil. Gil nodded again and whispered, "Slow, please? You're a big guy."

Tom got behind Gil, lubed himself and slowly entered him. All the way in Gil quietly mumbled, "Yes... yes... " Joe's man opened his eyes and watched them intently, holding Joe's head still on his dick. When Tom was completely inside

Gil he began a slow withdrawal. When Tom pushed in again, rather faster than before, Joe's man thrust up, into Joe's mouth and let out a whoop.

"You okay?" Tom whispered into Gil's ear.

Gil didn't answer but squeezed down on Tom, let up and squeezed down again. Tom pushed in as deep as he could go, making Gil gasp.

On the other bed, the man had pulled Joe up until Joe was straddling his chest and then pulled him forward until his nose was buried in Joe's pubic hair. Tom and Gil could see his throat muscles working but even if they couldn't they would have known what he was doing just by the look on Joe's face.

Joe got off first but not much ahead of both Tom and then Gil. A little later, as they were straightening the beds, they agreed that the pleasure had been extraordinary, perhaps because they had shared it.

As they were leaving Joe quietly asked Gil to come back on Friday with him. Gil agreed.

· · · · · · · · · · · · · · ·

On the last Monday of the month, when Tom got to the office, he found Sue already there. She'd brought in coffee and donuts. "So what's this all about," Tom said, accepting a cup of coffee from her.

Sue smiled. "It's about Mr. Diggs. You remember him don't you? Offered you a job?"

Tom laughed. "Yes, I remember him well. What about him?"

Sue's voice dropped almost to a whisper. "Well, I have this new boyfriend. He's a real keeper and," she grinned, "he really is a keeper."

"All very nice, Sue but what does this have to do with Mr. Diggs?" He sampled one of the donuts.

Sue laughed. "No, I mean he really *is* a keeper. He works down at County Hospital as an orderly, kind of like a glorified guard. In the psycho ward." She paused to let this sink in.

"Mr. Diggs is in the psycho ward? I don't believe it."

Sue nodded. "Kelly, that's my boyfriend, Kelly says that the cops brought him in last Wednesday with the DT's. He was in a straight jacket and everything."

Tom wrinkled his brow. "What are the DT's?"

"Kelly says it's what you get when you've been living in a bottle for too long. You know, too much alcohol over too long a time? Evidentially Mr. Diggs had given up food in favor of booze for the past month or two and it got him. He was seeing all kinds of weird bugs and snakes and stuff and wasn't making any sense."

"Well I'll be damned. You must have been right, all those allergy attacks..."

"Were hangover's," she finished for him. Then, looking up at Tom she said, "You know? I feel kind of sorry for him. I think maybe he was in over his head and was afraid of drowning."

Tom smiled at her. "Sue, you have the understanding of a woman three times your age."

She nodded. "That's what Kelly says. He thinks I should go to nursing school."

"So do I," Tom said, "but I'd sure miss you around here if you did. Have you told Miss West about Mr. Diggs?"

"No. Should I?"

"I think you should. Mr. Simms might already know but I'm sure if he does, he hasn't shared it with any one else." He grinned. "Well, maybe with his wife, Mrs. Simms."

Sue laughed. "He is so funny that way, So formal." She picked up the donut box and offered Tom another one. "I'll take these down and offer them to Miss West. I can mention Mr. Diggs when I do, keep it casual."

Miss West reacted about as expected, saying, "Yes, I should have expected that. Please Miss Lynn, don't spread this around more than you have to. He is, after all, a human being, just as you and I."

"Will you please mention it to Mr. Simms? I think he ought to know."

"Yes of course, Miss Lynn, although he may already know. Real estate is a close knit community here and mot much escapes notice." She turned to her typewriter but quickly turned back. "Thank you for the pastry, it's most welcome this morning. May I take one for Mr. Simms?"

"Oh, of course, please do." She laughed. "The fewer there are in the box, the less fat I'll get."

Back at her desk, Sue repeated the conversation, adding," You know, I really like her, Tom but I have this horrible urge to say *shit* to her, just once, just to see if she'd know what it meant."

Tom laughed. "I'm sure she does, Sue, but I'll bet she's never said it, even to herself. Now, get me the Latham file, will you? I'm hoping to close that one today."

. . . .

On Wednesday morning Charlie called and asked Tom if he could be at 323 at noon. "We need to discuss something."

"Don't tell me someone's in trouble again?"

Charlie laughed. "No, nothing like that. Just a little house meeting, that's all."

When Tom got to 323 the other three guys were already there. When everyone was settled with a sandwich and Coke, Charlie began.

"Okay, guys, by my reckoning every one of us has been with Gil at least once. Gil has expressed an interest, a great interest, in joining up with us and becoming a renter. He says he's lost out on any number of, uh... opportunities in the past because he didn't have any place to take a guy and he thinks this is the perfect setup. So... what do I tell him?"

Joe raised his hand. "I've only gotten to be with him once but that thing of his... well, it sure is handsome."

"It is that," said Ray, "and he knows how to use it like a pro. What about you, Tom, you like being with him?"

Tom laughed. "What's not to like? He's versatile and enthusiastic about all of it." He shrugged. "Why not?"

"I feel the same way," Charlie said. "So it looks like each of us is suddenly going to have an extra twenty dollars a month in his pocket."

"Let's not do that yet," Tom said. "Lets leave it at a hundred, for him too, and build up a little housekeeping fund. We could maybe get the place painted or fix up that back storeroom or something. Once we've done what we need to, we could lower our cost or better yet use the extra for a party once in a while."

"Hey," Ray said, "that's good. We do need to fix a couple of things and I doubt the landlady has the money to do it. I like the idea."

The rest agreed so the rent remained at a hundred dollars a month and Gil became a paying part of the group. Charlie said he'd call Gil and have a set of keys made for him. Tom was to tell Mrs. Tan that there was another renter when next he saw her.

"Hey, wait a minute guys, that's today," Tom said. "I knew there was something I was forgetting. I've got to go upstairs and pay the rent." He looked around the group. "No fair having an orgy while I'm gone." He emptied the flour canister, counted the money and went upstairs.

He knocked at Mrs. Tan's door and she called out to him to come it. She was sitting in the same chair in the living room and looked to Tom like she was a little pale. He put the money in the desk drawer as he always did and went over to her.

"How are you, ma'am?" he asked taking her hand.

"I don't know," she answered, "a little tired perhaps." She smiled. "I didn't even make tea. Shame on me."

Tom patted her hand. "Would you like tea? It's about that time, isn't it? Let me make you some."

She smiled. "Oh, would you? And maybe a few of those little cakes in the box on the counter? That would be very nice."

Tom made the tea and noted that the little cakes were the next thing to stale, probably three or four days old. He served them anyway because there wasn't anything else.

Sitting with a cup of tea at her side, Mrs. Tan seemed to perk up and be something of her old self. When Tom told her there would be another tenant in the apartment her only question was whether or not he would be staying nights. Tom told her no but hedged his bet by adding "not regularly." He figured you never knew what would happen down there.

"Well, then, that's fine, dear. As long as you're not too crowded." She took a bite of one of the little cakes and made a face. "These are stale aren't they? I'm so sorry."

"Could I get you some fresh ones, ma'am? I'm sure..."

"No, no. Wong will bring something when he brings my groceries. He's late is all. He's often late because he has so many deliveries to make for the store. You know," she said, suppressing a yawn, "I've gotten so very lazy lately. I can't seem to do what I used to. I suppose it's just age but it's so annoying." She smiled at him. "Don't laugh young man. It'll happen to you, too. I just thank my stars that I have people like you to come and visit me, and sometimes make the tea."

"I'm happy to make the tea any time, I hope you know that. Now it looks to me," he consulted his watch, "like it's nearing time for a nap. Let me pick up the tea things and then you can enjoy a nice afternoon's sleep."

He was true to his word and by the time he had washed and dried the little cups and plates, Mrs. Tan was fast asleep in her chair. Tom gently draped a light blanket around her and took his leave. 323 was empty when he looked in so he went back to work.

. . . .

A couple of weeks later Dan phoned and said he had to be in The City for a morning seminar and unfortunately had to go back to Palo Alto late in the afternoon. He suggested that they could at least have a drink together while he was in town, perhaps lunch.

"I'd like that," Tom said, "but I have maybe a better idea. Why don't you let me show you around that apartment I was telling you about, 323? If you're hungry we could get a sandwich at Whiskers and take it up with us."

There was a long chuckle from the other end of the phone. "Should I be frightened that you can read my mind, Tom? A visit to that place is exactly what I had in mind."

. . . .

They met Wednesday, outside Whiskers. Neither one of them was particularly hungry so they skipped getting sandwiches and went right up to the apartment. Inside they found Charlie, all by himself.

"You alone, Charlie? No sweet young thing needing his daily relief?"

Charlie nodded. "His boss needed him for a last minute meeting. At least he called and didn't just not show up like some of them do. But Ray's in the bedroom with someone."

Tom smiled. "Your guy work the same place you do? Always in a meeting?"

Charlie laughed. "No, he's the guy who takes the notes. Keeps everyone honest afterward." He looked at Dan. "So who's your friend?"

"Oh, I'm sorry. Charlie, this is Dan. You know, the guy I spent New Year's Eve with. Dan, this is Charlie, the one who brought me here the first time."

Dan put out his hand but Charlie swept him into a hug. "Nice to meet you, Dan." Then he kissed him. Tom could tell that Dan was momentarily taken aback but quickly adapted and kissed Charlie back, long and deep.

When they moved apart Tom could see that both of them were well on the way to an erection. He looked questioningly at Dan and got a slight nod. "Hey Charlie?" he said, "You want to join us?"

Charlie grinned. "Oh, God, I thought you'd never ask. Out here or shall we go in and see what Ray's up to?"

"Oh, by all means in the bedroom. That's where the show is."

They undressed in the living room. When Dan took his underwear off Charlie took hold of his erection and gently ran his hand the length of it. "Just like yours, Tom." He grinned, "Well, maybe just a little bigger but they could be brothers."

Tom glanced at Dan. "They are. More."

When they stepped into the bedroom Ray looked up from the dick he was sucking. "Oh, thank God, reinforcements." The man he was sucking put his hands on Ray's head, pushing him back down and said, "Not now. It's just getting good."

Tom put Dan on the other bed and spread his legs for him. "Show him your talent, Charlie. Like you did me." Then he straddled Dan's chest and laid the head of his dick across Dan's lips. Dan looked up at him and winked. When he sucked in his breath and let out an "Oh, yeah!" Tom knew Charlie had taken him in and his nose was now buried in Dan's wiry hair.

It didn't take long before both Dan and Tom were on the edge and somehow Charlie sensed it. He looked over and caught Ray's eye. Ray nodded and grinned, well, as much as a guy *can* grin with a dick in his mouth.

"Hey, what're you doing?" Ray's man asked as Ray let him go and climbed off the bed.

"Change of guard," Ray said. "And believe me, you're getting the best of the deal."

Charlie settled down between the man's legs and took him in. He got the same reaction as he had from Dan: a long intake of breath and an "Oh, yeah!" The man was, in two words, blown away.

On the other bed Ray took Dan's balls in his mouth and then moved lower, causing Dan to shiver and moan around Tom's dick. Tom knew exactly what was happening and, when he felt Dan's knees against his back he gently pulled out of Dan's mouth and turned himself around. Once they'd rearranged themselves Dan floated up to heaven with Ray inside him, Tom's dick in his mouth on his dick in Tom's mouth. The groans coming from the other bed only served to heighten the pleasure. It turned out to be a better afternoon than any of them had expected.

Later, on the way back to the office where Dan's ride was picking him up, Dan said, "How often does *that* happen. Not every day!"

Tom laughed. "No, not even every month. In fact, *that* has never happened before."

"But I thought all you guys..."

"Oh, yeah, we do get it on sometimes but never like that. I mean, we were all tuned in to the same station today and I guess the stars were aligned just right. You have fun?"

Dan stopped. "Yeah, I did. I never realized how much real fun you can have with sex." They started walking again. "It's different from, oh, I don't know, from the sex we have. That's for... Well, I don't know what it's for yet but it's more than fun. Maybe it's on a higher plane or something. But what we just did, that was great."

. . . .

All through June, when Tom went to see Mrs. Tan, she seemed somehow frail to him although he couldn't put his finger on what made her seem that way. Nearly always there were fresh cookies to go with the tea and she always seemed very pleased to sit and talk with him. Once she even asked him to change a couple of light bulbs in her hall which he happily did.

On Tuesday, in the second week of July, on his lunch hour, Tom saw a man in the coffee shop where he was having lunch who, for some reason, really turned him on. After a lot of meaningful glances and smiles Tom, not knowing what else to do, went over to the man and said, "Don't I know you from somewhere?"

The man grinned and said, "Doesn't matter. I think we should get to know each other better."

Tom nodded and looked at his watch. "Tomorrow? Lunch time? I have a place."

The man reached out, took Tom's hand and shook it, his middle finger curled against his palm. "Yes. Tomorrow. Lunchtime. Where?"

"In front of Whiskers. That sandwich shop over on Kearny?"

"I'll be there, twelve sharp. I'll also be thinking about you, tonight, when I… Well, you know." He looked pointedly at Tom's crotch. "Yeah, you know." He stood and faced the wall, rearranging himself.

As they were leaving the sandwich shop the man quietly said, "I doubt that I'll be able to wait until tonight so I guess I'll have to hit the men's room, probably around three. Think about me." He turned and walked off, up the street.

Tom was pretty distracted all afternoon too, but not enough to drive him to the men's room. He'd long ago decided that there weren't enough men on any of the floors in the building that he could get lost in some sort of anonymity. Sometimes he really wanted to go into a stall for some quick relief but so far he hadn't done it. That night, in bed, was a different story.

· · · · · · · · · · · · · ·

When he got up the next morning he found his dad sitting at the kitchen table with a cup of coffee and a cheese Danish. "Hey, Dad, what are you doing home?"

His dad grinned. "Coffee on the stove, rolls in that box on the counter." When Tom had helped himself and was seated at the table, his dad grinned. "Time for my annual physical so I thought I'd sleep in and have a leisurely breakfast. Don't have to be there until nine thirty."

"Well, good luck with the exam, Dad. You look pretty healthy to me but you know, old guys can have hidden problems."

Matt threatened to throw his Danish at Tom but took a bite of it instead, mumbling under his breath, "Old guys indeed."

When Tom left for work he kissed his dad on the cheek and said, "Say hello to Dr. Norris for me."

Tom's morning dragged and, thinking about it later, he didn't get very much done. He was very horny. Finally, just before noon he left the office. Wonder of wonders, walking over to Kearny Street, he didn't once worry that the guy wouldn't be there; he was pretty sure the guy was as anxious as he was. Sure enough, when he got to Whiskers, there the guy was, pretending to read the menu posted in the window.

Tom went up and stood next to him. "What looks good?"

The man turned and looked at him with a perfectly straight face. "Kisses to start. A small helping of blow-jobs. Fucking for the main course. You?"

Tom laughed. "All of the above. Listen, I have to tell you, there may be a few other guys in the room with us. Don't worry, they're there for the same reason as we are."

"If there are, can we watch them? Will they watch us?"

"Yes to both. Come on."

Tom let them in and lead the way up the stairs. All the way up, the man kept his hands on Tom's ass. Just outside the door to 323 Tom kissed the man and said, "By the way, I'm Tom. I don't know who you are."

The man nodded. "Blaine." He grinned. "My mother was reading an English novel while she was carrying me and I think it marked her."

Inside there were gentle groans coming from the bedroom. Blaine's eyes lit up. "Do we just burst in on them?"

"No. We get undressed first and go in quietly."

They kissed while they undressed. When they were naked Tom went down to his knees and said, "Second course. Just a taste." Blaine's dick fit perfectly in his mouth.

After a minute or two Blaine pulled Tom to his feet and returned the favor. Then he turned Tom around, pulled his buns apart and kissed his little brown pucker. Standing, he said, "You can't know how much I want to get in there. Please?"

Tom opened a drawer in an end table, took out a tube of KY and handed it to Blaine. "Come on."

In the bedroom the left bed was occupied by two men, one on his back and the other one ridding his dick. By his balls, Tom could tell that the one on his back was Ray.

"Can we do it like that?" Blaine asked quietly. Tom nodded.

Blaine laid down on the bed and Tom spread some of the KY over his dick and some more on his ass. Then he kneeled over Blaine and slowly settled down on his dick. As he did, Blaine let out a long sigh.

Ray caught Tom's eye and winked at him before giving him an okay sign. Tom smiled and blew him a kiss.

Unconsciously Tom matched the movements of the man riding Ray so they were almost perfectly synchronized. After ten or fifteen minutes the man turned to Tom and grinned. "Don't you just love this, kid?"

Tom nodded and squeezed his ass down on Blaine's dick, making him groan.

It was more the voice than the face and it took more than a minute before it came to Tom that the man ridding Ray's dick was his dad. He didn't have much time to react to that because first Blaine and then Ray went into the throes of orgasm.

A few moments later, when he was breathing more normally, Blaine pulled Tom forward and took Tom's dick in his mouth. Ray followed suit and it wasn't long before Tom and Ray's man—Tom's dad—were groaning through their own orgasms.

Afterward, when they were cleaned up and getting ready to dress, Ray said, "Where are my manners? Tom, this is Matt, Matt, Tom and… "

"Blaine," Tom said. Turning to Blaine, Tom introduced Ray. They shook hands all around.

"Oh, hell," Ray said. "Naked guys who've just watched each other fuck don't just shake hands. It's too civilized." He pulled Blaine into a hug and kissed him; then he did the same to Tom, whispering into his ear, "Isn't he neat? Nearly as pretty as you."

Matt pulled Blaine into a hug and kissed him quite thoroughly. Then he turned to Tom, almost imperceptibly shrugged his shoulders, pulled Tom into a hug and kissed him. Tom kissed him back and gave him a long, thorough grope, eliciting a little chuckle from Matt.

Getting dressed Blaine looked at Tom and Matt and said, "You guys must shop at the same place. You've got identical underwear." He looked from one to the other again, this time more carefully. "You look alike too. Enough to be brothers. You're not, are you?"

Matt, who seemed to be over the initial shock said, "No, we're not brothers," looking at Tom, "are we?"

Tom shook his head. "I don't think so. But we probably do shop at the same place. David Stephens?"

"You got it," Matt said, pulling on his pants. "Good stuff there."

When they were dressed and about to leave the apartment, Blaine said, "We gonna do this again,?" He was presumably talking to Tom but he was looking at Matt.

"Yes, young man," Ray said, patting him on the back. "I think that's a sure thing."

Back in his office, Tom didn't get a lot done that afternoon. He kept going over and over what had happened at lunchtime and wondering if it had really happened at all. His dad? He couldn't quite believe it.

About three, Sue came into his office and said, "I don't know what's gotten into you Tom, but you might as well go home. You're not really here anyway."

Tom looked up. "Is it that obvious?"

"Yes, Tom. It's *that* obvious.: She smiled and patted his hand. "Anything I can do? You need to talk or something?"

Tom shook his head. "No, I don't think so. It's pretty personal." He smiled at her. "Maybe I should go home and talk to my dad about it. Think you can hold down the fort for the rest of the afternoon?"

"Are you kidding? Who do you think runs this place when you're out inspecting or with clients?"

Tom laughed. "I know, I know. I'm just not thinking, that's all. I'll see you tomorrow."

CHAPTER 13

. . . .

Tom's brain kicked into analytical mode on the way home and he tried to find something, anything, in his life that might have told him that his father was gay. *Or maybe not,* he thought. *Maybe he isn't. Maybe he was just very horny and Ray took advantage of him.* As soon as the thought occurred to him he knew it was nonsense. His dad had enjoyed riding Ray's dick as much as he, himself, had enjoyed riding Blaine's, that was obvious, especially when he'd come. *He came! I watched my own father come! Now how many guys... There was a lot of it too, just like me. I guess like father, like...* He realized he'd given himself an erection, just thinking about watching his father come. His brain quietly shut down.

When he let himself into the apartment, his dad came out of the kitchen into the hall. Without a word he pulled Tom into a tight hug. "That sure was an educational lunch hour, wasn't it," he said, pulling back. All Tom could do was nod.

"Look," Matt said, turning serious. "We have three courses of action here. We can pretend it never happened, we can admit it happened and just go on with life, or we can talk about it. Which will it be?"

They looked each other in the eye for a long time and then, simultaneously, burst out laughing. "When have we ever swept something under the rug and *not* talked about it?" Tom asked. "Of course we'll talk about it."

"Tell you what," Matt said, "you go get changed, I'll make us a drink and we'll meet in the living room. Okay?"

A few minutes later, sitting in facing chairs, drinks at their sides, Tom said, "I gotta tell you Dad, I didn't have a clue. Not one."

"You? How about me? I'm the dad here, I'm the one who's supposed to pick up on stuff like this and counsel you about it but I didn't have a clue either. Nothing. Nada." He laughed. "And here I thought you were this big stud-about-town." He stopped and took a sip of his gin and tonic. "Now that I think about it, though, I guess you are. I just didn't know who you were servicing."

Tom ignored this. "When, Dad? When did you start... Well, start with men?"

Matt pulled up short. Tom's tone of voice indicated this to be an important question. It required an honest, serious answer.

"Not while I was with your Mother, Tom. I guess I'm a late bloomer or something but my very first time with a man was only a couple of years ago, when I came to San Francisco to check out the office here, see if I wanted to move here."

"How'd it happen?"

Matt sighed. Did all fathers tell their sons stuff like this? He guessed maybe they did, if they were going to have a completely open and honest relationship with their sons. It then occurred to him that he'd get to ask Tom the same questions and only if he was honest with Tom would Tom would be honest with him.

"Well, when the company sent me out they were saving money by not having expense accounts. They just gave you a certain amount of money for each day's expenses. You were in college and I figured every dime I could save would put us that much better off. So instead of staying at a nice hotel like the Mark Hopkins or the Fairmount, I checked into the YMCA. Twenty dollars a night rather than ninety."

"How long before..."

"The very first evening. I went down to the showers to clean up and there was a guy in there who kept looking at me. I finally figured out that he was looking at my..." He looked up at Tom. "You really want to know all this? I mean, I don't think other dads tell their kids this stuff."

Tom grinned. He knew that he was now going to have to tell his dad the very same stuff about himself and that he'd probably be terribly embarrassed about it but he was fascinated to know his dad this way. "They probably don't. And their kids probably don't know their dads as well as I'll know you. They lose, I win."

Well, I'll be damned! "Okay, well, the guy kept looking at me until he shut off his shower. Then he walked over to me and said, 'You want some help with that thing?' I didn't know what he was talking about until I looked down and saw I had a hard... uh, an erection."

"That's okay," Tom said. "I know what a hard-on is. I know *all* those words."

Matt laughed. "I know you do, son. It's just... Hell, I don't know *what* it's just. Okay, so I'm hard and he wants to help me take care of it. I'll admit, I wasn't quite sure what he meant, what he intended to do, but I nodded and said, 'Sure.' He bent down and took my, uh, my dick in his mouth. I'd never felt anything like it in my life. Never. And then I thought, what if someone comes in, what if we get caught? I was scared to death but his mouth felt so good on me and he was doing things..." He stopped and took a drink of his gin and tonic.

"Well?"

"Well, true to form, someone came in, this tall, skinny guy, and he just stood there, watching us. That did it. I came and had possibly the strongest orgasm I'd ever had and it just wouldn't stop." He looked over at Tom and grinned. "I kept pumping this stuff out and when I looked down I saw the guy wasn't keeping up with me and it was running out the corners of his mouth and dripping on the floor. Finally he spit it out, into his hand, and spread it on his dick. That's all it took, just one stroke and he was shooting cum all over the place. The tall, skinny guy I guess had been jerking off because suddenly he was shooting all over this guy and me. God, what a mess. You need a refill?"

Tom got up and took his dad's glass. "I'll do it." His dad noted that he had an erection.

Matt chuckled. "No fair jerking off in the kitchen." From Tom's expression he thought doing that might have been somewhere in the back of Tom's mind.

When Tom came back, Matt said, "Okay. So now you know more about my first time with a guy than you ever wanted to. Now it's your turn. What was your first time like?"

Tom looked off into the distance. "Not like yours, that's for sure. It was at college, my second year. I had a roommate named Tyler and he was pretty open about stuff like jacking off. I mean, he said everybody did it so why hide it. We sort of got to doing it together, at first just lying on our beds and watching each other. Then one evening he came over and got on my bed with me. Then we started jacking each other." He looked over at his dad. "I told you this wasn't nearly as interesting as yours. Anyway, one Saturday afternoon we were jacking each other and Tyler asked me if I'd go down on him. Heck, I didn't even know what 'going down' was. He showed me. He took my dick into his mouth and when he ran his tongue around the head I thought I was going to come. He pulled off before I did and asked me to do it to him. I gotta tell you, Dad, taking that dick in my mouth was a real surprise. I mean, I liked it, from the very beginning. I liked the taste, I liked the feel of it against my tongue, all of it."

He looked up. "That happen to you? I mean, the first time you went down on a guy? Did you know you liked it, that you liked doing it and wondered why you hadn't done it before?"

"Hey, this is your story. I'll tell you mine later."

"Well, all that happened to me. I don't suppose I was very good at it but Tyler seemed to like it. I got so wrapped up in it that I didn't think about the end of it, that Tyler would have to come at some point. But then he did and I liked that, too. He finally had to pull me off of him, you know, when his dick got too sensitive to be touched. Then he said he'd finish me off but he did it with his hand, not his mouth." Tom smiled at the recollection. "It took about three strokes and I let go. After, when I was cleaning it up I realized that I'd shot over my head and hit the wall behind the bed, about five feet up."

Matt laughed. "Well, I've shot pretty far but not *that* far. Good for you. You guys do it a lot after that?"

Tom laughed. "I did but I could tell that Tyler didn't really like doing it, at least he didn't much like sucking on me. He loved it when I sucked him. Oh, he'd go down on me, sort of. You know, kind of lick at me, maybe put the head in his mouth for a second but I could tell his heart wasn't in it. He was only doing it so I'd do it to him."

"Kind of selfish, wasn't it?"

"Maybe. But not really. He could tell I was really liking it, going down on him, and he always finished me off with his hand afterward. So I guess we were kind of even—we both got something we wanted. Besides, it only lasted five or six months."

"What happened?"

"He met a girl named Brenda."

"I take it she offered something he liked better than your mouth?"

Tom laughed. "Let's put it this way: I don't think he ever jacked-off again, at least not for the rest of that school year. He told me once that she worshiped his dick and said it was the only dick that had ever made her come. He also said that she regularly came three and four times every time they had sex."

"So, you find someone else to play with?"

"No. I figured Tyler had just been a lucky find and there weren't a whole lot of guys who would like having another guy go down on them." He grinned. "I hadn't been to San Francisco yet."

"So what happened here?"

"I met Mario."

Tom went on to explain about Mario and how he'd taught Tom about sex and making love, and the difference between them. As he talked, Matt thought, *Thank you Mario. These are things a man can't teach his son, yet things his son needs to know in order to be a man. The good man he obviously is.*

"You still see him? Mario?"

"Oh, yeah. He comes up to 323 on his day off sometimes to play with whoever might be there. Sometimes I'm there and we get to play." Tom thought for a moment. "It's better, though, when it's a weekend and his aunt is visiting with her friend in Marin. Sometimes we spend the whole afternoon in bed."

"You serious about this Mario?"

"Huh?" Tom had to think for a moment, figuring out what his dad was getting at. "Oh. No, not really. I guess I probably was, once, but not any more. He's older," he looked his dad up and down, "maybe your age, and he doesn't think that would be good for either of us." He shrugged and Matt read the added 'but I do' in it. He kept his own counsel.

"So tell me about this apartment, 323."

Tom nodded. "You need to understand the apartment, dad. It's simply a place for the guys to take guys for play. No strings, no emotion, just fun sex. The first time I was there was with Charlie." He stopped and took a sip of his drink. "You know who Charlie is?"

Matt shrugged. "Sport, I don't know who anyone is, except you and Dr. DeWolf. Oh, and that kid you were with, Blake was it? Where'd he come from?"

"Blaine. And he came from a coffee shop over on Sutter Street. We cruised each other and one thing lead to another."

"Okay, I'm beginning to see. But tell me, who's apartment is it?"

"Well, let's see. Charlie. Gil, Joe, Ray, that is, Dr. DeWolf, and mine."

"Yours? What…"

"Wait, dad. We, the guys I named and me, we pay the rent on it and we all use it. If we find a guy, like I did with Blaine, we have a place to go for a little lunch hour play. The guys we take up there, well, I'd guess you'd say they are all fair game for all of us so some of them are around a lot."

"And you? Were you 'around a lot?'"

Tom cocked his head and looked at his dad. Where was this going?

Matt caught Tom's look and smiled. "No, Sport, this isn't some sort of judgment. After all, I was taken up there and I was asked to come back so maybe I'll be 'around a lot.'"

"I get your point. Yeah, I was around a lot, so much that Charlie even gave me a key to the place. I was passed around, too." He had a sudden thought. "As you will be."

"Me? You think I'll be, as you put it, passed around?"

Tom laughed. "Think about it, Dad. You're handsome, you have a big dick, you seem to really like sex and you're versatile. Of course you'll be passed around. If you want to be."

Matt thought for a few moments and then smiled. "Yeah, I guess I do want to be. But then, I sure did like today, with Dr. DeWolf. I'd sure like…"

"Dad, his name is Ray. If you call him Dr. DeWolf no one will know who you're talking about. In the apartment, probably not even him." He paused and thought for a moment. "By the way, how did you come to be there? I thought you had your physical today, with Dr. Norris."

"Oh, yes, well, it seems that Dr. Norris is sunning himself down in Mexico for the week. His nurse said he got a really cheap ticket so he passed his appointments out to some other doctors and took off. I drew Dr. DeWolf who, by the way, gave me a very thorough going over. Thorough enough that I got hard in his hand and gave the show away."

Tom laughed. "Yes, the man can be quite thorough when he wants to be." He looked at his drink, which was nearly empty. "You want another or are you hungry?"

Matt finished the last of his drink. "Now that you mention it, I'm starved. I'm also tired so if you don't feel like cooking, we're going out."

"And just when," Tom asked, "would it be that I feel like cooking? Where do you want to go?"

"How about a place called The P.S., down on Polk Street? The food's good and I think we'll both appreciate the waiters."

It took Tom a moment to process that last. "Appreciate... It's gay?" He thought for a second. "Yeah, I guess we could go to a gay place now that... now that we're out to each other."

In the cab, on the way to the restaurant, Tom turned to Matt and said, "You know, coming home this afternoon, a lot of things went through my head, about how it would be, you knowing about... well, about me. But I forgot, you're my friend, too. Friends, real friends, don't judge."

Matt smiled. "Uh... Don't forget, your friend had his secret too. And he worried just as much about how you'd react as you did about him." He laughed. "You know, Sport, being friends has some real advantages."

"Yeah. It does," Tom said with a grin.

In the restaurant, with dinner ordered and martinis in front of them, Tom said, "I wonder how long it's going to take before the guys at the apartment figure us out. I mean, that you're my dad."

Matt took a sip of his drink and found the gin both good and cold. "Not long, I expect. Dr. De... that is, Ray, has my full name and I'd say he's a pretty bright guy so he'll figure it out pretty quick. Whether he'll tell the others, well, I can't call that one. Don't know him well enough yet."

Tom noticed the 'yet' but kept it to himself. "Well, it'll be interesting, running into you and Ray, or whoever, in the apartment. Fun to watch."

Matt thought about that for a bit, unsure how he felt abut it. Finally he just pushed it to the back of his mind, to be contemplated at a later time. "I doubt you'll learn anything new," he said, "or see anything you haven't done yourself."

They sat quietly, sipping their drinks, each lost in thought. The waiter interrupted, clearing away the empty glasses and asking if they wanted another round. Tom shook his head so they ordered a bottle of wine instead. When the waiter left Matt looked at Tom and said, "I have a question. It's probably out of line and maybe impertinent so feel free to tell me to mind my own business, okay?"

Tom looked him in the eye. "I'll tell you anything you want to know, Dad. You know that."

"Well, I…"

He was cut off by the waiter, bringing the salads, placing them just so in front of them and then going through the fresh pepper ritual with a peppermill the size of a tennis racket. When he was gone, Tom said, "You wanted to know…"

"Growing up, did you ever wonder what your dad, that is, what I, looked like… having sex?"

"Huh?"

Matt rushed on, "I know, I know, but *I* did. My whole adolescence, when I looked at your Grandpa, I wondered how he looked when he was, you know, *doing* it. And *how* he did it, too. Quick? Slow? Lights on? Naked?" He quietly laughed. "No, I wasn't exactly obsessed with it, I just wondered. I think maybe I was afraid I wouldn't know how to do it the right way when I had to do it." He picked up his fork and attacked his salad. "Forget it."

They ate in silence for a while, until Tom pushed his salad plate away.

"Yeah, I did" Tom said quietly. "All the time, and I think for the same reason. I wanted to do it right, the first time, and I knew that if anybody did it right, it was you. And I wanted to see you hard, too. To compare."

"I never thought about that," Matt said, putting his fork down and wiping his lips with his napkin. "Of course you did. Just like I wanted to see Grandpa." He smiled. "You know, Son, I never in my whole life saw your Grandpa naked, never saw what I thought of as *his equipment*. That's why I made sure we were so… so free around each other. Well, at least after your mother died. She was a little prudish about that sort of thing."

A very handsome busboy appeared and claimed their full attention while he cleared away the salads. He was an equal opportunity busboy, too, making sure he rubbed his crotch against both of them and gave both of them the same dazzling smile. Whatever portion of the tip he got, Tom figured he earned it.

As soon as the table was cleared the waiter appeared with their entrees, sole for Matt, scallops for Tom. They ate in silence except for comments about the food and exchanges of small portions. By the time they finished they had agreed that the sole was marginally better than the scallops but the butter sauce on the scallops had more garlic in it, thus making it the better sauce.

"I appreciate the freedom, Dad. When I was young it never occurred to me that I wouldn't have... well, a big one like you and I couldn't wait for it to grow." He laughed. "Comparing was even more important once I began to grow. It let me see where I was and how far I had to go. But I sure did want to see how big you got when you were hard."

"Well, I'm sorry about that, Sport. If I'd realized... Well, it's a little late for that now. I guess you've seen all there is to see."

Tom smiled. "Yeah, I guess. Or at least most of it."

"Now what's... " Matt was interrupted by the waiter, asking about dessert. They both opted for brandy.

Once the brandy was served, Matt looked Tom in the eye and said, "There's one thing we need to talk about." He sniffed his brandy and nodded. "You'll like it, I think."

Tom sniffed his and then tasted it. "You're right, Dad. It's a good one." They enjoyed their brandy for a moment before Tom said, "Something we need to talk about?"

"Oh, yeah. Look, you said that I'll probably be invited back to that apartment and I sure would like to be. You also said I'd probably be, as you so delicately put it, passed around. Well, I'd like that, too."

"So what's the problem?"

"I didn't say there *was* a problem. But how are you going to feel about it, occasionally finding me in the other bed, like you did today, having sex with one of the guys or maybe someone who's being passed around too? That going to bother you?"

Tom sipped his brandy, thinking. "I think the answer depends partially on you. That is, I'm going to be doing the same thing. How will you feel about that? Especially if he's older?"

"Older? How much older?"

Tom laughed. "*That* would make the difference? Okay, say he's *really* old, like your age. Would that bother you?"

"No, I guess not. I mean, I'm not *too* far over the hill."

"Okay, say he's as old as Grandpa."

Matt looked off into space, thinking. After a few minutes he took a sip of his brandy and looked directly at Tom. "Damn it, I hate it when you do that to me, make me really think about something. Okay, okay, nineteen or seventy-nine, it's all the same thing, isn't it? It's you, having sex with another man, nothing more and nothing less." He sipped his brandy again. "No, it won't bother me. I'll probably watch pretty closely at first, until I get used to it. But you'll be doing that too, I suspect so if it doesn't bother you, it won't bother me."

"So no problem." He drank the last of his brandy. "You want another?"

Matt looked at his watch. "I don't think so. It's getting late and I have to be up early tomorrow. Gotta make up for lost time."

At home, in bed, lulled by the foghorns, Tom figured he'd fall asleep right away but the image of his father sitting on Ray, ridding him, drove his hand directly to his dick which was hard and impatiently waiting for it.

CHAPTER 14

. . . .

The next day Tom ran into Charlie on the cable car and even before he climbed up between his legs he could tell he was horny. As soon as Charlie's hand moved along the grab-rail and settled on his crotch, looking for his dick, Tom grinned at him and said, "Twelve-thirty?"

Charlie smiled and nodded. "I've been missing you." He looked up at the gray sky. "God, I wish this fog would go away. Look at them," he nodded towards a man and a woman, both clad in shorts and tee shirts. "I swear, they ought to be turning blue by now."

"Not to worry, Charlie," Tom said, pressing firmly against Charlie's hand. "September will be here soon and we'll all be complaining about the heat."

When they got off at their stop, Tom held his newspaper in front of him. "Thanks for the hint, Charlie," he said, "I carry this every day now. Just in case I run into you."

Charlie looked closely at the paper and laughed. "What the hell? That paper's from May. You're a little out of date, you know? I mean, today's July 13."

"I didn't say I read it, Charlie, I said I carried it. It's for camouflage, not information. See you at twelve-thirty."

A little after nine he was negotiating with a man who was trying to lease a property Tom had listed. The man was trying to get it on the cheap and Tom was trying to show him that it already was cheap at the asking price and, furthermore, it was exactly right for the man's needs. As he was repeating his point for the third time, Sue put a note in front of him.

Miss West on 2. Simms

Wants you. Now?

Tom shook his head and scribbled on the note

Not now!

Sue shrugged her shoulders, took the note and left.

It took another half hour but Tom finally managed to convince the guy he had to have the property and that it was a very good deal at the offered price. He even got the guy to ask him to try and get an additional two years on the lease. When he went out to Sue's desk he was justifiably proud of himself.

"So what was all that nonsense about Simms?"

Sue sighed. "How come I always get the dirty jobs around here? She's not easy to deal with, you know, and when she wants something, she wants it now!"

Tom raised an eyebrow. "Maybe we should change places. You argue with that idiot over the price of that building and I'll sweet talk Miss West."

Sue laughed. "Okay, so I do have the easier calls. But still, Miss West..."

"So, Simms wants me?"

"Just as soon as you get off the phone. Like right now."

Tom walked down the hall, wondering what could be so important that he was wanted *immediately*. When he got to Mr. Simms outer office Miss West simply waived him in saying, 'He's expecting you."

Inside the office, Mr. Simms, as always, offered him the cigarette box and when Tom waived it away, pointed to a chair. "You know, Mr. Braden," he said, lighting a cigarette, "as I have said before, the real estate community is a tight knit group here in The City and, as such, we tend to take care of our own. It's the right thing to do, taking care of our fellows, especially as we might need some care ourselves, at sometime in the future. Now, I've spoken with my wife, Mrs. Simms, about this and she agrees that we must offer help." He paused, contemplating the smoke rising from his cigarette while Tom presumably contemplated his words. Tom, of course, had no idea what he was talking about.

After a suitable interval, Mr. Simms went on. "As you know, our colleague and former employee, Mr. Diggs, has had a bit of bad luck with his health. As a result he finds he must move to Arizona and it's dryer climate. To this end he finds that he must close his offices here and sell his business assets. He has asked that you help him to put them in order and assist with their valuation."

The only thing that Tom could think of to say was, "Me?"

"Yes, you, Mr. Braden. Mr. Diggs feels that you understand the way that he does business and keeps his files. He had a secretary to assist him for a brief period but she was let go when he found that he was unable to go to the office for a time."

"Uh... Well, sure, I'd be happy to help out but my..."

"Your work here, of course, must not suffer from this task, but I'm sure that you could somehow balance both for a week or so. Mr. Diggs is offering a very generous remuneration for your time and I, of course, will continue your salary uninterrupted. You will do this?"

From Tom's point of view there wasn't any choice. "Yes, Sir, of course I will."

"Excellent. You'll begin on Monday morning. Mr. Diggs will be expecting you at eight- thirty sharp." Mr. Simms stood and extended his hand, signaling that the interview was over. As Tom was approaching the door, Mr. Simms said, "Oh, and though we will be thinking of perhaps buying Mr. Diggs' assets, I admonish you to value them fairly. Do you understand?"

"Yes, Sir. You know I could do no less."

Mr. Simms nodded. "Thank you, Mr. Braden."

Back in his own office Tom told Sue what had just happened.

"Oh, yeah, Kelly told me he'd heard that Diggs was being sprung from rehab. I wonder how he'll be? Kelly said that he's gotten pretty weird in the way he dresses."

"Well, we'll see on Monday."

The rest of the morning was spent clearing up some long-pending files and anticipating a lunchtime session with Charlie. By the time he left for lunch, Tom had to carry his paper with him.

When he got to 323 he found Charlie in the living room, his tie off and his shirt half unbuttoned. "Well, well, here's the man now," he said as Tom let himself in.

Tom took Charlie in his arms and kissed him. "I've missed you, Charlie."

Charlie ran his hands over Tom's crotch, finding his dick mostly hard. "And I've missed you." he squeezed Tom's dick, "This too. Got a question for you, but after, okay? For now I just want this thing down my throat. Both beds are taken so we're left with the couch."

They undressed each other and stood for a moment, hugging and rubbing their hard dicks against each other. Then Charlie sat Tom down on the couch, pulled a pillow down to the floor and kneeled on it, between Tom's legs.

"Go slow," Tom said, "let's make it last."

To their credit, they tried but it's very difficult to make it last when your dick is down someone's throat so far that the someone can nibble gently at it's base. And when he swallows...

Charlie was holding Tom's balls in his hand, not only because he liked the feel of them but also because he could tell when they began to pull up into Tom's crotch. Once they did he slowly pulled off, which in itself pushed Tom closer to his edge.

They changed places and did it all over again, except that Tom couldn't get Charlie's dick as far down his throat as Charlie could his. Nevertheless, Charlie came up fast and it wasn't long before he pulled Tom off of him. They stretched out on the couch then, kissing and playing with each other.

"So who's in the bedroom?" Tom asked.

"Well, that's kind of what I wanted to ask you about. I think it's Ray and your dad, but I'm not sure. I mean, I'm sure it's Ray but the other guy..."

"Who else?"

"No one. But I thought, if it is... Well, you might not want... Oh, hell, I don't know. You suppose it is? Your dad?"

Tom laughed and kissed Charlie. "I imagine it probably is. It was yesterday so why not today, too?"

Charlie pulled back so he could look at Tom. "Your dad? Yesterday? How…"

So Tom told Charlie about taking Blaine into the bedroom the day before and finding Ray and his dad. "I tell you, Charlie, it was quite a surprise. I hadn't a clue that he played with guys. Not a clue. By the way, how do you know it's my dad in there now?"

"Ray called me this morning. Told me about it. Said he'd invited the guy up for lunch today. That's why we're out here. I thought you might be… I don't know, shy about it or something. He's really your dad?"

Tom laughed. "Yeah, Charlie, he's really my dad." He had a sudden thought. "And sometime I want you to show him that little trick you do with your throat, okay?"

"You wouldn't mind if I… That is, if he…"

Tom reached down and ran his hand along the length of Charlie's dick. "He's not my lover, Charlie, he's my dad. I want only the best for him and believe me, you're the best."

Just then the door to the bedroom opened and Ray and Matt came into the living room. Both of them were naked.

"Hey, Charlie," Ray called. "You seen any stray clothes around there?" His eyes swept the room and lit on a jumble of shirts and pants. "Never mind. Here they are. I guess we were in a little bit of a hurry." He turned to Tom's dad. "We were, weren't we, Matt? Have you met Charlie?"

Charlie sat up and Matt took a step towards him, extending his hand. "Glad to meet you, Charlie." He glanced at Charlie's dick which hadn't softened very much. "Very glad to meet you."

Tom laughed, seeing where his dad's eyes were fixed. "Don't worry, Dad. I've already fixed you up with him. All you guys have to do is pick a date and time."

"Well, thank you, my boy. I'll return the favor—if I ever run across someone you haven't had already."

Ray cleared his throat and handed Matt his pants. "We gotta get on with it, Matt. I don't know about you but I have a patient in ten minutes."

Matt pulled on his shirt. "And I have a client who'll be seeking your services if I don't get there and calm him down."

When they were gone Tom and Charlie claimed one of the beds and made each other about as happy as a man can be, getting a blow job.

. . . .

The next day, Friday, Tom had a call from Dan who said he had to be in town the next morning but would be finished with his talk around eleven and didn't have to leave until Sunday afternoon. Even better, the guy he stayed with would be in L.A. again so, if Tom was interested, they'd have the place to themselves."

"Interested? Of course I'm interested. We can have lunch and then find something to entertain us until dinner. And then maybe breakfast."

Dan laughed. "Is that all you think about? Eating?"

"You? Yes." He blushed and checked again to be sure his door was closed. "Hey, I've got an idea, let's take my dad to dinner. I think it's about time you met him, don't you? We'll go to the Waterfront, the food's pretty good there."

"Tom? Uh… The Waterfront's gay, you know."

"So's my dad."

"What?"

"Yeah, it's a long story. I'll tell you on Saturday."

Tom didn't go up to 323 that day. Matt did, though, and for the first time experienced what Charlie could do. He was amazed, and very pleasantly so.

. . . .

The next day Tom got to the flat where Dan was staying about eleven-fifteen. When he rang the bell, Dan answered the door, naked. After a long look up and down Tom put his arms around Dan and kissed him. "You know," he said, a little breathless from the kiss, "I do believe this is the first time I've ever seen you naked and without a hard-on." He stood back slightly and looked Dan up and down again. "Well, you didn't have one when you answered the door."

"Get in here!" He pulled Tom into the hall and ran his hand over Tom's crotch. "I guess I'll never get to see you that way. Oh, well." He pulled Tom towards the bedroom. "Let's see if we can think of something to do with these things."

It didn't take a lot of thought.

Later, curled up together, Dan asked Tom is he was hungry.

"No thanks. I just ate."

"So did I but, substantial as it was, I don't think it'll keep me 'till dinner. Besides, I stopped at the food court in the Emporium and picked up a few things we might like."

Tom nuzzled him under the chin, licking his Adam's apple. "What's his name?"

Dan let out a low moan. "I forget. And if you don't stop that I won't remember my own name."

"Don't worry. It's Dan. I'll never forget it."

It was another hour before they found time to eat the *Marcel et Henri* pâté and sample the *York Mountain* burgundy Dan had bought. They found both to be very good but not nearly as satisfying as making love to each other.

After a short nap they finally found time to talk in sentences that actually made sense.

"So your dad is gay? How did *that* come out?" Tom grinned and ran his hand over Dan's chest. Dan removed it and just to be sure, intertwined their fingers, effectively stopping Tom from moving it. "No, really, I'm interested."

"Okay." Tom relaxed and snuggled up to Dan. "It was, let's see... Wednesday. I can't believe it's only been three days! Anyway, I had picked up this kid, Blaine I think was his name, and took him up to 323. Someone was in the bedroom so we undressed in the living room and then went in. On one of the beds there was this guy, riding Ray's dick. We laid on the other bed and I started riding him. It was a nice dick, too. Not all that big but... "

"Okay, okay. Get on with the story."

Tom leaned in to him and gave him a kiss. "Well, there's not much more, actually. The guy and I are riding along, pretty much at the same pace, and he turns to me and says something like 'Isn't this fun?' I agreed and he turned back, looking at Ray." He began to chuckle.

"What's funny?"

"Me, I guess. I didn't see it for the longest while. I mean, it's my own dad riding Ray's dick and talking to me and I didn't recognize him." He laughed. "I just didn't recognize him. Isn't that weird?"

"Not really. You wouldn't expect to see him there so he doesn't exist there and it takes the brain a while to recognize that in fact he is there." He gave Tom a kiss but pulled back when Tom pushed his tongue into his mouth. He wanted to hear the rest of the story. "So what happened?"

Tom shrugged. "Nothing really." He pulled Dan over, so he was resting on Tom's chest. "Oh, yeah, one thing happened. I got to grope him."

Dan pulled back so he could see Tom's eyes. "Your dad? You groped your dad?"

Tom grinned. "Yeah. Before we got dressed Ray went around introducing us and then said something about guys who watch guys having sex ought to kiss so we did. Ray groped the guy I was with so I groped the guy he was with. It's just that he was with my dad."

"Oh, God, I can't imagine that. Was everyone shocked? I mean, that you groped your own dad?"

"Well, Ray—and Blaine, for that matter—didn't know he was my dad. I guess Ray does now, though. I was up there with Charlie the next day and he knew. Said Ray told him."

"So how is it now? At home, I mean. Isn't it kind weird? I mean, both of you…"

"No, it's nice. He's my dad and it's nice to be who I am with him. And for him too, I think. I mean, I can invite him to dinner with the handsomest man I know and not worry that he'll think something is wrong."

Dan glanced at the bedside clock. "Well, if we're going to have dinner with him, we'd better get with it. Unless you want to shower alone."

"Not a chance."

When they got to the restaurant they found Matt sitting at the bar, drinking a martini. By the time introductions were over and they'd been shown to their table, Tom knew that at some point Dan and his dad were going to bed each other. And, being the son, he'd no doubt be left out.

Dinner was good. The chef was feeling frisky that night which meant several small dishes of things appeared at the table with complements of the kitchen. Things like crab cakes and bacon wrapped chicken livers and roasted garlic cloves. On top of a really good dinner they were almost too much.

Conversation was good as well. Matt and Dan hit it off and talk among the three of them flowed freely, as did the cocktails and wine. At the end, sipping their brandy, Dan asked Matt what he was going to do for the rest of the evening.

"Well, after that dinner, I should probably just go home and go to bed." He looked around the room and grinned. "But I don't think so. I think I'll go to the baths instead, at least for a while."

Tom looked at both Matt and Dan. "You ever been there, to the baths?"

Both Matt and Dan nodded.

"You haven't?" Dan asked. At Tom's shake of the head, he said, "We'll go sometime. It can be lots of fun, right Matt?"

"Yeah, it can. I haven't been a lot but my times there have always been good."

They finished their brandy and Tom picked up the check. "My treat, guys."

"Okay," Dan said, "Then I'll buy breakfast."

Matt just smiled, proud that his son was taking him out to dinner and wondering if there might be some other reason Tom wanted him to meet Dan.

The rest of the night went well for all concerned. None of them got a lot of sleep but all of them were well satisfied.

The next night, over cocktails in the den, Matt thanked Tom again for dinner and said, "That Dan is quite a guy, isn't he? You see a lot of him"

Tom nodded. "Some. He's teaching some sort of class for one of the banks in town so he gets up a couple of times a month."

"He ever been to that apartment of yours?"

Tom grinned. "Yeah, once or twice. You want me to take you up, the next time he's in town?"

Matt took on a serious expression. "Would you mind?"

Tom crossed to his dad, pulled him out of his chair and gave him a hug. "No, it hasn't gone that far yet. But thank you for asking, I really appreciate that." He went back to his chair, sat and grinned. "I can't believe this. I'm pimping for my own dad."

CHAPTER15

· · · · · · · · · · · · • • • • • • • • • • • • • · · · · · ·

Monday morning, when Sue got to the office, she found Tom at his desk, going through some files. "Hey, I thought you were supposed to be over at Diggs office. What're you doing here?"

"Just checking to see if there's anything I really need to deal with this morning, before I go." He tossed the file he was reading on the desk. "I guess there isn't."

"No, there isn't. And there won't be. I can take care of things here so go."

Tom got up from his desk and grinned at her. "Yes Ma'am!"

The Russ building was only a block and a half up Montgomery Street so it didn't take Tom long to get there. He took the elevator up to the fifth floor and found *Diggs & Associates* nearly at the end of the hall. The door was open.

"Thomas. Thank you for taking the time to help me with this. You always were good at figuring out what I was doing." Mr. Diggs was wearing button fly Levi's, a dark brown shirt, boots and, Tom couldn't help noticing, a very large, very obvious bulge at his crotch. Mr. Diggs caught him looking.

"Oh, since I'm not doing actual business, I decided I could wear my more casual clothes. I hope you don't mind," he said.

"No, not at all," Tom said, thinking he perhaps had underestimated the man. "Shall we get started?"

They spent the morning organizing files, weeding out the closed ones that probably would never be reopened and setting aside any that required active attention. While they worked Mr. Diggs would periodically rearrange himself in his jeans. Finally, around eleven, he said, "I'm sorry for all this plucking at myself, Thomas, but the underwear I'm wearing is most uncomfortable. If you don't mind, I think I'll call it a day, go home and change it." He dug a key out of his pocket. "Here, please lock up when you leave." He smiled. "The key will get you in, in the morning. I may be late."

With that he was gone and Tom sighed. He'd liked looking and, in his mind, speculating on just what was creating that bulge but he was glad not to have the distraction. He got more done in that last hour than he had all morning.

Back in his own office he found a neat pile of phone messages, stacked in order of importance. He started at the top and had cleared quite a few of them when Sue came in from lunch. She was carrying a pink box from one of the bakeries on Grant Avenue.

"What's this?" Tom said as she put the box on his desk.

"*Char Siu Bao*," she said. "You know, steamed pork buns. I thought you might be skipping lunch."

"My dear, you are a life saver. How'd you know these were my favorite?"

"I didn't. They're my favorite, too." She smiled. "I had them for lunch."

Tom sampled one of the savory buns and gave a sigh of contentment. "They're wonderful. What do I owe you?"

She shook her head. "Nothing. They're on me and don't argue."

"Well then, thanks. You're a good person." He turned back to his stack of phone messages.

The next day, true to his word, Mr. Diggs didn't come into the office until ten-thirty. He was again dressed in Levi's, this time with a skin tight Western shirt and, of course, the boots. The one thing Tom noticed was that the big bulge was gone, replaced by a thick hose hanging down his right leg, topped by what were obviously two quite good sized, egg shaped objects. Mr. Diggs caught him looking, again, and laughed.

"Yes, Thomas, the underwear is gone. It's much more comfortable this way. I don't know why I didn't think of it long ago. Now, let's get to work."

By eleven-thirty they had organized quite a few files, including three that Mr. Diggs had no recollection of ever opening.

"You know, Thomas," Mr. Diggs said as they put another file in the "Closed" drawer, "I think it's time for lunch. Come on, my treat."

They went up California Street to the *Big Four*, an expensive and very good restaurant. When they were seated, the waiter brought tall glasses of iced tea along with the menus.

"As you can see," Mr. Diggs said, "I eat here quite often. My therapist at the center said I had to eat three meals a day." He laughed. "And not just canapés to accompany cocktails."

"Probably good advice," Tom said, squeezing the lemon wedge into his tea.

"Oh, they gave me lots of good advice there," Mr. Diggs said. "For example, you have noticed that I dress differently?"

Tom was saved from saying anything by the waiter, asking for their lunch orders. Mr. Diggs had a steak sandwich with fried potatoes and salad. Tom followed suit.

When the waiter had gone, Mr. Diggs said," As I was saying, they gave me lots of good advice and a lot of insight as well. One thing they... well, I guess 'harped' is not exactly the word but it certainly seemed like it at the time. Anyway, they told me my, uh, problem may have come from me trying to be something I'm not. They encouraged me to find my, as they put it, my inner man. I'm supposed to let him out, to be that man. So that's what you see," he spread his arms, "my inner man."

They were interrupted by the waiter, placing large platters in front of them. They ate in silence for a while, enjoying the good food. After a while Mr. Diggs began to chuckle quietly. When Tom looked up at him he pushed his plate away and leaned back in his chair.

"I'll bet you're wondering just who this inner man might be. I mean, he dresses funny and he says things you might not expect. Well, I'll tell you, Tom. I'll tell you because you put up with a lot of shit from me when you worked for me and because I respect you. I like you, too. That makes all the difference.

"See, for a while, the therapist—and I—thought I might be gay, might actually like men rather than women. So I bought some new clothes and set out on a quest to find out if my inner man was queer." He grinned at Tom. "You can't imagine what an interesting quest that was and, actually, how much I learned about men. And myself."

The waiter refilled their iced tea and, looking at their plates, said, "I'll have these put up in a box for you."

Mr. Diggs gave Tom a long look. "Are you interested in what I learned? I really don't want to bore you but I thought maybe, it might explain," he held his arms out again, "me. Or at least what you see of me."

Tom nodded. "Yes, Sir, I'm very interested. I think because I like you, too. Maybe not so much when you're in one of those black moods, but mostly."

"Well, the first thing I learned was, my inner man not withstanding, I don't much like the… well, the sex part. With men. It's okay, I guess, if they want to, shall we say, pleasure me but the other way around, not on your life. Give me a woman every time." He grinned. "And that, Thomas, is the voice of experience speaking. I tried all that, more than once, and it just didn't… I don't know, it just didn't *do* anything for me. Or my inner man."

Tom nodded. "Then why the…"

"Why the clothes? Well, Thomas, it turns out that my inner man is something of a serious exhibitionist. He wants others to look at him, men and women. He's got something he thinks is very special and he wants people to know it, look at it and, in the case of women, fondle it. Men not so much, although a gentle, what do you call it? A grope? Yes, a casual grope from a man is not unappreciated as long as he doesn't expect anything else or anything in return." He took a drink of his iced tea. "Is any of this making sense, Thomas?"

Tom was a while in answering. Finally he said, "I think it does, Sir. It explains some of what went on in the office and it certainly explains your new wardrobe. Which, I might add, is actually quite becoming on you. You look good in it and I'll bet, especially in this town, you do get a few gropes, from both men and women."

When they left the restaurant Mr. Diggs hailed a cab. "Come on, Thomas, I'll give you a ride back to the office." Then, on the way, he said, "I have a few things to set up in Phoenix so I'll be over there for the next couple of days. I'll be back Friday and you can tell me about what I have then. Okay?"

Tom did a few quick calculations in his head and nodded. "Yeah, I think I'll be finished by Friday. Have a good time in the desert."

That night he told his dad about Mr. Diggs and the changes he'd undergone. "Really. Dad, he's a whole new guy. And you should see him in his new clothes. Nothing from David Stephens, I guarantee."

Matt grinned. "And he's showing himself off? To everyone?"

"Well, he was in the office, and in the restaurant, too. Man, I thought you—we—were well endowed but he makes us look like twelve-year-olds. Really."

"Well, if it gets results, why not? But I'd be embarrassed to show myself off like that."

Tom blushed. "Me, too, I guess. Heck, I'd be hard all the time, walking around like that. But I have to say, on him it looks good."

. . . .

Two nights later, on Thursday, both Matt and Tom were late getting home so they decided to go to Momma Giordano's for dinner. As always, it was like a family reunion when they walked in. Once they were settled down at a table and the martinis had been served, Matt said, "Charlie says you haven't been around 323 lately. Working through lunch?"

Tom toasted his dad with his drink. "Yeah, mostly. There's a lot to do, Dad, putting all those files together in some sort of order. But it's going to be worth it. Mr. Diggs is going to pay me for doing it and Mr. Simms is still paying my salary. Besides, I think we, that is, Mr. Simms, is going to buy most of the business which means a lot of it will come right back to me. Best to put it into good shape now, while I'm being paid twice."

"You know? You're the smartest kid I had."

Tom laughed. "Also the only, if I remember correctly. Or is there something I don't know about?"

"Not a chance. You were too good to try for another."

Just then one of the Giordano daughters—Tom could never keep them apart— came to take their order. When she'd gone Tom said, "You mentioned Charlie. You been up at 323 a lot?"

Matt blushed. "You might say that. Man, Tom, those guys are so good to me. And fun!" He was quiet for a moment and then said, "Oh, and I met your Mario. Nice guy."

From the look on his dad's face Tom knew right away that he'd done more than just meet Mario. Matt was spared further interrogation by the young lady serving the salads.

. . . .

On Friday, Tom was nearly finished with his review when Mr. Diggs walked into the office.

"Hello, Thomas. How's the work going?" He was wearing the tightest white pants Tom had ever seen. He was also wearing white socks, white patient leather loafers, a very pale, teal blue shirt and a dark blue blazer.

"Excuse me for just a moment," Tom said. He went into the back storage room where there was a sink, and washed his hands. He carefully dried them and went back to Mr. Diggs. "You are gorgeous," Tom said, pulling him into a tight hug. Then he carefully, thoroughly—and slowly—groped him.

"I hope your inner man doesn't mind," Tom said, "but I've wanted to do that since Monday." He grinned. "It was worth the wait."

Mr. Diggs leaned in and kissed Tom briefly on the mouth. "So have I," he said, "and yes, it was worth it."

They looked at each other for a long time and then stepped apart. "So," Mr. Diggs said, "What's your opinion?" When a slow grin appeared on Tom's face he added, "Of the files, Tom. Of the files."

Tom nodded. "Good. Frankly, as assets, they're better than I expected." He took a folder off the reception desk. "I've prepared an analysis and recommendation." He suddenly grinned. "You have no idea how I was grilled about that report yesterday, both by Mr. Simms *and* by Miss West. I told them both it was yours to read first."

Mr. Diggs laughed. "That old fraud. He carries on about 'good business practices' and 'ethics' but ignores both when they might inconvenience him. Thank you for the courtesy, Thomas." He sat in the receptionist's chair and slowly leafed through the report, occasionally re-reading a paragraph or two.

"Miss Lyn type this?"

"Yeah... Why?"

"It looks like her work. Neat, accurate, correct." He looked up. "Hang on to her, Thomas. She's good." As an after thought he added, "Like you."

An hour later Tom handed the report to Mr. Simms after declining Miss West's offer to deliver it. Then he went back to his own work but not until he had fully described Mr. Diggs outfit to Sue, who seemed to know all about Mr. Diggs' inner man.

"Well, Kelly, my boyfriend, kind of stayed in touch with the guys at the rehab center because he knows I used to work for Diggs. Kelly wasn't sure, though, if he's really gay or not. What do you think?"

"I think it's probably none of our business but I also think he's not. Now, let's get to work."

At four Miss West called to say that Mr. Simms would like to see Tom, at his convenience. Her words were quite casual but her tone of voice, according to Sue, who took the call, was *Right Now*, with capital letters.

"Good afternoon, Mr. Braden," Mr. Simms said, six minutes later. "Thank you for dropping by so promptly. Cigarette?"

Tom waived away the cigarette box and wondered if Mr. Simms would ever figure out that he didn't smoke. He took the offered chair.

"Well, I must say, your report," he tapped a fingernail on the one folder on his desk, "is not only well done but seems quite complete and well thought out. But I want to ask you, is this figure for the value of the assets yours or Mr. Diggs?"

"Mine, Sir. I doubt that Mr. Diggs had any idea what the assets were worth. Quite frankly, I doubt that Mr. Diggs had any idea what the assets *were*. He seemed quite surprised when he read the report."

"Yes, I imagine so. You know, Mr. Braden, Mr. Diggs is an excellent salesman but he has no idea how to complete a sale after it is agreed upon. I must say, I hope he will find an assistant as well organized as yourself when he gets to Arizona." He paused, perhaps giving the powers that be instructions to find that person.

"Now then, I have not as yet discussed your report with my wife, Mrs. Simms, but I'm sure she will agree with my conclusions. For planning purposes, you should assume this firm will buy Mr. Diggs' assets, probably at a figure slightly below what you suggest, and integrate them into our own. This will require a bit of extra work on your part but will be quite advantageous to us in the future."

He stood, indicating their meeting was concluded. Tom shook his hand and left.

Back in his own office, Tom sent Sue home and then went home himself. He found a note on the hall table saying his dad would not be home that night. Tom smiled to himself and thought, *and he thinks I'm a stud around town!*

He heated up some leftovers and went to bed, tired from the long week.

. . . .

The last day of the month was a Monday and at one o'clock Tom knocked on Mrs. Tan's door. When she called for him to enter, he went in and found her in the wing chair in the living room just as he'd expected. He put the money in the desk drawer before crossing the room and giving her a kiss on the cheek.

"Shall I make tea?" he asked.

"Oh yes, that would be lovely. There are some fresh cakes, too. One or two of those would be nice."

Tom went out to the kitchen and found the tea things laid out on the counter, ready for him. He thought that was a good sign."

"You're feeling better," he said with a smile as he set the tea tray down on the little table next to her. "Last month it was the every-day china."

She grinned at him. "You are a most observant boy, Tom. Yes, I'm feeling better. I ascribe it to that new tonic the doctor has given me."

"Well, you keep taking it. It seems to be doing you a world of good. I'm glad you went to the doctor, too. He found nothing really wrong?"

She sighed. "Nothing but a little tiredness. That's what the tonic is for." There was a slight pause and then, with a little laugh, "I don't suppose there's one for old age, now is there?"

"I'm afraid not," Tom said. "It's just something you do. Now, let's have tea."

They chatted for a while but Tom could see, in spite of the tonic, she began to tire quickly. He watched her eat a part of one of the little cakes and then put it down as though it was too heavy to hold. As soon as he could he began to clear away the cups and plates. When he returned from the kitchen, having washed the dishes, he found Mrs. Tan with her chin on her chest, snoring softly. He let himself out, making a mental note to check on her in a few day's time.

He wanted to stop in at the apartment but thought it was a little too late. Mr. Simms was having a meeting with Mr. Diggs this afternoon and he wanted to be there when it was over. He idly wondered what Mr. Diggs would wear to the meeting and how Mr. Simms would react to it. He never did find out.

CHAPTER16

. . . .

During the month of August his dad seemed to be away from home more than he was there. He spent Most weekend nights away as well as one or two during the week. Tom avoided asking him what he was doing and the even more interesting question of who he was doing it with. Matt didn't offer any information but Tom knew he would when he was ready.

Tom was also busy that month, both at work where he was integrating Mr. Diggs files with both his and Mr. Simms, and at 323 or with Dan who was in town more and more.

He was also busy with Mrs. Tan whom he visited every couple of days and who appeared to be deteriorating rapidly. On the last Monday of the month he found her on the floor, conscious but making no sense. He found her address book on her desk and called her doctor.

The doctor sent an ambulance and, in fact, arrived with it. Mrs. Tan became quite docile as soon as she saw him and allowed the ambulance guys to strap her onto a gurney with a minimum of complaint. When they took her downstairs and put her in the ambulance she seemed to go to sleep. Tom remained behind to lock up. He also called Sue and told her he'd be late getting back. Then he went downstairs.

It was late and only Ray and a very handsome, tall black man were there. Both were naked and obviously just finished with what must have been a very pleasurable time for both.

"Tom. Good to see you. Meet Clark."

The black man held out his hand and gave Tom an appraising look. "Glad to meet you, Tom." Based on the look, the length of the handshake and the fact that he flexed his dick a couple of times, Tom was fairly sure they would meet again, under better circumstances. He was already looking forward to it.

"Tom? You..." Ray nodded at the bedroom.

"No, sorry, guys, I've got to get back to work."

Clark dug his watch out of his pants and looked at it. "Holy shit, me too! My boss is going to be pissed off as it is." He pulled on the pants and grabbed a shirt off the chair.

"Where..."

Clark looked up and smiled. "Down Post Street, almost to Market."

Ray shook his head. "Well, I guess we're all out of luck. I've got a patient. Three minutes ago."

"Okay, I'll make this fast," Tom said, handing Ray his pants. "I was just up to Mrs. Tan's, and she's pretty sick. Ambulance came and took her to the hospital."

Ray looked at Clark. "So that's what all that commotion out in the hall was." He turned to Tom. "We were, ah, shall we say, pretty busy just about then and didn't go see what was going on."

"Yeah," laughed Clark, patting Ray's ass. "We were busy alright." He finished tying his shoes, picked up his coat and headed for the door. "We going to do this again?" he said, opening the door. "It sure was fun." He disappeared out the door.

"You want me to check on her?" Ray asked. "Who's the doctor?"

"Chinese guy named Lee. Would you?"

"Sure. I'll call you tomorrow." He glanced at his watch. "We better go."

True to his word, Ray called the next morning. "It's maybe not as bad as it looked," Ray said. "She's diabetic and her blood glucose was somewhere around two hundred which put her well out of things. They gave her some insulin which really helped."

"How long…"

"A week, maybe two. The doc wants to watch her for a while, somewhere where they can keep track of her glucose and what she's eating. But she'll be okay."

"Can I…"

"Yeah, but not for a couple of days. She's in French Hospital, out on Geary. Give her until Thursday at least." There was a pause and then he said, "I guess you pretty much saved her life, Tom. The doc says 'thanks.'" Another pause. "Me too. Gotta go." He hung up.

Busy as it was in the office, Tom took Thursday afternoon off and rode the bus out Geary Street to French Hospital, armed with a large bouquet of flowers. Her room was on the fifth floor and when he got there he was carefully questioned at the nurse's station, making sure he hadn't brought candy. Or anything else to eat. Once convinced he was clean of any food a nurse took the flowers to put them in water and directed him to a room down the hall.

It was a short but happy visit for both of them. Mrs. Tan was elated that Tom had come to see her and Tom was pleased that she looked as good as she did and that she seemed to be accepting of her condition. After a few minutes, though, she drifted off. The nurse, bringing in the flowers said that this was normal. Mrs. Tan was growing stronger and this was part of the process. She assured him that she would tell Mrs. Tan that he had brought the flowers and sent him on his way.

Back downtown, he was saved from going back to the office by Blaine, who was looking in the window of a bookstore.

"Well, hello Blaine. What are you doing out here at this hour? Looking for a book to read?"

Blaine looked up and grinned. "Not quite. I'm cruising that guy in there. The one pretending to read that book? We've been making eyes and… Uh oh."

"What?"

"That woman. See? Heading down the aisle?" He paused for just a moment. "I knew it, I knew it. I'll bet she's his wife. Damn."

"Aww, poor Blaine. Wives can be such an inconvenience."

Blaine suddenly broke out in a grin. "They can be, that's for sure. You don't have one by any chance, do you?"

"A wife? No, but I have a place we can go and fuck. Will that do?"

"Let's go!"

The apartment was empty when they got there and they had the place to themselves.

A half hour later, when they were at that point where it was either be distracted or fall over the edge, they decided to distract each other with conversation.

"So, Blaine, how come you were out cruising on a Thursday afternoon?" Tom pulled back, leaving half his dick still inside Blaine.

"Don't do that, Tom, or you'll make me come." He was quiet for a moment, gathering control. "Well, they're doing something to the street in front of my building and managed to chop into some sort of communications cable. Since my job is mostly running the Teletype and the Telex, my boss told me to just take the rest of the day off. How about you?"

"Had an errand to do so I took the afternoon off." He moved again, pushing in.

Blaine countered his move by squeezing down on Tom's dick. It felt pretty good so he did it again. "Hey, Tom? That guy, the one who looks like you? You said you weren't brothers but I figure you have to be at least cousins. I mean, he looked just like you."

Tom very slowly pulled back until just the head of his dick was inside Blaine and that was tugging at his sphincter. "Actually he doesn't look like me. I look like him." He pushed back in, all the way.

"Oh, man, Tom! Do that again, real slow."

Tom did and Blaine let out a long sigh. "Oh, yeah. Now stop for a minute, please?" He lay quietly, trying not to think about how good Tom felt inside him. "What'd you mean? It's all the same, isn't it?"

"Think about it this way: a father doesn't look like his son, his son looks like him." Tom stroked once more, this time scraping along Blaine's prostate.

Blaine let out a strangled cry. "I'm gonna come," he said in a raspy whisper. "Oh, yeah, big time!"

Tom pulled back and stroked in fast. He did this all the while Blaine was thrashing around the bed with his orgasm. Then he had his own and they thrashed around together for a while.

A little later, cleaned up and getting dressed, Blaine stopped buttoning his shirt and gave Tom an amazed look. "Your dad? He's your dad?"

Tom nodded. "Yeah, he's my dad. And you know something? I didn't know, hadn't a clue, until that afternoon when he said, 'Isn't this great, kid?'" He laughed. "But that's okay because he didn't have any idea about me, either."

Blaine sat on the edge of the bed. "Your own dad? And you got to watch him have sex, get fucked by that guy? Oh, man..."

Tom sat next to him and put his arms around him. "Yeah, that was interesting but the best part was seeing him hard. I never had and I really wondered how he'd be, hard."

Blaine turned so he could look at Tom. "Hell, I've never even seen my old man naked, much less hard. You are one lucky guy."

Tom smiled. "Yeah, I guess I am. To have him as a dad." There was a long pause and then he said, "Come on, let's straighten up the bed. I need to get home."

At home Tom looked to see if there was anything on their family calendar. There wasn't but looking reminded him that it was the last day of the month. *Oh, well,* he thought, *she won't care if I take the rent up one day late.*

When his dad came in he suggested dinner out. They decided on a place called *The Yacht Club* on Polk Street.

"You know," Matt said in the cab on the way to dinner, "one good thing about being, what do you call it? out? yeah, out to each other is that there are so many interesting gay restaurants around that we never got to try before."

Tom smiled at him. "Yeah, and they're generally cheaper than the others. Think about *that* for a while."

They had a martini at the bar before being lead to a quiet table in the back. Their waiter, a handsome little stud named Jack, didn't even ask. Fresh martinis appeared on the table as if by magic.

"I'm a little curious, Dad. What—or more likely *who*—has been taking up all your time lately? You hardly ever sleep at home."

Matt laughed. "You keeping score?" He laughed again. "Okay, okay, I know I've been out a lot and... well, I guess I haven't said a lot about it because... because he's sort of a friend of yours and I haven't known how to approach you about it."

He was saved yet again from approaching it by the appearance of the waiter, anxious to reel off the list of specials. Matt and Tom listened attentively and then ordered from the menu.

"Damn he's a cute little thing," Matt said when he'd gone.

"Yeah," Tom agreed, "I'd do him."

"I'm sure," Matt said with a shrug. "But then, so would I."

They sipped at their drinks in silence, until Tom said, "You gonna tell me or make me guess?"

Matt sighed. "Hey, it's no big deal but I've been, ah, spending a lot of time with Mario, that's all."

Tom feigned horror. "But Dad, he'll teach you all the secrets he taught me! I won't be the only one who can do those things."

Matt laughed. "I think you may be a little late, my boy. In this town, everyone, it seems, knows how to do those things. And does them very well." He finished his martini. "So you don't mind?"

Tom followed suit. "No, I don't mind. I think it's wonderful. Mario was never really into one night stands and as for me... well, he thinks I'm a bit young."

Their salads were served and then the main course, rare steak for Matt (*gotta keep my strength up*) and shrimp in garlic sauce for Tom (*I'm not going anywhere tonight*). They skipped dessert in favor of brandy.

"Where have you guys been going?" Tom asked as he sniffed his brandy. "I mean, his aunt hasn't moved out, has she?"

"No, she's still there most of the time. We've been renting a hotel room mostly."

"You know, Dad, maybe it's time we rethink our agreement about taking people home. Now that we're... well, on the same wavelength, I don't think it'd be a problem if you brought some guy home once in a while. Same for me." He smiled. "Not every Tom, Dick or Harry maybe, but guys... Well guys like Mario. Guys you see more than once."

Matt thought about it for a few moments. "You may be on to something there, Tom." He chuckled. "It'd sure be cheaper."

"Yeah," Tom said with an attempt at an evil grin, "and I'd get to see who you're sleeping with."

Matt laughed. "Works both ways, Tom. And as the more mature man I just might attract... uh, some interest."

"Attract away, Dad. We've shared guys before, although we mostly don't know who they are."

"Yeah, I'll bet there are more lurking out there than either one of us knows. Probably for the better, too."

. . . .

The next day, Friday, the first of September, Tom dug the rent out of the flour canister and took it up to Mrs. Tan's apartment and put it in the desk drawer. It felt strange, being alone in Mrs. Tan's apartment and he didn't linger.

After work he rode the bus out to the hospital. The nurse at the fifth floor station said he could see Mrs. Tan but asked that he not stay long. "She's still weak but her glucose level is way down. We may be able to take her off the insulin over the weekend," she said.

Mrs. Tan was awake but Tom thought she did look weak; and just a little pale. She didn't move much either but did present her cheek for a kiss. "Thank you for coming, Tom. I do appreciate it."

They talked about the hospital routine for a few minutes and how much she hated it but the talk seemed to tire her even more so it wasn't long before Tom took his leave, saying he'd be back tomorrow to see her.

"Oh, Tom, you don't have to come every day. Please. I know how busy you young people are these days." She thought for a moment, "And it's the weekend. Please, come back on Monday. I'll be more rested then and we can have a good visit."

When he left he mentioned to the nurse what she'd said. The nurse thought it was an excellent idea. "She does need rest, perhaps more than anything else. Let her be until Monday. We'll know more then, too."

. . . .

On Monday they did, in fact, know more. First of all, Mrs. Tan wasn't diabetic after all. Her blood glucose had been up so high because she'd had a stroke, evidentially early Monday morning, the day Tom had found her on the floor.

Secondly, she'd had another stroke over the weekend. A fairly bad one they said, and it had affected her memory to the point that she didn't know who anyone was. Tom went in to see her anyway.

The first words out of her mouth were, "Oh, Tom, I'm so glad you're here. All these people, I don't know..." She squinted, first at the nurse and then at Dr. Lee. "Well, I do know him. He's... She stuttered around for a moment and then smiled. "Dr. Lee. What are you doing here?"

Dr. Lee stepped around the bed and took her hand. "I'm here to help you, Mrs. Tan. Do you know where you are?"

She slowly looked around the room. "No, I... Wait. I'm in the hospital, aren't I? I... I've had a stroke? That's what everyone says." She squeezed his hand. "Is it true? Have I had a stroke?"

He said she had and asked if she would mind answering some questions. He didn't wait for her answer but started by asking if she knew who she was, who was president, what day it was. From her answers it quickly became evident that she was well oriented in both time and place but had completely lost the past week. She could remember nothing of coming to the hospital, Tom's visits or anything else that had happened since the previous Monday.

Tom realized that he had to leave if he was going to get any work done that afternoon. But when he said his goodbye's, Mrs. Tan asked him to stay just a moment longer because she had a favor she wanted to ask of him. She then shooed everyone else out of the room.

When they were alone she asked Tom if he would go down to Whiskers and collect the month's rent. "They usually send one or another of the folks that work there up with it but of course I wasn't there. Just ask for Mr. Beard and tell him I have asked you to collect it for me. Can you find a pen and paper? I'll just write him a little note."

Tom gave her his pen—not the gold one he used only for his signature—and one of his business cards to write on. She took the card but didn't know which hand to hold the pen with. Once he got it in her right hand she looked up at him with a confused expression on her face and told him she didn't have any idea how to write. She knew what writing was, she just didn't know how to do it. The really strange thing, at least to Tom's mind, was that she didn't seem the least concerned about it.

Tom excused himself and went out to find Dr. Lee who shook his head but wouldn't offer any opinion. In the end, Dr. Lee wrote a short note on the back of the card, stating that he was Mrs. Tan's doctor and that Tom was acting at her request. Tom went back to Mrs. Tan, kissed her on the cheek and took his leave.

. . . .

The next day Tom took an early lunch hour and went over to Whiskers. He asked for the manager and was directed to a large, bearded man standing behind the counter making egg salad. When Tom got the man's attention he came around the counter and shook Tom's hand, introducing himself as, "William Beard. Oh, yes, Beard, but not the famous one," he said, fingering his short, nearly white beard. "That would be my cousin James, the one who really knows how to cook."

Tom, who, thanks to his father's occasional forays into cooking, knew who James Beard was, said, "I'll bet his egg salad isn't as good as yours. I'm Tom Braden, Sir, from upstairs."

"Up... Huh?"

They both laughed. "I guess that is a little unclear. I'm one of the guys who rent the apartment above you."

Mr. Beard nodded. "Oh, yes, that social club or whatever it is. What can I do for you, Mr. Braden?"

"Well, Mrs. Tan, our landlady... "

"I know who Mrs. Tan is. What about her?"

"Well, she's in the hospital, Sir, with a stroke. I... I found her on the floor, unconscious, when I took our rent up to her so I called... "

"So that's what all the commotion was about. Jenny, one of the kids who works for me, said she thought it was Mrs. Tan who was carried out. How long do you suppose she'll be in the hospital?"

Tom shook his head. "Don't know, Sir. Maybe a while. I saw her yesterday and she didn't know who anybody was but me. Then she started to remember a little... "

"Son, why are we standing here in the middle of the floor? Come on." He waived towards the little tables by the window. "Coffee?" He didn't wait for an answer, calling out, "Maggie? Coffee over here."

"So, I'm here," Tom said, when they were seated, "because Mrs. Tan asked me to collect your rent for her. She can't write but," he pulled out the business card, "Dr. Lee, her doctor, wrote this note for her."

Mr. Beard looked at the card carefully, then turned it over, read the name there and then looked closely at Tom, as though comparing him to his name. Satisfied, he asked the pretty young girl pouring coffee to run into the back office and bring him the package on his desk. They sipped their coffee in silence until she come back with the package. Taking it from her, he handed it to Tom.

"Handle it with care," he said. "It's easily lost."

Tom shook his head. "I know. Ours, too. I'll put it in her desk right away." He frowned. "What I'd rather do is put it in a bank somewhere but..." He shrugged his shoulders.

"I know, me too. What do you suppose she does with it? Surely she doesn't gamble or do drugs."

Tom laughed. "Doubtful, Sir. On both counts. Thank you for the coffee."

Once the money was in Mrs. Tan's desk, Tom had thought he'd go down to the apartment for a little while and see who might be there. Instead, he walked to a hardware store a few blocks away and bought two new deadbolts and several window locks. These he installed in Mrs. Tan's apartment. He debated what to do with the keys but in the end he put them in Mrs. Tan's key case and put that in his pocket.

He was late to work.

. . . .

For the rest of the week he visited Mrs. Tan daily, sometimes at noon, sometimes after work. And every day it was apparent that she was going downhill. On Friday, when he went out to see her at noon, she seemed to be awake but didn't seem aware that he was in the room.

That afternoon he had a call from Dan who said he'd be in town the next day and suggested dinner Saturday and breakfast Sunday. Bob, the man who owned the place Dan stayed, would be home so they'd have to be a little quiet but it would be okay.

"Wait!" Tom said. "Why annoy Bob when we can just as well annoy my dad? We talked about it and agreed that we could bring a guy home as long as he was a special guy." He laughed. "If you aren't special then nobody is."

Dan was a little reluctant but in the end agreed that staying at Tom's was the better plan. "I'll make reservations," he said, "for three. You and your dad like Indian food? I mean, like curry and lamb and stuff?"

Tom had no idea. They'd never had Indian food. "But if you like it, we'll like it. Oh, and make the reservations for four. Dad, I think, will have a friend along."

Dan chuckled knowingly and said he would.

Saturday at the hospital was Friday all over again. The nurses convinced Tom not to bother visiting on Sunday. He was hesitant so one of the nurses took his phone number and promised to call him if Mrs. Tan was anywhere near awake, or even the least bit responsive.

Dan arrived at four Saturday afternoon, breathless and bearing gifts, good gin for Matt and flowers for Tom. While Tom and Dan were in the shower together, Matt chilled glasses and got out the olives and pickled onions, this last for Mario who was quite fond of Gibsons.

By the time Mario arrived, Tom and Dan were out of the shower and in the bedroom dressing—well, in the bedroom anyway—so Matt and Mario had their turn in the shower. Finally clean and dressed—and, if the truth be known, mutually satisfied—the four of them met in the living room and toasted one another with icy gin and vermouth.

Dinner, at India House was wonderful. They had Chicken Tikkas, Seekh Kibab and hot, curried rice. For dessert, a platter of cooling fruit. Back at home, sitting in the living room with their brandy, they agreed that the food had been good but perhaps a little more spicy than what they were used to. They also agreed that the clear sauce which looked like water was actually liquid fire.

Later, lying in bed holding Dan, Tom looked around his room and chuckled quietly.

"What?"

"You. Us. You're the first man who's ever been in this bed, or, except for my dad, in this room for that matter. Well, the first one who wasn't just a figment of my imagination." He ran his hand along Dan's flank and across his buns. "You're lots better than the figments were."

Dan turned his head and kissed him. "Yeah, especially because I can do this for real." He turned over in Tom's arms and then, with another kiss, turned Tom over. Being their second time, Tom was still lubed and Dan went easily into him.

. . . .

In the morning Tom woke to find Dan, his head cupped in his hand, looking at him.

"Hi."

"Hi." Dan leaned down and kissed him.

"What are you thinking?"

"I was wondering what would happen if I told you I love you."

Tom was quiet for a few moments before he said, "Well, I guess it would give me the courage to tell you that I've been thinking of you that way for a while."

They were silent for a long time, each taking in what the other had said. Then Tom whispered, "You know what? I gotta pee so bad I can taste it."

Dan grinned. "You mean, you have to get out of bed?"

"That's exactly what I mean. Come on, you can help me."

Dan wasn't exactly a lot of help but sure did make the whole process fun.

The four men went to Sears for breakfast, happily standing in line with the other hungry people and enjoying the warm September sun. Afterward they walked up Nob Hill and down to Fisherman's Warf.

When he left that afternoon, Dan said he'd be back the next Saturday.

CHAPTER 17

. . . .

The following week was a very difficult one at the office. Tom spent a lot of time with several of Mr. Diggs clients, straightening out some misunderstandings—and perhaps some downright lies. He also went out to see Mrs. Tan every day, even though she seldom recognized him when he was there.

Then, Thursday morning, Dr. Lee called. Mrs. Tan had had another stroke, early in the morning, and she hadn't survived this one. It was good, Dr. Lee said, because now she was in a better place, one without pain. Tom was touched by the thought. When he asked about final arrangements, Dr. Lee said his instructions were that the body was to be cremated and that Mrs. Tan wanted no service of any kind.

At noon Tom went up to 323 and found Charlie, Joe and Gill there. Charlie and Gill were with guys in the bedroom but Joe was alone in the living room so Tom told him the news.

"Oh, that's too bad," Joe said. "You know I never met her and I don't think she even knew I was part of the group."

"Sure she did," Tom said. "I told her about you your first month, when I took the rent up to her."

"Well, I'm sorry she's gone. I suppose they'll raise our rent now, whoever inherits the place. I mean, it's pretty cheap rent."

Tom sighed. "Yeah, I suppose so but I don't know who that might be. She always said she didn't have any family and all of her husband's people, out to third cousin or so, were also all gone so... Well, we'll see. I understand that there is a will so somebody must get the place."

About then Charlie came out of the bedroom. Tom was surprised to see he was with Jonesy.

"Well, hi, Tom. Haven't seen you in a long time," Jonesy said, pulling him into a hug and then kissing him.

"Hi, yourself, guy. Still got that hole in your pocket?"

Jonesy took Tom's hand and pushed it into his right hand pocket. All Tom found in there was a very warm, slightly damp dick. He fondled it for a moment before withdrawing his hand. "We gotta get together," Tom said. "I haven't seen you around for a while. Where have you been?"

Jonesy pulled himself up straight and grinned. "Got myself promoted. More money and a training class in New York for a couple of months. Man! Now there's a big place for you. But you know what? They still like to do the same things we like to do out here. No better than us, either."

Charlie cut in. "You okay, Tom? You look a little pale."

Tom shook his head. "No, I'm okay. It's just that, well, Mrs. Tan died this morning and I'm a little... You know."

Charlie pulled him into a long hug. "You were kind of fond of the old lady, weren't you?" He gave Tom a long but gentle kiss.

"Yeah, I was," Tom said, when they broke. "She was... I don't know, she was nice."

Jonesy was pointing at his watch and looking from Charlie to the door and back, the way a dog might when he needs to go outside and pee.

"Look, I promised David here I'd give him a tour of my shop so he could see how my guys are organized and we don't have a lot of time. You be around, ah, Monday?"

Tom nodded, gave Joe a hug and a kiss, and they all left together.

. . . .

That night Matt could tell Tom was upset about something so he took him to dinner at Momma Giordano's. When they were seated with their usual martinis he asked Tom what was bothering him.

Tom looked up and Matt was pleased to see that his eyes were clear. "I guess it shouldn't get to me so much but Mrs. Tan, you know, the landlady at 323? Well, she died this morning, had a really big stroke and... and just... you know, just stopped living."

Matt reached across the table and put his hand over Tom's. "You were pretty fond of her, weren't you Son?"

Tom looked up. "Yeah, I guess I was. She was so interesting and such a strong woman. I mean, she lost both her sons in the War and then her husband not too long after."

"No family?"

"That's the really bad part. She didn't have anyone, not even an aunt or cousin or anything. And her husband's family, they said she was an outsider and never even spoke to her."

"They... Really? I thought the Chinese were very much into family."

Tom laughed a little, which Matt took as a good sign. "But see, she wasn't family. She was married to their son, sure, but *she* wasn't Chinese. She was *English* for God's sake!"

"I see the problem. So they didn't accept her?"

"No. She once told me that her mother-in-law had never been in her home. Never. She only saw the boys when her son took them to her house. And then she didn't really accept them either. Dad, she didn't even say she was sorry when the boys were killed. No one else did, either."

"Excuse me, please." Momma Giordano stood at the table, holding a tray. "You seemed so deep in your conversation that we didn't want to bother you so I just brought you something." She placed a large soup plate of steamed clams in front of Tom and a platter of Chicken Parmigiana in front of Matt. She set a basket of garlic bread on the table between them. "I hope it's okay."

Matt smiled up at her. "Yes, I think it's okay," he said with a grin. "It's exactly what we would have ordered. Thank you. And thank you for your kindness."

Momma Giordano smiled broadly and nodded before moving off, back to her kitchen.

After sampling the food, Matt looked up and said, "Boy, with treatment like that, I think I'd have packed up and gone back to England."

"She said she thought of that, after Mr. Tan died," Tom said, wiping his fingers on one of the white linen napkins Mamma Giordano had left on the table. "She didn't do it because, as she herself said, she's stubborn and she wasn't going to let those heathen people run her out. Her words."

They continued eating and, when she came to check that everything was satisfactory, asked the daughter to thank her mother again for her thoughtfulness.

"I guess she was a little strange, too," Tom said, sopping up the last of the clam juice with the last of the garlic bread. "She didn't believe in banks. We paid the rent on the apartment in cash and so did the sandwich shop."

"Really? Hard to keep records that way." Matt poured the last of the wine in their glasses.

"Not only that, where did she keep the money?" He sipped his wine. "I put the rent in a desk drawer but where did it go from there? Her mattress?"

Matt grinned. "Surely not. But it is a good point. I hope she had good locks on her door."

"Oh, speaking of that, when I collected the rent from downstairs and put it in the desk I got nervous so I changed the locks on the doors and windows." He shrugged. "I didn't know what else to do."

"Oh, I think you did the right thing. You never know who might have had a key to her place. Who'd you give the keys to?"

Tom looked blank for a moment. "Give the keys... Nobody. They're on my—or rather her— key ring."

"Don't you think *someone* might like to get in there? Like whoever inherits the place?" He could practically see the light go on in Tom's head.

"Didn't think of that, Dad. Never crossed my mind. Now what do I do?"

Matt shook his head. "Did she have a lawyer? If she did, he'd be the logical choice."

"I have no idea. But she did have an address book, I saw it on the desk. I'll check it tomorrow. You want a brandy?"

. . . .

Tom did check the address book on Friday and did indeed find a lawyer listed. When he called, the man's secretary was rather abrupt and set an appointment for a week from Monday.

As long as Tom was at 323 anyway, he went down to the apartment, just to see who was there. It turned out that the place was fairly crowded. Joe was being undressed in the living room by an oriental looking man who spoke with a very soft accent and obviously excited Joe greatly; Gil was sitting on the couch alone and, like Tom, looking to see if anyone needed help. Through the open bedroom doors Tom could see Charlie with a new guy he'd picked up on the cable car that morning. Ray, on the other bed and bent almost double over a couch cushion and two pillows, was taking everything Russ, the giant cable car gripman, had to give. His facial expression was easily translated: *Bliss.*

Tom went into the bedroom with the intention of, at last, getting to kiss Russ, whom he'd lusted after for more than a year. Russ was having none of it, though, and when Tom bent down Russ shook his head and said, "Don't do that. Sorry." His hand left Ray's ass for a moment and patted Tom's. "Sure would like to do this, though," he said. "Often thought this was a fine one." He looked up at Tom with a grin. "You gonna wait?"

Tom was tempted. Very tempted. "Can't, so you just take your time here. Make it a good long one, so he'll shoot off every time he even thinks about you."

Russ slapped Tom on the ass, a real slap, not just a pat. "One day?"

"Oh, yes. One day soon." Tom tweaked Russ' nipple and went back out to the living room. Ray grinned at him as he passed.

He flopped down on the couch next to Gil and groped him. Gil was already hard. "So how's it going," he said, not removing his hand.

"Good," Gil said. Then he laughed. "Good and horny."

"Yeah, me too. You want to take care of it?"

Gil didn't answer, just moved around so he and Tom were face to crotch. They opened each other's pants and fished around in each other's underwear until they found what they wanted. It didn't take long but was pleasantly pleasurable nonetheless.

Tom was late getting back to work so to make up for it he gave Sue the rest of the afternoon off. She was delighted because she and Kelly were going out to dinner that night and she *really* needed a new pair of shoes.

Alone in the office, Tom surprised himself by how much he got done. So much so that he spent another six hours there the next day.

. . . .

At ten-thirty Monday morning Tom found himself sitting in a marginally comfortable leather chair in front of the desk of C. Wilson Bernat, Attorney at Law. C. Wilson Bernat, in the flesh, wasn't nearly as impressive as his name. He wasn't tall, perhaps five feet six or so, and he wasn't big, perhaps a hundred forty-five pounds. He also looked to be about sixteen years old and probably didn't need to shave every day. Tom also thought he was kind of cuddly, the wedding ring on his left hand notwithstanding.

"So you are Mr. Braden." He grinned and Tom immediately liked him. "I'll tell you frankly, I thought you'd be much older." Tom laughed and thought about pots talking to kettles about color. "Mrs. Tan said you are a successful real estate executive?"

"Not exactly. I mean, I do work in real estate, for *Bay Holdings Group*. But..."

"You know a guy named Diggs? Warren Diggs?"

Tom nodded. "Yeah. I worked for him when he was at bay holdings."

"You know what happened to him?"

"Last I heard, he was opening an office in Phoenix."

"No, no, not that. I mean... the clothes and stuff. What was that all about?"

Tom laughed. "His inner man got out, I guess, and his inner man liked to dress that way."

Mr. Bernat laughed. "Well, if I was as big as he is, maybe I'd dress like that too. I don't think so, but never rule anything out. Now," he turned serious, "we need to discuss Mrs. Tan. She was greatly taken with you, Tom. You know that?"

Tom shrugged. "Not really. I was very taken with her, I know that. We talked a lot, and drank tea."

Mr. Bernat grinned. "Yeah, she talked and you drank tea. But it was good tea, I'll say that. You know, I advised her against doing this."

Huh? "You advised her against doing what?" This wasn't going at all as Tom had thought it would and he was both intrigued and... He couldn't quite put his finger on it but it was an emotion he wasn't accustomed to having.

"Didn't she ever talk to you about any of this? I mean, her will, her last wishes, anything like that?"

Tom shook his head. "Nothing. We didn't talk about death much, except for her sons and her husband. Why?"

"Well, I told her to. Really. I did." He let out a deep sigh. "I guess I should have known she wouldn't." He looked Tom in the eye. "Understand, I couldn't talk to you about it. She wouldn't give me permission and I couldn't do it on my own. It wouldn't have been ethical."

Tom hated beating around the bush in real estate deals and he hated it everywhere else, too. "Can we get to the point here? What the hell are we talking about?"

Mr. Bernat said, in even tones and without emotion, "We're talking about you being Mrs. Tan's sole heir, that's what we're talking about." He paused to let that sink in. "There isn't a lot really, at least that I know about. There's maybe a thousand dollars or so in her purse. Maybe a little more hidden in the sugar bowl. No, it's the building mostly. 323 Kearny Street? I guess you know the place, since you live there. Anyway, it's yours now. Lock, stock and that hippy who lives on the fourth floor. All yours."

It took a few moments for it all to sink in and, when it did, Tom didn't know what to say and C. Wilson did nothing to help him out.

"See? That's one of the reasons I advised her against it. You don't even know what to say. You hardly knew her. Oh, yeah, you went around there, buttering her up, getting on her good side. Why?" He stood behind his desk and looked at Tom with defiance in his eyes. "Why? Because she was old and was happy for any little tidbit of attention and because you knew she had to kick off pretty quick anyway? That's probably why you live there. That and the fact that she didn't charge you any rent. What a nice guy you were." His voice dropped an octave or two. "What a con."

Tom jumped up and glared at him. "Just who are you calling a con, Mr. Bernat? Me? Because I took an interest in that sweet lady? Because I found her life interesting?" He raised his voice. "Because I went to the hospital every fucking day to see her, to make sure she was getting the best care they could give?"

"No, I…"

Tom was on a roll and ignored him. His voice dropped to just above a whisper. "I don't think so, Mr. Bernat. No, I wonder if you didn't covet that building for yourself, try to talk her into leaving it to you and now you're angry at her and taking it out on me." He had more to say but was sidetracked when the secretary stuck her head in the door and asked if anything was wrong.

"No, Miss Day, nothing is amiss. Mr. Braden—and I—let ourselves stray from the business at hand. But as long as you're here, perhaps Mr. Braden would like a cup of coffee. I know I would."

Miss Day looked at Tom, assessing his potential for violence. Tom nodded, smiled and said, "Black."

The two men slowly sank into their respective chairs, their eyes never leaving each other's faces. They sat in silence until Miss Day brought the coffee, in a china mug for Mr. Bernat and a paper cup for Tom. Before she could leave Mr. Bernat reached across the desk and traded cups with Tom. Miss Day sniffed, turned on her heel and left the room.

"I think, Mr. Braden, that we have better things to do than scream at one-another. I apologize for my behavior and for that of my secretary."

Tom lifted his cup and made a gesture of toasting Mr. Bernat. "I apologize as well, Sir. As my father would be, I am appalled at my behavior. Please forgive me."

"Forgiven." In that one word Tom knew he and Mr. Bernat would never have other than a distant business relationship. Some little part of him was sorry for that.

The rest of their meeting went more smoothly. Tom signed a lot of papers, many of which Miss Day notarized, without speaking a word to him. Mr. Bernat showed Tom the letters he'd written to Social Security and the company who sent her pension check. An hour later and a hundred dollars lighter Tom left the office. It would take several months to become official, Mr. Bernat had said, but Tom was now the owner of 323 Kearny Street.

Tom went back to the office and spent the rest of the day on the phone with new clients and solving problems for old ones. He thought about going up to 323 but couldn't quite make himself do it just yet. In the end he called Charlie and asked him to set up a meeting for Wednesday afternoon. Then he told Sue he was taking Wednesday off.

CHAPTER 18

On Wednesday morning Tom went up to 323 with the idea of taking the rent money out of Mrs. Tan's desk and putting it in the bank. When he opened the drawer and started to take things out of it, he got quite a surprise.

His last rent payment, and that of Mr. Beard from the sandwich shop, was there but so was that of the month before. Below that was a good sized box with a note taped to the top.

> *Dear Tom, it said, I know you'll think me a little daft and perhaps I am. But you have been so kind to me, always making tea and bringing those little cakes, and especially listening to me run on about The Boys and Mr. Tan, I want to do this for you. You are a very sweet man and, I expect, you will always be.*
>
> *Yours,*
>
> *Beatrice Tan*

Inside the box was all the rent payments that had been made on the apartment.

There was another box with another note.

Dear Tom, This is for Henry, the man on the top floor. I know he's a little strange but I think he's what is called a Hippy or a Hoppy (I've never been sure which). He has been good about sweeping the floors and doing little things around the place and I know he hasn't much money so this will help him out.

Thank you,

B.T.

There was a similar box and note for Mr. Beard.

The only comment that came to Tom's mind was: *Well, I'll be damned!* He even said it aloud, although he knew Mrs. Tan wouldn't approve of such language.

He took the box for Henry and went up to his apartment. He had to wait for what seemed a long time after he knocked but eventually Henry answered, peering around the door.

"Yeah? What?"

Tom realized that he and Henry had never met before. "Hi. My name is Tom, Tom Braden. I'm one of the renters in the second floor front."

"Well, if you're one of them then I guess you've seen a naked man before." He laughed and opened the door. He was indeed a naked man, and very much of a man, Tom noted. He gestured Tom into the apartment and closed the door. "What can I do for you?"

Tom thrust the box out to him. "I don't know if you know yet but Mrs. Tan passed away a week ago. She left you this."

"Dead?" He shook his head. "Well, I guess we all have our time but I'm sorry to see that sweet old lady go. What's this?"

"I have no idea," Tom said, although he suspected he did. "Open it and see."

When he did, Henry's only comment was, "Well, I'll be fucked. Money."

Tom smiled at him. "That's what I said, although I used slightly different language."

Henry looked him up and down. "Yeah, I guess to you guys, being fucked is a good thing." He grinned at Tom. "Hey, I'm okay with that. Don't much like it myself but a lot of guys do. You want a joint?" He picked up a cigarette box and offered it to Tom."

"Uh, no. Thanks." He giggled, suddenly visualizing Mr. Simms standing behind his desk, offering up the cigarette box. Naked. "Sorry," he said and laughed again. At Henry's cocked head he added, "My boss does that same thing every time I go into his office only he's got clothes on." He wanted to say, *and I'm sure he's no where near as hung as you are,* but he didn't. "Oh, yeah, and the cigarettes in the box are Marlboros."

Henry helped himself to a joint and while he was lighting it Tom looked around the room. It was furnished in contemporary thrift store and there was a plant on every flat surface. On closer inspection he saw that all the plants were marijuana.

"Yeah, there's a lot of it, isn't there. I deal some, mostly so I can buy food and pay the little bit of rent Mrs. Tan gets. The rest is for me. I guess I'm a little overly fond of the stuff but... What the hell, it's like sex; some guys can't go two hours without whacking off or screwing some chick," he winked at Tom, "or some guy, but me? A little weed keeps me happy." He took a long toke of his joint and held it for what Tom thought was a very long while. When he'd let it out, he said, "Don't get me wrong, I like getting my rocks off as much as the next guy but I'm not driven by it the way some guys are."

Tom shrugged. "To each his own, I guess." He glanced at his watch. "Hey, I gotta get going," he said, putting out his hand.

"No, wait," Henry said. "What now? I mean, with Mrs. T gone who do I pay the rent to?" His eyes darted around the room and stopped on the box of money. He chuckled. "Specially now that I got the money to pay without scratching around and selling my best stuff."

"I don't have the answer to that just yet but I tell you what. Just hold on to the rent money and I'll find out. Okay?"

"Yeah, okay, man. That's good." He took another long drag on his joint. Then he scratched his balls and Tom saw that his dick was rapidly growing. "Look, I think I gotta... Well, I haven't had any for a long time and talking about sex and all has got me..." He looked at Tom. "You want to watch? Some guys do, I know."

Tom laughed. "Yeah, I'm one of those guys I guess. But I have a lot to do so I'll take a pass. Maybe next time?"

Henry was fully erect now and he wrapped his hand around it. Tom noticed that his thumb and forefinger didn't go all the way around all the way and there was room for at least one more hand on it. "Okay. Yeah, next time. You'll see." He laughed.

Tom was half way down the hall before he got the joke.

Back in Mrs. Tan's apartment he sorted the rent money into five stacks and put each in an envelope. Then he went down to Whiskers and bought an assortment of sandwiches and things.

Gil was the first to arrive, followed by Ray and Joe. Charlie was late, saying he got held up at a meeting.

"Charlie told us the old lady died," Joe said. "Who do you suppose will be the landlord now? Probably raise the rent, too."

"Yeah, you seem to be plugged into all this, Tom. What's going to happen?"

"Well, Ray, I can't say for sure but I have some ideas. As to the rent, I can practically guarantee it won't get raised so you can stop worrying about that." Tom picked up the envelopes from a side table. "I've got something for you guys."

He passed out the envelopes and the consensus was: *What the hell?*

"That," Tom said, "is all the rent we've paid on this place. It's a gift from Mrs. Tan, who, by the way, thought we are some sort of social club."

"Well, aren't we?" asked Charlie. "I mean, we do social things."

"I'm not sure cock-sucking is exactly social," Ray said with a shrug. "Not the way you do it. With you it's more of a great art."

They joked around a little more before it occurred to someone to ask Tom how he came to have all the rent money. Tom told them about his visit to the lawyer, Mr. Bernat.

"That must have been fun," Ray said. "Was he acting like a prick?"

"Good description, Ray. Although I've yet to meet an actual prick who behaved that badly. But yeah, he was acting like a jerk. That is until..."

"You stood up to him," Ray finished for him. "He's like that, I think because he's so short and juvenile looking. Tries to establish control but can't maintain it when someone stands up to him."

"You know him?"

"Professionally. So don't tell him I said so. Oh, and don't tell him I said he's hung like a large horse, either, but he is. Got the balls for it, too. So why were you seeing him?"

"Evidentially I turned out to be Mrs. Tan's best, perhaps only, friend. So she left 323 to me. Everything. Including a box containing all the money we've ever paid in rent." He laughed. "Thus the guarantee the rent won't go up."

"Well, who better to leave it to than a real estate man," Charlie said. Then, turning to Tom, "You going to sell it?"

Tom thought for a long time. "You know, I haven't had time to think about that, Charlie, but my first reaction is no, I don't think I will. Heck," he said with a grin, "I may live here."

They talked for a while longer, until Charlie had to leave for a meeting and Joe had to go and see a client. The three left eventually fell into a sort of puppy pile which sorted itself out to Gil and Tom in a sixty-nine with Ray fucking Tom until he was right on the edge and then switching to Gil for the big finish. And a big one it was, with lots of groans and pleasure.

When Tom told his dad about 323 that evening, his dad's first comment was made in a perfectly terrible Jewish accent, "Well, well, my son, a man of property." Over dinner they decided that Matt, who had only seen the one apartment, would get a tour of the entire place the next afternoon.

After his tour, which included Mrs. Tan's and the empty apartments but omitted Henry's because he wasn't in and Tom didn't have a key, Matt convinced Tom to hire a good contractor to make an assessment of the whole place.

. . . .

On Saturday, Dan, who was back in town for the weekend, got the same tour, but including Henry's.

That evening Matt had decided to cook since Mario would also be there and Matt was trying to impress him with his skill in the kitchen. Lamb steak, twice baked red potatoes and salad seemed to fill the bill.

While Matt was in the kitchen, Mario asked Tom to sit with him at the little round, inlayed table in the bay window. He poured some of the very good scotch he had brought with him and they sat across from each other, rather formally Tom thought.

When Mario started it was obvious that he wasn't skilled in these kinds of conversations, even if Tom couldn't figure out just *what kind* of conversation it actually was.

"Uh, Tom, we, I mean you and I, we've, uh, been close for a long time, right? I mean, we've shared good things together and, well, we've even made love together. I know you think... you've thought that you were, that is, that we were... attuned to each other and... Well, I think maybe you thought you wanted to, ah, have more together than we did. But... I told you that, well, that you are a bit too young for me."

Tom nodded and wondered just where this was going. Did Mario have a new... Then it hit him and he found it very hard to keep a straight face. He decided to help Mario out.

"I guess I finally figured that out, Mario. I think I was probably in love with you that summer when you taught me about sex and making love. Maybe all guys fall in love with the first man who treats them like a man, a sexual man. And some of us will never forget that man, will always remember him with great affection. But we have to move on, both of us. It's hard, but it has to be done."

Mario had a look of great relief on his face. "Yes, Tom, that's it: we have to move on. What we, uh did, no, what we had was, I think, good for both of us but... "

Tom smiled. "That was then, this is now. It's time to move on. But you know something Mario? I've grown to think of you as part of my family, sort of a big brother, and I'd be very happy if it stayed that way, however you move on, if you stayed part of my family."

Tom was sure he could see the light go on just above Mario's head.

"Would you like it if I was, oh, say, a sort of dad? Not like Matt, I mean, your actual dad, but kind of in that same position?"

Tom stood and went around to Mario's side of the table where he pulled him up, out of his chair and kissed him. Not a son and dad kiss, not a lover's kiss but something in between. It was close enough to a lover's kiss to make them both begin to get hard, though.

"I hope," Tom said, "that you and my dad will be very happy together." Then, pulling back and looking Mario in the eye, "Because if he's not, you will have me to answer to."

In the meantime, in the kitchen, Dan was helping Matt prepare the salad by chopping the onions and crumbling the cheese. "You know, Sir, I just love this kind of cheese in a salad."

Matt rapped his wooden spoon sharply against the pot he was stirring and turned to face Dan. "I wish you wouldn't call me sir, Dan. They call me that at work and even there it makes me feel old. From a boy no older than my son, the word makes me feel ancient."

Dan held Matt's eyes. "Then is it okay if I call you Dad?" He didn't blink but Matt was sure he saw a bit of moisture there.

"What would your, uh, your actual father think about that?"

Dan made a sound that wasn't laughter but wasn't a cry either. "I don't have one of those."

Matt took a step towards him. "How is that, Dan?"

Dan laid down the chopping knife. "He left when I was three. Mom couldn't take care of us so I had a long series of foster parents. None of the men stick in my mind as a dad."

Matt crossed the room and gathered Dan into a tight hug. After a long moment he said, "Of course you may call me dad. And, if you don't mind, I'll treat you as a son, my son. Okay?"

It took a long moment for Dan's head to come back to that kitchen, to that man now known as his Dad. "Thank you, Dad. With all my heart, thank you." He gave Matt a rather un-son-like kiss but that was all right; Matt understood exactly what was being communicated. They went back to their various duties, changed men.

While Matt was putting the lamb steaks on the grill, Dan, standing next to him and observing, said, "Dad, I'd like to ask you something else but it's kind of delicate now. I mean, I came in here with the intention of asking you for permission to ask your son to live with me and see if I can make him as happy as he makes me."

"I'd like nothing better. But what's the difficulty?"

Dan grinned. "Well, he's my brother now. I mean, isn't that incest?"

Matt laughed. "That it is, Son, of the very best kind." Then he got very serious. "Thank you for asking me, Son. You have no idea how happy that makes me, that you have the courtesy, and good sense, to ask." He kissed Dan, then, and swatted him on the butt. "Now go out there and tell those lazy guys that they'll get well done lamb if they don't hurry up.

Dan went out to the living room, truly a changed man.

The next morning, stretched out in bed, Tom kissed Dan and said, "That was a very touching speech dad gave last night and I don't think I've properly welcomed you as my brother, yet."

Dan kissed him back. "If what you did to me last night wasn't a proper welcome, I doubt that I'd survive the real thing."

"Really? Want to try, anyway?"

He did.

After, when they were basking in the glow of energy well spent, Tom said, "You know? I had a very sweet conversation with Mario last night. He was, in his own way, asking for permission to... I don't know, to pursue my dad, I guess. To ask him to live together." He chuckled. "It was so Mario, so proper."

"I think that's wonderful, that he did that. Did you give him permission?"

Tom smiled and kissed Dan. "Yeah, I gave him permission. And then I thought about us, about living together when you graduate in December. After Dad's speech, I guess maybe I'd better ask him. I mean, you're his son now, too."

Dan grinned at him. "Don't sweat it, Tom. I took care of it last night."

THE END

Wait! you say. *That was then, 1961, and this is now, 2009. What happened to them all? Surely they didn't just... stop!*

No, they didn't just stop. They went on to live full lives. Tom and Dan formed an enduring partnership and actually got married in 2008, when it became legal in California. Tom was seventy and Dan was seventy-one. They made a charming couple.

Matt and Mario, too, formed an enduring, and, surprising to Matt who didn't really believe men could do such a thing, monogamous partnership which lasted until 1999 when Matt died at the age of eighty-one. Mario lived only a month longer and died of a broken heart.

Mr. Simms and his wife, Mrs. Simms, retired in 1968, after selling *Bay Holdings* to Tom and Dan. They moved to Sun City, Arizona, where they became fairly large cogs in a fairly small wheel, advancing to President and Treasurer, respectively, of the Home Owners Association. Unable to give up smoking, they died within a month of one another in 1969.

Mr. Diggs became quite successful in Phoenix real estate and often gave lavish parties at his estate in the adjoining town of Scottsdale. He was active in the community theatre where his tendency toward exhibitionism fit right in. He passed away quietly in 1985, disappointing a number of ladies in town whose husbands had lost either the interest or the ability to satisfy their needs.

Sue left *Bay Holdings* in 1962 to marry Kelly, who put her through nursing school. They worked their entire careers at San Francisco General Hospital. Today, they're retired in, of all places, Cancun, Mexico, where they spend their days on the beaches and nearly always have tacos for lunch.

The renters kept the apartment for several years although, with the advent of the plague, it became a closed social club where only the members took care of the members. It was informally disbanded after Gil died of cancer and Joe moved, with his wife, to Ft. Lauderdale.

Mr. Barnet became quite active in California politics. He's still active—and powerful—in the California State Senate.

And, finally, Henry, the hippy marijuana farmer, still lives quietly on the fourth floor of 323. He lives with a man named Eric whom he befriended—and protected—during a brief stint in county jail. Eric was so thankful for the protection that he willingly gave himself to Henry who found, after a remarkably short time, that he liked sex with Eric as much as he liked it with a woman. Besides that, Eric is always eager and always enjoys it as much as Henry does. They both think nobody knows they are lovers.

ABOUT THE AUTHOR

Greg was born in Glendale, California, grew up in San Luis Obispo, California, and came out in San Francisco, California. He lives in Palm Springs with his partner and the most stubborn Wire Hair Terrier on the planet.

www.ingramcontent.com/pod-product-compliance
Lightning Source LLC
Chambersburg PA
CBHW071158260626
47162CB00003B/1097